Christmas on Peppermint Lane

Excerpt

Santa found her there, gently knocking on her door with the kind of patience that comes from centuries of understanding human hearts. "You know," he said, settling into her grandmother's old rocking chair, "some of my favorite Christmas memories started with things going completely wrong."

Holly looked up, her eyes red-rimmed but curious. "Even you make mistakes, Santa?"

His belly shook with a gentle laugh. "Oh, Holly. The year I delivered presents in a thunderstorm, or when the reindeer got tangled in the Northern Lights – those aren't mistakes. They're the moments that make magic real. Just like Jingles and his wonderful chaos."

The mention of his name made her heart ache. "But the gingerbread house—"

"Was never about perfection," Santa interrupted softly. "It was about bringing people together. And look what Jingles did – he brought more joy to this town in a few weeks than all the perfect frosting roses in the world could manage."

Through her window, Holly could see movement in the town square. Curious, she moved closer, Santa joining her with a knowing smile. There, in the gently falling snow, the entire town had gathered. Elves and townspeople alike were working together, carrying armfuls of gingerbread panels and buckets of icing. They were rebuilding the house.

Mrs. Peppermint, the town's oldest resident, was directing traffic with her candy cane cane, while young elves darted between adults' legs with bags of candies and sprinkles. Even grumpy Mr. Icicle, who hadn't participated in a town event since the Great Blizzard of '82, was carefully placing gumdrops along a roof panel.

"They're doing it all wrong," Holly whispered, but there was no judgment in her voice – only wonder. The walls weren't perfectly aligned, the frosting dripped in places, and someone had clearly let the kindergarten class decorate one entire side with what appeared to be a rainbow explosion of candies.

It was beautiful.

Holly's feet were moving before she realized it, Santa's warm chuckle following her out the door. The townspeople looked up as she approached, their faces showing not judgment but joy. Little Timmy, face covered in frosting, ran up to her with a candy cane. "We're fixing it, Miss Holly! We remembered how you said the secret ingredient is love!"

That's when she saw it – the magic she'd been missing all along. It wasn't in the perfectly piped borders or the mathematically precise angles. It was in the smudged fingerprints of children helping to hold panels steady, in the slightly crooked windows that somehow made the house look like it was winking at passersby, in the way the whole town had come together.

"Jingles," she breathed, suddenly realizing what she needed to do. "Has anyone seen Jingles?"

"He's heading to the Santa Express," called out an elf. "Said something about giving Frostyville back its perfect Christmas."

Holly's heart leaped into her throat. Without a word, she turned and ran, her boots slipping on the icy streets. She could hear the train whistle in the distance, its mournful sound echoing off the snow-covered buildings. Twice she nearly fell, but she didn't slow down. She couldn't.

The platform was empty except for one figure, his familiar mismatched socks visible beneath his coat. "Jingles!" she called out, her voice carrying on the winter wind.

He turned, suitcase in hand, his usually bright eyes dim with sadness. "Holly? What are you doing here?"

She stopped in front of him, breathing hard, snowflakes catching in her eyelashes. "Making the biggest mistake of my life," she said, "by letting you leave."

"But the gingerbread house—"

"Is perfect," she interrupted, taking his hand. "Not because of straight lines or proper proportions, but because it's filled with love and laughter and yes, a little bit of chaos. Your chaos."

Reaching into her pocket, Holly pulled out a handful of the magical edible glitter that had started everything. "You know what I realized? Life isn't about following recipes exactly. It's about adding your own ingredients." She blew the glitter into the air, where it caught the light and danced around them like stars.

"The town is rebuilding the house right now, and it's wonderfully, perfectly imperfect. Just like us." Holly took a deep breath, her heart racing but her voice steady. "Which is why I have a very important question to ask you."

Patti Petrone Miller

For Tessa my beloved loyal, loving baby 12/28/2006-11/20/2023

Christmas on Peppermint Lane

Christmas on Peppermint Lane
Written by **Patti Petrone Miller**

Copyright © 2024 by **Patti Petrone Miller**
All rights reserved.

No part of this book may be reproduced, distributed, or transmitted in any form or by any means, including photocopying, recording, or other electronic or mechanical methods, without the prior written permission of the publisher, except in the case of brief quotations embodied in critical reviews and certain other noncommercial uses permitted by copyright law. For permission requests, write to the publisher at the address below.

Published by **AP Miller Productions**

This book is a work of fiction. Names, characters, businesses, places, events, and incidents are either the products of the author's imagination or used in a fictitious manner. Any resemblance to actual persons, living or dead, or actual events is purely coincidental.

Cover design by **Cover Coven**

Printed in the United States of America
First Edition: 2024

For more information, visit **pattipetronemillerexecutiveproducer.wordpress.com**

Patti Petrone Miller

CHRISTMAS ON PEPPERMINT LANE

Author Book List

Accidental Vows
A Krampus Christmas
Sin Takes A Holiday
Barking Up The Wrong Bakery, Thankgiving
Barking Up The Wrong Bakery, Christmas
Best Served Dead
Bewitching Charms
Christmas at Hollybrook Inn
Christmas on Peppermit Lane
Krampus
Hex and the City
Love in Stitches
Pies and Perps
Spectres and Souffles
Mamma Mia It's Murder
Once Upon A Christmas
The Fatman
The Frosted Felony
The Purr-fect Suspect
The Boogeyman
The Gingerdead Men
Vikings Enchantress
Welcome to Scarecrow Hollow
The Pendleton Witches
The Cabinet of Curiosities
Christmas In Pine Haven
Love in the Stacks
Once Upon A Christmas

Author Social Media Links

https://www.facebook.com/pattipetronemiller/
https://www.instagram.com/pattipetronemiller/
https://bsky.app/profile/pattipetronemiller.bsky.social

CHRISTMAS ON PEPPERMINT LANE

By Patti Petrone Miller

Christmas on Peppermint Lane

Praise For Author "Patti Petrone Miller's books hit different from your typical feel-good stories. Sure, Hallmark's got their formula down pat, but Miller brings something fresh to the table - authentic characters that actually feel like people you know, dealing with real-life stuff while still keeping things wonderfully uplifting.

I honestly get the same warm fuzzies reading her books as I do curling up with hot cocoa for a Hallmark marathon, but without all the predictable plot points we've seen a million times. She's nailed that sweet spot between heartwarming and genuine that's super hard to find these days. If you're looking for stories that'll leave you smiling but don't make you roll your eyes at how perfect everything is, Miller's your girl. She's got that special touch that makes you feel like you're hanging out with friends rather than just reading about characters. Move over, Hallmark - there's a new queen of wholesome in town!"

Dear Gentle Readers,

   If you purchased this book, I thank you from the bottom of my heart. First let me say, my books are not explicit. They are like a warm fuzzy blanket you wrap around you while curled up in your favorite comfy place. Holly and Jingles are very much like us. They have drama, flaws and pure emotions.
   The setting is in the fictional North Pole with all the holiday trimmings filled only with hugs and chaste kisses.
   So, if you are searching for explcit scenes and obscene language, this is not the book for you. If you are looking for a Hallmarky type read, than this is the book for you.
   That being said, I have made several changes to the original copy and added lots of goodies in here for you.
   I hope you enjoy this version along with the chapters at the end for the next two books in Holly and Jingle's journey.

   Now let's dive into the story...

Gingerbread Cookies

Ingredients:

- 3 cups all-purpose flour
- 3/4 cup brown sugar
- 3/4 tsp baking soda
- 1 tbsp ground ginger
- 1 tbsp ground cinnamon
- 1/2 tsp ground cloves
- 1/2 tsp salt
- 1/2 cup unsalted butter, softened
- 3/4 cup molasses
- 1 large egg
- 1 tsp vanilla extract

Instructions:

1. In a large bowl, whisk together flour, brown sugar, baking soda, spices, and salt.
2. Add softened butter and mix until crumbly.

3. Stir in molasses, egg, and vanilla until the dough comes together.
4. Divide dough into two portions, wrap in plastic, and chill for 2 hours.
5. Preheat oven to 350°F (175°C).
6. Roll out dough on a lightly floured surface to 1/4-inch thickness. Cut with cookie cutters.
7. Place cookies on a lined baking sheet and bake for 8-10 minutes.
8. Let cool before decorating.

Gingerbread House Recipe

Ingredients:

Dough:

- 5 1/2 cups all-purpose flour
- 1 tsp baking soda
- 1 tsp salt
- 2 tsp ground ginger
- 2 tsp ground cinnamon
- 1/2 tsp ground cloves
- 1 cup unsalted butter, softened
- 1 cup brown sugar
- 1 1/4 cups molasses
- 2 large eggs

Royal Icing (for glue):

- 3 large egg whites
- 4 cups powdered sugar
- 1 tsp lemon juice

Instructions:

1. Whisk flour, baking soda, salt, and spices in a bowl.
2. In another bowl, cream butter and brown sugar until fluffy. Mix in molasses and eggs.
3. Gradually add dry ingredients to wet ingredients, forming a firm dough.
4. Chill dough for 2 hours.
5. Preheat oven to 350°F (175°C). Roll dough to 1/4-inch thickness.
6. Cut out house shapes using a template (walls, roof, etc.) and bake for 12-15 minutes. Cool completely.
7. Prepare royal icing by beating egg whites and adding powdered sugar gradually until stiff peaks form.
8. Assemble house using icing as glue. Let set before decorating.

Sugar Cookies

Ingredients:

- 2 3/4 cups all-purpose flour
- 1 tsp baking soda
- 1/2 tsp baking powder
- 1 cup unsalted butter, softened
- 1 1/2 cups granulated sugar
- 1 large egg
- 1 tsp vanilla extract
- 1/2 tsp almond extract (optional)

Instructions:

1. Preheat oven to 375°F (190°C). Line baking sheets with parchment paper.
2. Whisk flour, baking soda, and baking powder in a bowl.
3. Cream butter and sugar until light and fluffy. Beat in egg and extracts.
4. Gradually mix dry ingredients into wet ingredients.

5. Roll dough into 1-inch balls and place on baking sheets.
6. Flatten slightly with a glass. Optional: Sprinkle with sugar before baking.
7. Bake for 8-10 minutes until edges are set but not browned. Cool on wire racks.

Snickerdoodles

Ingredients:

- 2 3/4 cups all-purpose flour
- 2 tsp cream of tartar
- 1 tsp baking soda
- 1/2 tsp salt
- 1 cup unsalted butter, softened
- 1 1/2 cups granulated sugar
- 2 large eggs
- 1 tsp vanilla extract

Cinnamon Sugar Coating:

- 1/4 cup granulated sugar
- 1 1/2 tsp ground cinnamon

Instructions:

1. Preheat oven to 375°F (190°C). Line baking sheets with parchment paper.
2. Whisk flour, cream of tartar, baking soda, and salt in a bowl.
3. Cream butter and sugar until fluffy. Add eggs and vanilla, mixing well.
4. Gradually add dry ingredients to wet ingredients.
5. Combine cinnamon and sugar in a small bowl.
6. Roll dough into 1-inch balls, then roll in cinnamon sugar to coat.
7. Place on baking sheets and bake for 9-11 minutes until edges are set.
8. Cool on baking sheets for 5 minutes, then transfer to a wire rack.

This is my favorite recipe for Hot Chocolate! Give it a try!

Golden Moon Hot Chocolate
A rich and creamy hot chocolate infused with spices, a touch of citrus, and a golden shimmer that makes it truly magical.

Ingredients (Serves 2)

      2 cups whole milk (or a non-dairy alternative like oat milk for creaminess)
      1/2 cup dark chocolate (70% cocoa or higher), finely chopped
      1/4 cup coconut cream (optional for extra richness)
      1 tbsp cocoa powder
      1 tbsp honey or maple syrup (adjust to taste)
      1 tsp orange zest
      1/4 tsp ground cardamom
      1/4 tsp ground cinnamon
      1/8 tsp cayenne pepper (optional, for a subtle warmth)

      1/2 tsp vanilla extract

Optional Toppings: Whipped cream, marshmallows, or a sprinkle of cinnamon (I use cinnamon and whiped cream)

Instructions

1. **Warm the Milk Base**: In a medium saucepan, heat the milk and coconut cream over medium heat until warm but not boiling. Stir frequently to avoid scorching.

2. **Add Chocolate & Cocoa**: Lower the heat and whisk in the dark chocolate and cocoa powder. Stir until completely melted and smooth. (Make sure it's not lumpy or too watery)

3. **Infuse Spices & Sweetener**: Add honey (or maple syrup this gives it a better flavor), orange zest, cardamom, cinnamon, and cayenne pepper. Whisk well and let the mixture simmer on low heat for 2-3 minutes to blend the flavors.

4. **Add the Magic Touch**: Stir in the vanilla extract

5. **Serve**: Pour the hot chocolate into clear mugs (or your favorite mugs) to showcase the shimmer. Top with whipped cream, or marshmallows, and sprinkle a little edible gold dust or cinnamon on top for a finishing touch.

Pro Tips:

For an even creamier texture, blend the hot chocolate in a blender for 30 seconds before serving.
Experiment with different spices like nutmeg or a pinch of ground ginger for your own magical twist.

Enjoy your Golden Moon Hot Chocolate, a warm hug in a mug with a bit of sparkle!

Classic Homemade Eggnog

A creamy, rich, and festive holiday drink with a touch of nutmeg.

Ingredients (Serves 6-8)

4 large eggs (You can use egg beaters in the carton)
1/3 cup granulated sugar (adjust to taste)
2 cups whole milk
1 cup heavy cream
1/2 teaspoon vanilla extract
1/4 teaspoon ground nutmeg (plus more for garnish)
Optional: 1/3 to 1/2 cup bourbon, rum, or brandy for an adult version

Instructions

1. **Beat the Eggs and Sugar**:

    In a medium mixing bowl, whisk the eggs and sugar together until light and creamy.

2. **Warm the Milk**:

In a medium saucepan, heat the milk over medium heat until it's warm (not boiling). Stir occasionally to prevent scorching.

3. **Temper the Eggs**:

    Slowly pour a small amount of the warm milk into the egg mixture, whisking constantly to temper the eggs. This prevents them from scrambling.
    Gradually add the rest of the milk while whisking continuously.

4. **Cook the Mixture**:

    Pour the mixture back into the saucepan. Cook over medium-low heat, stirring frequently, until it thickens slightly (about 160°F or when it coats the back of a spoon). Do not let it boil.

5. **Finish with Cream and Vanilla**:

    Remove the saucepan from heat. Stir in the heavy cream, vanilla extract, and nutmeg.

6. **Cool and Serve**:

    Let the eggnog cool to room temperature, then chill in the refrigerator for at least 2 hours. Stir in your choice of alcohol before serving (if using).

7. **Garnish and Enjoy**:

    Pour into mugs or glasses, sprinkle with a pinch of nutmeg, and serve with a cinnamon stick or whipped cream for extra flair.

Tips for Success

If you want an extra-thick eggnog, use an electric mixer to whip the heavy cream separately and fold it into the cooled eggnog.

For a dairy-free option, use almond milk and coconut cream instead of milk and heavy cream. Eggnog can be stored in the fridge for up to 3 days.

Chapter 1: The Magic of Christmas Baking

Holly Sugarplum stood at her workstation in the North Pole Bakery, her delicate fingers moving with practiced precision as she piped intricate snowflake designs onto the sugar cookies laid out before her. Her brow furrowed in concentration, wisps of chestnut hair escaping from her festive red and green cap, which was adorned with tiny silver bells that chimed softly with each movement. The warm, sugary air was filled with the hum of holiday tunes and the clatter of baking trays, creating a symphony of seasonal cheer that usually set her heart at ease. Ancient recipes passed down through generations of Christmas bakers lined the walls in gilded frames, their parchment pages glowing with a subtle magical shimmer.

The bakery itself was a marvel of Christmas architecture, a testament to centuries of North Pole craftsmanship. The building had been grown rather than built, coaxed from magical sugar crystals by the legendary Sugar Crystal Singers of the First Christmas. Its candy cane-striped support beams weren't merely decorative – they were actually crystallized peppermint that helped purify and strengthen the Christmas magic flowing through the building. The windows, frosted with intricate patterns that seemed to dance and shift in the golden light, were made from sugar glass that had been enchanted to display scenes from Christmas stories when the light hit them just right.

Ancient copper pots and pans hung from the ceiling, each one with its own story and magical properties. There was Old Copper Bottom, a massive cauldron that could multiply any recipe tenfold without losing its flavor, and the Whisperwhisk Pan, which would softly hum holiday tunes that made anything baked in it taste better. Their polished surfaces reflected the warm glow of the enchanted ovens – masterpieces of magical engineering that had been designed by Santa's own grandfather and never burned a single cookie.

The air sparkled with what the elves called "sugar dust" – tiny motes of magical energy that helped ensure every treat baked within these walls carried a touch of Christmas wonder. Holly had learned that this dust was actually crystallized joy, created naturally whenever Christmas magic and baking talent combined. It settled on everything in fine layers, giving the whole bakery a subtle shimmer and infusing every creation with a spark of happiness that would spread to whoever ate it.

The bakery's layout itself was a magical marvel, with rooms that shifted and rearranged themselves according to the needs of the day. The ingredient storeroom could expand infinitely to accommodate new shipments of magical supplies, while the proof room existed in a special time bubble where dough could rise for exactly the right amount of time, regardless of how long it actually spent there. Even the floor contributed to the magic, its tiles made from compressed sugar crystals that helped regulate the temperature and humidity to create the perfect baking environment.

With a final flourish, Holly set down the icing bag – a special silver instrument passed down to her by Cinnamon Sparklecake herself – and leaned back to scrutinize her handiwork. The cookies were beautifully adorned with lacy patterns of sparkling white icing, each one a unique frosty masterpiece that seemed to capture the essence of winter itself. The icing wasn't ordinary sugar and water; it was made with crystallized moonlight collected during the winter solstice, giving each pattern an ethereal glow that would never fade.

And yet, doubt wiggled at the back of her mind like an unwelcome guest, persistent as the winter wind that whistled beyond the bakery's enchanted walls. Unlike her fellow bakers – immortal elves who had centuries to perfect their craft – Holly had only been at the North Pole Bakery for three years, ever since that fateful Christmas Eve when she had discovered her gift for magical baking. She remembered it clearly: she had been working late at her family's small bakery in Minnesota, preparing cookies for the local children's hospital, when her gingerbread had suddenly started to glow. Each cookie she'd decorated that night had somehow captured a piece of Christmas magic, bringing smiles and joy to every child who tasted them.

That was the night Santa himself had appeared in her kitchen, his eyes twinkling with recognition of a rare talent. He'd explained that every few centuries, a human baker was born with the ability to channel Christmas magic through their creations. These special individuals were called "Sugar-Blessed" by the elves, and they brought fresh creativity and innovation to the ancient art of magical baking.

The transition hadn't been easy. Moving to the North Pole meant leaving behind her family's generations-old bakery, though Santa had arranged for her younger sister to discover a sudden talent for baking that would keep the family tradition alive. And while most of the elves had welcomed her warmly, there were some, like Frosting Fairweather III, who still viewed human bakers with skepticism, clinging to centuries-old traditions and techniques.

"Are they festive enough?" she murmured to herself, tilting her head as she examined a cookie from every angle. The snowflake patterns caught the light from the enchanted lanterns floating overhead, casting miniature rainbow reflections across her workspace. "Maybe I should have added more silver dragées for sparkle." These weren't ordinary dragées either, but tiny spheres of compressed starlight, each one containing a spark of joy that would spread warmth through anyone who tasted it.

As Jingles approached her workstation, his boots leaving tiny trails of glowing footprints that sparkled briefly before fading away, Holly couldn't help but smile. The head toy designer's presence always brought an extra dose of creativity to the bakery, and today, with the challenge of the Christmas Eve parade's centerpiece ahead of her, she had a feeling she would need all the inspiration she could get.

The magical timepiece on the wall – its hands made of peppermint sticks and its numbers of spun sugar – chimed the quarter hour, reminding Holly that in the North Pole, time itself moved differently, dancing to the rhythm of Christmas magic. The clock had been crafted by Father Time himself as a gift to Santa, designed to keep pace with the special temporal flow of the North Pole, where a single night could stretch long enough to deliver presents to every child in the world.

"Holly!" Jingles called out, his voice carrying the melodic quality of sleigh bells. He adjusted his wire-rimmed spectacles, which were frosted at the edges with tiny snowflake patterns. "I've been hoping to catch you. Those toy soldier cookies you made last week have given me the most wonderful inspiration for this year's mechanical toys."

Jingles reached into his coat – a magnificent creation of shifting colors that seemed to capture the aurora borealis in fabric form – and pulled out a series of sketches. His fingers left trails of sparkling inspiration in the air, a common side effect of working with magical toy designs for centuries. The sketches showed intricate mechanical soldiers that looked remarkably similar to Holly's cookie designs, right down to the frosted buttons and candy cane swords.

"You see," he continued excitedly, "the way you decorated their uniforms with that special peppermint-infused icing gave me an idea for a new kind of mechanical joint that moves as smoothly as your icing flows. And look here—" he pointed to a particular gear mechanism, "this whole assembly was inspired by your snowflake piping technique!"

Holly felt a warm glow of pride spread through her chest. This was what she loved most about the North Pole – the way magic flowed between all their different crafts, connecting toy-making, baking, and every other Christmas art in an endless dance of creativity and wonder. She remembered her first week at the Pole, when she'd been amazed to discover that toy designers regularly consulted with bakers, and wrapping paper patterns were often inspired by cookie decorations.

"That's incredible, Jingles," she said, leaning in to study the sketches more closely. The papers seemed to hum with magical potential, and she could almost hear the tiny gears turning. "I never imagined my cookies could inspire something like this."

"Oh, but that's not all!" Jingles practically bounced with excitement, causing the bells on his collar and hat to chime in harmony. "When I heard about your commission for the

Christmas Eve parade centerpiece, I had another idea. What if we collaborated? A gingerbread house that doesn't just look magical, but actually is magical!"

Holly's eyes widened as Jingles pulled out another sketch, this one showing a gingerbread house with tiny mechanical elements integrated seamlessly into its sugary architecture. There were miniature toy soldiers marching along its candy walkways, tiny elves that popped out of candy windows, and a magnificent clockwork star for the top that would spread sparkles of real Christmas magic over the crowd.

"We could combine your baking expertise with my mechanical knowledge," Jingles explained, his eyes twinkling with possibilities. "The sugar glass windows could be enhanced with my special toy-maker's magic to show scenes from Santa's workshop, and the candy cane columns could actually rotate! Just think of the children's faces when they see it!"

As Holly listened to Jingles's enthusiastic description, her mind was already whirling with ideas. She thought about the special gingerbread recipe handed down by generations of Christmas bakers – the one made with spices ground by Father Christmas's own windmills and honey gathered from flowers that bloomed in eternal summer at the heart of the North Pole. Combined with Jingles's mechanical magic, it could create something truly unprecedented.

"But there's more," Jingles lowered his voice conspiratorially, glancing around before pulling out one final sketch from his seemingly bottomless pockets. "I've been working on a new type of candy – sweets that can move and change on their own. Imagine sugar plum fairies that actually dance, or chocolate reindeer that prance through the air!"

Holly gasped as she watched the drawings on the page shift and move, the magical ink bringing the concepts to life before her eyes. This was the kind of project she'd dreamed of when she first arrived at the North Pole – a perfect fusion of culinary artistry and Christmas magic that could create genuine wonder.

She took a deep breath, drawing in the comforting scents of cinnamon, vanilla, and that indefinable essence of joy that permeated every corner of Santa's realm. The challenges ahead were daunting, but they were also thrilling. This wasn't just about making a centerpiece anymore; it was about pushing the boundaries of what Christmas magic could achieve.

"Jingles," she said, straightening her festive cap with determination, "I think this could be the beginning of something extraordinary. When can we start?"

The head toy designer's face lit up like a Christmas tree, and he immediately began spreading his sketches across Holly's workstation, their enchanted pages casting warm, twinkling lights across the freshly decorated cookies. As they began to plan, neither of them noticed Mrs. Claus watching from the doorway, a knowing smile on her face as she watched two of her favorite creators embarking on what promised to be a magnificent adventure.

Chapter 2: A Lesson in Patience

The workshop doors burst open with such enthusiasm that several nearby elves jumped, sending a cascade of ribbons floating through the air like festive confetti. Jingles bounded in, his signature silver bells creating a symphony of cheerful chimes that echoed through the cavernous space. Each bell had been carefully chosen and polished to perfection, their melodious tones a reflection of his perpetually optimistic spirit.

"Hello, hello my festive friends!" he called out, his voice carrying the warmth of fresh-baked cookies. His smile, dazzling enough to rival the Northern Lights, spread across his face as he surveyed the bustling workshop. "Ready to jingle all the way through this Christmas crunch?"

Several elves looked up from their workstations, their expressions a mix of amusement and mild apprehension. They knew Jingles well enough to recognize the telltale signs of his excitement - the slight bounce in his step, the way his pointed ears twitched with barely contained energy, and that particular gleam in his bright blue eyes that often preceded one of his "brilliant" ideas.

The workshop itself was a masterpiece of organized chaos, a whirlwind of activity that had been perfected over centuries of Christmas preparations. Ribbons in every shade imaginable twisted and curled through the air, caught in the gentle draft from the ventilation system that kept the space comfortably cool despite the dozens of busy elves. Wrapping paper in patterns both traditional and innovative lined the walls in neat rolls, their surfaces catching the light from the enchanted lanterns that floated near the ceiling.

Jingles bounced on the balls of his feet, his custom-made boots (complete with tiny bells on the laces) barely touching the ground. The scene before him was a feast for his innovation-hungry mind - toys in various stages of completion, each one representing a potential opportunity for "improvement."

"Oh boy, the toy assembly line is really humming along!" He clapped his hands together, the sound mixing with his jingling bells in a festive cacophony. His mind was already full to the brim with new ideas, each one more elaborate than the last. "I wonder if there are ways we could make things even more efficient this year..."

He darted over to the nearest table, his movement causing a slight breeze that ruffled the papers on nearby desks. Snickerdoodle, a veteran elf known for her impeccable attention to detail, was carefully dressing a collection of porcelain dolls. Each tiny button was being fastened with precision, each ribbon tied with perfect symmetry.

"Looking snazzy, Snickerdoodle!" Jingles leaned in close, his nose nearly touching the delicate fabric of a doll's dress. "I bet we could rig up a contraption to button those tiny dresses in a snap. Ooh, maybe something with rotating mechanical arms..." His hands moved animatedly as he described his vision, nearly knocking over a jar of buttons in his enthusiasm.

Snickerdoodle chuckled, the sound warm and patient like a mother addressing an overexcited child. Her fingers never stopped their careful work as she responded, "If anyone could dream that up, it's you Jingles. But maybe we should stick to the methods on Santa's nice list for now, hmm?" Her eyes crinkled at the corners, softening the gentle rebuke.

Undeterred, Jingles flitted to the next station like a hummingbird searching for nectar. Here, Whistleworth, an elf with a magnificent mustache that curled at the ends, was assembling intricate model trains. Each tiny component was being fitted together with mathematical precision, the resulting locomotives perfect miniatures of their full-sized counterparts.

As Jingles watched, the gears in his head turned faster than the wheels on the toy trains. There had to be a way to help his fellow elves work more efficiently. His talents - his wonderful, sometimes misunderstood talents - could really make the North Pole shine! He could already picture it: the workshop running like a well-oiled machine (quite literally, if he had his way), productivity soaring to unprecedented heights.

In his mind's eye, he saw himself standing triumphant amidst a sea of completed toys, his fellow elves cheering his name in gratitude. Santa would beam with pride, his jolly laugh booming through the workshop as he declared Jingles Employee of the Month. Maybe he'd even get an extra candy cane - one of those special ones with the sparkly sugar that only Santa could make...

"Focus, Jingles," he muttered under his breath, giving himself a small shake that set his bells tinkling. His reflection in a nearby ornament showed a determined elf with slightly disheveled auburn hair and a smattering of freckles across his nose. One step at a time. He just needed to find that first opportunity to lend his skills, to prove that his knack for "improving" things could pay off.

Jingles continued his circuit of the room, his bells creating a gentle melody that mixed with the whirring of machines and the cheerful chatter of his fellow elves. Each workstation was a miniature world unto itself, filled with the particular tools and touches of the elf who called it home. Tinker Tom's bench was neatly organized, his tools arranged by size and function. In contrast, Maple Sugarplum's area was a riot of color, with inspiration boards covered in drawings and swatches of fabric pinned haphazardly to every available surface.

"Maybe if I just tweak the conveyor speed a little," Jingles mused aloud, his fingers practically tingling with the urge to tinker. The massive conveyor belt that ran the length of the workshop was the beating heart of their operation, moving toys from station to station in a carefully choreographed dance. In Jingles' mind, he could already see the toys gliding by at a brisker pace, production numbers soaring. "No harm in a tiny adjustment, right?"

He waited until the other elves were absorbed in their work, the sounds of sawing, hammering, and cheerful humming creating the perfect cover. With exaggerated casualness, he tiptoed over to the control panel, his movements reminiscent of a cartoon character trying to be stealthy. The panel itself was a masterpiece of engineering, covered in dials, switches, and buttons that controlled every aspect of the conveyor system.

With one final furtive glance around, he reached for the main speed control. The dial was cool under his fingers as he turned it ever so slightly to the right. The conveyor's steady hum increased in pitch, almost imperceptibly at first. Toys began to move faster along the belt, and the elves at their stations quickened their pace to keep up.

"Trust me, it'll be great!" he called out, trying to project confidence as he noticed some concerned looks. His voice carried a slight tremor of uncertainty that he tried to mask with enthusiasm. "Just give it a minute and you'll see how much faster we can—"

His words were cut short by a sound that would haunt his dreams for weeks to come: the distinctive whoosh of a stuffed bear achieving lift-off. The toy sailed through the air in a graceful arc, followed immediately by an entire battalion of toy soldiers, their tiny painted faces seeming to share Jingles' expression of horror.

The workshop erupted into chaos as elves abandoned their posts to dive for the airborne toys. Workstations became impromptu shelters as more and more items gained momentum and took flight. Tinker Tom's meticulously organized tools scattered like pickup sticks as he ducked behind his bench to avoid a barrage of building blocks.

"Oh no, oh no! I can fix it, just—" Jingles' voice cracked with panic as he lunged back toward the control panel. His bells jangled frantically as he fumbled with the dial, but in his haste, he only managed to make things worse. The conveyor belt's speed increased further, and the situation devolved into complete pandemonium.

An elf named Twinkle stumbled backward into a towering stack of carefully packed gift boxes, setting off a chain reaction that sent them toppling like festive dominoes. Pepper Peppermint, usually the most graceful dancer at the North Pole's holiday parties, lost her footing on a runaway marble and went sliding across the floor, taking out a display of stuffed animals like a bowling ball hitting pins.

"Stop! Hold on!" Jingles shouted, his voice barely audible over the cacophony of chaos. With trembling hands, he finally located the emergency stop lever - a bright red handle that until now had never needed to be used. He yanked it down with perhaps more force than necessary, and the conveyor belt ground to a halt with a sound like a disappointed sigh.

The workshop fell into an eerie silence, broken only by the soft thump of the last few airborne toys finding their landing spots. Dozens of eyes turned to fix their gaze on Jingles, ranging from mildly annoyed to outright furious. He swallowed hard, feeling his face flush as red as Rudolph's nose.

"Um... sorry?" The word came out as more of a squeak than actual speech, his usual confidence deflated like a balloon that had met a pin.

Just then, a deep, jolly laugh echoed through the workshop, startling several elves who were still in defensive crouches. "Ho ho ho! What have we here?"

Santa Claus himself stood in the doorway, his impressive frame filling the space with both physical and magical presence. His eyes, twinkling behind wire-rimmed glasses that sat perfectly on his nose, took in the scene before him. Scattered toys littered the floor like debris after a particularly festive storm. Elves in various states of dishevelment were emerging from their makeshift shelters. And in the middle of it all stood Jingles, looking very much like he wished he could disappear into his jingling boots.

Santa strode into the workshop, each step measured and purposeful despite his considerable girth. His red suit, trimmed with the finest white fur, seemed to glow with its own inner light. He reached up to stroke his snowy white beard, a gesture that every elf knew meant he was deep in thought.

"Jingles, my boy," Santa said, his voice warm and booming yet somehow gentle. The sound wrapped around

Jingles like a cozy blanket, despite the circumstances. "I appreciate your enthusiasm, but remember: the road to the naughty list is paved with good intentions."

The words hit Jingles like a snowball to the heart. His shoulders slumped, and the bells on his hat gave a dejected little tinkle. "I just wanted to help, Santa. I thought if we could finish the toys faster, everyone would have more time to enjoy Christmas." His voice was small, but sincere.

Santa moved closer, navigating around scattered toys with surprising grace for someone of his size. He placed a warm, mittened hand on Jingles' shoulder, giving it a gentle squeeze that seemed to transfer some of his endless wisdom and compassion directly into the young elf's heart.

"Speed isn't everything, Jingles," Santa said, his eyes twinkling with understanding. "It's the care and love we put into each toy that makes them special. Every stitch, every brushstroke, every carefully placed gear - that's what creates the magic that brings joy to children on Christmas morning. Take your time, and the joy will come."

Around them, the other elves began to relax, some even nodding in agreement with Santa's words. Tinker Tom straightened his bow tie and offered Jingles a small smile. Maple Sugarplum had already started humming quietly as she retrieved scattered fabric scraps.

"Now," Santa continued, clapping his hands together with such enthusiasm that his belly gave a jolly shake, "how about we all take a cocoa break? On me."

A collective cheer went up at these words, and the remaining tension in the room melted away faster than a snowman in spring. The promise of Santa's special hot cocoa - made with chocolate that had been aged in candy cane barrels for a hundred years - could lift any spirit. Elves began filing out of the workshop, their chatter turning to excited discussions of marshmallow-to-whipped-cream ratios.

Jingles hung back, his eyes scanning the chaos he had created. Toys lay scattered like autumn leaves after a storm, the conveyor belt sat silent and reproachful, and several workstations looked like they had been hit by a miniature tornado. He knew he had a lot to learn, but Santa's words had planted a seed of understanding in his heart.

"Come on, Jingles," called Pepper Peppermint from the doorway, any trace of annoyance gone from her voice. "Don't miss out on the cocoa!"

He took a tentative step toward the door, then paused. "You go ahead. I'll catch up." The words came out soft but determined.

Once the workshop was empty, save for the lingering scent of peppermint and sawdust, Jingles set to work. One by one, he picked up the scattered toys, handling each with a new appreciation for the craftsmanship that had gone into them. He imagined each one in a child's hands on Christmas morning - the sparkle of joy in their eyes, the gasp of delight, the careful way they would explore every detail.

As Jingles carefully placed each toy back on the conveyor belt, his usual frenetic energy gave way to something quieter, more thoughtful. The workshop's magical lighting cast gentle shadows across the floor, and the distant sound of laughter and clinking cocoa mugs drifted through the walls. Each item he picked up told its own story - a teddy bear with slightly uneven stitching that somehow made it more lovable, a wooden train with delicate hand-painted details that caught the light just so.

"One step at a time," he whispered to himself, his voice barely disturbing the peaceful silence. The words felt different now, weighted with new understanding. His silver bells chimed softly as he moved, creating a gentle melody that seemed to match his more measured pace.

When the last toy was back in its proper place, Jingles stood in the center of the workshop, taking in the scene with fresh eyes. The conveyor belt, now properly adjusted to its original speed, waited patiently for tomorrow's work. Each workstation stood ready, tools and materials arranged with care and purpose. Even the emergency stop lever seemed to gleam with a certain dignity, as if proud of its role in the day's events.

With a lighter heart, he headed toward the door, the sound of celebration growing louder with each step. Just as he reached the threshold, he paused and looked back at the workshop - the heart of Christmas itself. In the quiet emptiness, he could almost feel the magic that Santa had spoken of, the love and care that went into every toy.

"I'll make sure of it," he said firmly, his voice carrying new resolve. With that promise made to himself and the workshop, he joined his friends.

The North Pole's main hall was alive with warmth and cheer when Jingles arrived. Elves gathered around circular tables, their faces glowing in the light of floating candles that bobbed gently near the ceiling. The massive stone fireplace crackled merrily, sending the scent of burning pine throughout the space. Santa's special cocoa steamed in oversized mugs, topped with whipped cream that sparkled with magical sugar crystals.

Holly caught his eye from across the room, her green eyes bright with warmth. She gestured to an empty seat beside her, and Jingles felt his heart do a little skip. As he made his way over, weaving between tables and dodging the occasional floating marshmallow (someone had clearly been experimenting with levitation spells again), he noticed how the light caught the copper highlights in her hair.

"Saved you some cocoa," Holly said as he sat down, pushing a mug toward him. The whipped cream had been artfully swirled into the shape of a Christmas tree, complete with tiny candy cane decorations. "I added an extra sprinkle of cinnamon, just how you like it."

Jingles felt his cheeks warm, and not just from the steam rising from the mug. "Thanks, Holly. That's... that's really thoughtful of you."

"Well," she said, a slight blush coloring her own cheeks, "I know it's been a rough day. Sometimes a little extra cinnamon is all it takes to make things better."

The cocoa was perfect - warm and sweet, with just the right balance of chocolate and spice. As Jingles sipped, he felt the last of his anxiety melt away. The conversation around them flowed easily, filled with laughter and plans for the upcoming Christmas season.

"You know," Holly said softly, her fingers tracing the rim of her mug, "what happened today... it wasn't all bad."

Jingles nearly choked on his cocoa. "Not all bad? Holly, I turned the workshop into a toy tornado!"

She laughed, the sound like silver bells in winter. "Yes, but look around." She gestured to their fellow elves, all enjoying their cocoa break together. "When was the last time everyone took a moment to just... be together like this? Usually we're all so focused on our work, we forget to enjoy each other's company."

Jingles considered her words, watching as Tinker Tom attempted to balance a spoon on his nose while Maple Sugarplum cheered him on. Even Santa was joining in the fun, performing his famous candy cane juggling trick to enthusiastic applause.

"Maybe you're right," he admitted, a small smile tugging at his lips. "Though I probably shouldn't make a habit of causing chaos just to get everyone to take a break."

"Probably not," Holly agreed, her eyes twinkling with mischief. "But speaking of habits... I heard you might be spending some time in the bakery?"

Jingles' face lit up at the mention of the bakery, his natural enthusiasm bubbling back to the surface. "Yes! Santa thought it might be a good place for me to... um... channel my creative energy." He ran a hand through his auburn hair, making his hat tilt at a slightly crooked angle. "Though I have to admit, I'm a bit nervous. I've never really baked anything before."

Holly's eyes softened with understanding. "Well, you're in luck. I happen to be an expert at teaching nervous elves how to bake." She leaned in conspiratorially, lowering her voice. "Want to know a secret? I was terrible when I first started. Burned more cookies than I care to admit."

"You?" Jingles couldn't hide his surprise. Holly was known throughout the North Pole for her incredible confections. Her gingerbread houses were architectural masterpieces, and her sugar cookies were said to contain actual stardust (though no one had ever proven this theory).

"Oh yes," she continued, a reminiscent smile playing across her lips. "There was this one time I mixed up salt and sugar in a batch of snickerdoodles. Poor Santa was too polite to say anything, but his face turned the same color as his suit!" She giggled at the memory, and Jingles found himself chuckling along.

"So there's hope for me yet?" he asked, his blue eyes twinkling with renewed optimism.

"More than hope," Holly assured him, reaching across the table to straighten his crooked hat. Her fingers brushed against his hair for just a moment, sending a shower of sparkles through his belly that had nothing to do with magical sugar. "I think you might surprise yourself. Baking is a lot like inventing, you know. It's all about creativity and precision working together."

The next morning dawned crisp and clear, the kind of winter day that made the North Pole feel like a snow globe come to life. Jingles stood outside the bakery's door, his breath forming little clouds in the frigid air. The building itself was a masterpiece of gingerbread architecture, its windows glowing with warm light and its roof dusted with perpetual powdered sugar snow that never melted.

Through the frosted windowpanes, he could see shapes moving about - elves preparing for another day of holiday baking. The scent of vanilla and cinnamon wafted through the air, making his stomach rumble appreciatively. Taking a deep breath, he reached for the door handle, which was shaped like a rolling pin.

"Okay, Jingles," he whispered to himself, his bells jingling softly with will power. "Time for a new adventure."

The warmth hit him like a hug as he stepped inside. The bakery was a symphony of sounds and smells - the whir of mixers, the clatter of baking sheets, the hollow thump of rolling pins against marble counters. Every surface gleamed with well-maintained cleanliness, and the air was thick with flour dust that sparkled in the morning light.

"Well, well, well!" a voice called out, making Jingles jump. "Look who's finally decided to join the sweet side!"

Pepper Mintington, the head baker, emerged from behind a tower of cooling racks, her white apron already dusted with cocoa powder despite the early hour. Her silver hair was twisted into an elaborate bun held in place by two candy cane pins, and her eyes sparkled with good humor behind spectacles that were slightly fogged from the ovens' heat.

"Good morning, Miss Mintington," Jingles said, trying to stand up straighter. "I'm here to... well, to learn."

"Just Pepper, dear," she corrected, wiping her hands on her apron. "Miss Mintington makes me sound like a candy cane that's lost its stripe! Now, let's get you properly outfitted for bakery work."

She disappeared into a back room and returned with a pristine white apron, embroidered with tiny golden bells along the hem. "Holly mentioned you might be joining us, so I had this made special. Can't have you working without your signature jingle, can we?"

Jingles held the special apron reverently, his fingers tracing the golden bells embroidered along the hem. Each tiny bell was stitched with remarkable detail, catching the light just as his real ones did. As he slipped it over his head, the fabric settled around him like a warm hug, smelling faintly of vanilla.

"Now then," Pepper said, clapping her flour-dusted hands together, "let's start you off with something simple. Holly!" She called out toward the back of the bakery. "Your apprentice has arrived!"

Holly emerged from behind a row of industrial-sized ovens, carrying a tray of freshly baked sugar cookies. Her cheeks were flushed from the heat, and a dusting of flour streaked across her forehead like a wayward snowfall. When she saw Jingles in his new apron, her face lit up with a smile that made his bells tingle of their own accord.

"Perfect timing!" she exclaimed, setting down the tray. "We're just about to start the morning batch of candy cane cookies. They're a bit tricky, but I think you'll enjoy the process - lots of precise twisting and turning involved."

Jingles followed Holly to a large marble workstation, trying not to feel overwhelmed by the array of tools laid out before him. Rolling pins of various sizes gleamed in the warm light, alongside measuring cups, spatulas, and mysterious implements he couldn't even name.

"First rule of magical baking," Holly said, reaching for a bowl of glittering sugar, "is that every ingredient has its own personality. You have to respect each one, or they might decide to misbehave." She picked up a crystal that seemed to pulse with an inner light. "Take North Star sugar, for example. It only dissolves properly if you sing to it while stirring."

"Sing to it?" Jingles asked, his eyes wide with fascination.

"Mm-hmm. Christmas carols work best, but it's particularly fond of 'Silent Night.'" She demonstrated, her voice soft and sweet as she sprinkled the sugar into a mixing bowl. The crystals sparkled and swirled, creating tiny constellations before dissolving into the dough.

"That's amazing!" Jingles leaned in closer, his bells jingling with excitement. "What other magical ingredients do we use?"

"Well," Holly said, reaching for a jar filled with what looked like ordinary cinnamon, "this is Aurora spice. It's harvested from the northern lights themselves. Makes the cookies glow slightly when you bite into them. And over here..." She pointed to a bottle of vanilla extract that seemed to be floating slightly above the counter, "Cloudvapor vanilla. Collected from the highest, fluffiest clouds on Christmas Eve."

As Holly explained each ingredient, Jingles found himself drawn into the magical science of baking. It wasn't so different from his tinkering, really - just a different kind of invention.

"Ready to try making your first batch?" Holly asked, holding out a measuring cup filled with flour that sparkled like fresh snow.

"I... yes?" Jingles said, though it came out more like a question. He reached for the cup, trying to steady his slightly shaking hands.

"Don't worry," Holly reassured him, her hand brushing against his as she helped him hold the measuring cup. "I'll be right here to help. And remember - even if something goes wrong, we can always try again. That's the beauty of baking."

Under Holly's patient guidance, Jingles began measuring ingredients. His natural precision came in handy as he carefully leveled each cup of flour, though he did have a slight mishap with the Aurora spice that left him temporarily glowing like a Christmas light.

"Now for the tricky part," Holly announced, rolling out the candy cane dough into long strips. "We need to twist these together to get the proper stripe pattern. It's all in the wrist movement..."

Jingles watched intently as Holly demonstrated the proper technique for twisting the candy cane dough. Her hands moved with practiced grace, creating perfect red and white spirals that seemed to shimmer with holiday magic. The red dough was infused with crushed candy crystals that gave off a subtle peppermint aroma, while the white sparkled with that mysterious North Star sugar.

"Your turn," Holly said, stepping aside to give him room at the workstation. "Remember, gentle but confident movements. The dough can sense hesitation."

Jingles took a deep breath and picked up two strips of dough. His first attempt at twisting resulted in something that looked more like a pretzel than a candy cane, but Holly's encouraging smile kept him from getting discouraged.

"That's actually not bad for a first try," she said, adjusting his hands slightly. "Here, let me show you..." She stepped behind him, her arms reaching around to guide his movements. Jingles felt his cheeks flush warm enough to rival the ovens, very aware of how close she was standing.

"See? Like this," Holly continued, helping him create a perfect twist. "The red stripe needs to catch the light just right, or the Christmas magic won't activate properly."

"Christmas magic?" Jingles asked, trying to focus on the task and not on how his bells were chiming in harmony with his racing heart.

"Oh yes," Holly nodded, stepping back to let him try again on his own. "Every candy cane we make here has a specific purpose. Some bring sweet dreams on Christmas Eve, others help reindeer fly higher, and a special few..." she lowered her voice conspiratorially, "...can even make grumpy adults remember what it feels like to believe in Santa."

Jingles' next attempt at twisting came out much better, the stripes aligning perfectly. "That's incredible! I had no idea there was so much magic in baking."

"Most people don't," Holly said, beginning to shape the twisted dough into curved canes. "They think it's all just sugar and spice. But here at the North Pole, every cookie, every candy cane, every gingerbread house has its own special magic. It's not about how quickly you can make them - it's about the love and care you put into each one."

The words echoed Santa's advice from the day before, and Jingles felt something click into place in his understanding. He looked down at the candy cane in his hands, really seeing it for the first time - not as just another item to be produced, but as a vessel for Christmas magic itself.

"I think I'm starting to understand," he said softly, carefully placing his completed candy cane on a baking sheet.

The stripes seemed to glow faintly, responding to his newfound appreciation.

"Wonderful!" Pepper called out from across the bakery, where she had been quietly observing. "Because we have about three thousand more to make before Christmas!"

Jingles' eyes widened in alarm, but Holly just laughed, the sound as sweet as the treats they were creating. "Don't worry," she said, bumping his shoulder playfully with her own. "We'll make them all, one candy cane at a time. Quality over quantity, remember?"

As the morning progressed, Jingles found himself falling into a comfortable rhythm. His natural dexterity, usually applied to tinkering with gadgets, translated well to the precise movements required for candy cane crafting. The bakery filled with the scent of peppermint and warming sugar, and the sound of holiday music mixed with friendly chatter and the occasional jingle of his bells.

By mid-afternoon, Jingles had settled into a comfortable groove. His workspace was dusted with flour and sparkles of North Star sugar, and a respectable collection of candy canes lined the cooling racks. Each one might not have been perfect, but they all held that subtle glow of Christmas magic that marked them as genuine North Pole creations.

"Look at these!" Holly exclaimed, holding one of his candy canes up to the light. The stripes spiraled perfectly, and the curve was just right. "Jingles, these are wonderful! And do you see how they're glowing? That only happens when they're made with true holiday spirit."

Jingles felt a warmth spread through his chest that had nothing to do with the heat from the ovens. "Really? I thought maybe I'd gotten some extra Aurora spice on them or something."

"No, this is different," Holly said, her green eyes sparkling. "This is pure Christmas magic. Here, watch..." She took the candy cane and touched it gently to one of his bells. Immediately, a soft, melodious chime rang out - sweeter and clearer than any sound his bells had ever made before.

"How did you...?" Jingles started to ask, but he was interrupted by the arrival of a small group of young elves, their faces pressed against the bakery's window.

"Oh! It's time for the afternoon cookie delivery to the elfling school," Holly explained. "Want to help? It's my favorite part of the day."

Together, they loaded a cart with still-warm cookies, each one decorated with holiday scenes that moved and sparkled. Jingles watched in amazement as tiny frosting reindeer pranced across sugar cookies and miniature Christmas trees twinkled with edible lights.

As they pushed the cart through the snowy streets of the North Pole, Holly explained how each treat was specially designed to help young elves learn their Christmas crafts. "The gingerbread stars help with navigation lessons - they point true North, you see. And these peppermint swirls? They help with memorizing carol lyrics."

The elflings greeted them with unbridled enthusiasm, their small faces lighting up at the sight of the magical treats. Jingles found himself drawn into their excitement, demonstrating how his candy canes could make music when tapped against different surfaces. The pure joy in their laughter made his heart feel like it might burst.

Back at the bakery, the afternoon light was turning golden, filtering through the frosted windows and making everything glow. Pepper was teaching a group of elves how to make snowflake cookies that would float in hot cocoa, and the

Christmas on Peppermint Lane

air was filled with the scent of melting chocolate and warm spices.

"Thank you," Jingles said softly to Holly as they cleaned their workstation. "For today, for teaching me, for... everything."

Holly looked up, a smudge of flour on her nose making her look even more endearing than usual. "You don't need to thank me, Jingles. You belonged here all along - you just needed to find your way to it."

"Still," he insisted, reaching out to gently brush the flour from her nose before he could stop himself. "I've learned more today than just how to make candy canes. I think I finally understand what Santa meant about taking time and putting love into things."

Holly's cheeks turned pink, matching the peppermint swirls in her apron. "Well, you're welcome to come back tomorrow. We're making aurora borealis bonbons, and I could use a partner who knows how to make things sparkle."

Before Jingles could respond, there was a commotion at the front of the bakery. Santa himself had arrived, drawn by the scent of fresh baking and, if his twinkling eyes were any indication, more than a little curiosity about how his troublemaker elf was faring in his new role.

"Well, well!" Santa boomed, his jolly voice filling the space. "What's this I hear about musical candy canes?" He picked up one of Jingles' creations, examining it with expert eyes. "Remarkable! And look at that glow - I haven't seen candy canes with this much Christmas spirit since... well, since Mrs. Claus made them herself!"

Jingles felt his pointed ears turn red at the high praise. "It was all Holly's teaching, sir. She helped me understand how to put the magic in."

"Oh, I think you had the magic all along, my boy," Santa said knowingly. "You just needed to find the right way to let it out." He turned to address the entire bakery. "I do believe this calls for a celebration! Hot cocoa for everyone - with extra marshmallows!"

As the bakery erupted in cheers and elves rushed to gather around the big marble counter, Jingles felt Holly's hand slip into his. Her fingers were warm and slightly rough from working with dough all day, and they fit perfectly between his own.

"See?" she whispered. "Sometimes the best inventions aren't machines at all. Sometimes they're moments like this."

Jingles squeezed her hand gently, his bells chiming softly in agreement. Looking around at the joyful faces of his fellow elves, the warmth of the bakery, and the magic that seemed to float in the very air, he knew she was right. He had finally found his place in the North Pole's grand symphony of Christmas magic - not as a rushing innovator, but as a creator of sweet moments and magical memories.

And as Santa passed out mugs of cocoa, each one topped with a perfectly floating snowflake cookie, Jingles realized that this truly was going to be the best Christmas ever - just not in the way he had originally planned.

Chapter 3: The Glittery Encounter

Holly hunched over her design sketches, brows knitted in concentration. Her pencil danced across the page, bringing to life swirls of icing, gumdrop pathways, and intricate candy cane arches. She paused, tapping the eraser against her lips. *The roof needs more sparkle*, she mused. *But not too much. It has to be perfect.*

The bakery door burst open with a merry jingle, shattering Holly's focus. Jingles bounded inside, his cheeks flushed with cold and eyes twinkling.

"Hiya Holly!" he called, skidding to a stop beside her. "Whatcha working on?"

"Oh! Hi Jingles," Holly stammered, flustered by his sudden appearance. She self-consciously tidied her sketches. "Just some designs for the gingerbread festival. I want to make sure they're flawless."

Jingles leaned in, scrutinizing the drawings. His brow furrowed for a moment before breaking into a wide grin. "Holly, these are amazing! You've got a real talent."

A blush crept into Holly's cheeks at the compliment. "Thanks. I just hope I can do them justice in the actual houses."

"Are you kidding? With your baking skills, they'll be even better in gingerbread form!" Jingles proclaimed. He winked at her. "I bet they'll be the talk of Frostyville."

Despite her nerves, Holly couldn't help but smile at his infectious enthusiasm. *Maybe he's right,* she thought. *I shouldn't doubt myself so much.*

She took a deep breath, gathering her courage. "Hey Jingles, I could actually use a second opinion on these. Do you have a few minutes to take a look?"

Jingles' face lit up. "I'd love to! Let's see what sugary magic you've dreamed up."

As they huddled over the sketches together, heads bent close, Holly felt a warmth blossoming in her chest that had nothing to do with the cozy bakery. *There's just something about him,* she realized, sneaking a glance at Jingles' eager face. *Something special.*

Outside, snow began to fall, blanketing Frostyville in a fresh layer of glittering white. But inside the North Pole Bakery, a different kind of magic was stirring - the sweet, unexpected magic of two hearts drawing closer.

Jingles' eyes darted around the bakery, searching for a way to make himself useful. His gaze landed on a tub of edible glitter perched high on a shelf, just out of reach. A mischievous grin spread across his face as an idea took hold.

"I've got it!" he exclaimed, rubbing his hands together. "That glitter is just what these gingerbread houses need. A little extra sparkle to make them really shine!"

Before Holly could respond, Jingles was already scaling the shelf, his nimble fingers finding purchase on the smooth wood. He moved with the agility of a squirrel, his bells jingling merrily with each step.

Holly's eyes widened as she watched him climb higher and higher. "Jingles, be careful!" she called out, her voice laced with concern. "That shelf isn't meant to hold weight."

But Jingles was too focused on his mission to heed her warning. He stretched his arm out, fingertips grazing the edge of the glitter tub. "Almost... got it..." he grunted, tongue poking out in concentration.

Holly's heart raced as she saw the shelf begin to wobble under Jingles' weight. "Jingles, watch out!" she cried, rushing forward. But it was too late.

With a resounding crash, the shelf gave way, sending Jingles tumbling to the ground in a flurry of limbs and bells. The glitter tub flew from his grasp, spinning through the air in a dizzying arc.

Time seemed to slow as Holly watched in horror, her mind flashing to the hours of work she'd poured into her gingerbread sketches. *Not the designs!* she thought desperately, reaching out as if to catch the falling tub.

But Jingles was quicker. With a burst of speed, he lunged forward, snatching the tub mere inches before it hit the ground. He landed in a heap, glitter raining down around him like a shimmering curtain.

For a moment, the only sound was the tinkling of Jingles' bells and the pounding of Holly's heart. Then, slowly, Jingles sat up, a sheepish grin on his face. "Ta-da!" he said weakly, holding up the glitter tub. "Saved the sparkle."

Despite the chaos, Holly couldn't help but laugh. The tension drained from her body as she shook her head in amazement. "Jingles Evergreen," she said, trying to sound stern even as a smile tugged at her lips. "You nearly gave me a heart attack."

Jingles scrambled to his feet, brushing glitter from his hat. "Sorry about that," he said, his cheeks flushing beneath the dusting of sparkles. "I just wanted to help."

Holly's gaze softened as she took in his earnest expression. *He really does mean well*, she thought, feeling a tug of affection in her chest. Even if his methods are a bit... unconventional.

She sighed, offering him a small smile. "I appreciate the thought," she said gently. "But maybe next time, we can find a way to add sparkle that doesn't involve death-defying acrobatics?"

Jingles let out a relieved chuckle. "Deal," he said, extending his hand for a handshake. "Partners in shine, but with a little more caution?"

As Holly took his hand, she felt a spark of electricity pass between them. His touch was warm and steady, and she found herself lost for words. She swallowed hard, trying to ignore the way her pulse quickened.

Get it together, Holly, she scolded herself. *You've got gingerbread houses to build, not daydreams to get lost in.*

But as they stood there, hand in hand, surrounded by a sea of glitter, Holly couldn't shake the feeling that something special was unfolding - something sweet and unexpected and filled with the magic of the season.

Holly reluctantly pulled her hand away from Jingles', the lingering warmth of his touch leaving her fingers tingling. She surveyed the bakery, now transformed into a glittering wonderland, and couldn't help but marvel at the unexpected beauty of the chaos.

"Well," she said, brushing a stray lock of hair from her face, "I suppose we should start cleaning up. Can't have the North Pole Bakery looking like a disco ball exploded."

Jingles grinned, his eyes sparkling with mischief. "I don't know," he teased, "I think it adds a certain je ne sais quoi. But if you insist..."

He grabbed a broom and began sweeping the glitter into a pile, his movements exaggerated and comical. Holly couldn't help but laugh as she watched him work, his enthusiasm infectious.

He's like a breath of fresh air, she thought, surprised by the warmth blooming in her chest. *I've been so focused on perfection, on getting everything just right, that I've forgotten how to have fun.*

As they cleaned, they fell into an easy rhythm, their conversation flowing naturally. Jingles regaled her with tales of his misadventures in the workshop, his voice filled with self-deprecating humor and genuine

warmth. Holly found herself opening up in return, sharing her dreams for the bakery and her hopes for the future.

"You know," Jingles said, pausing to lean on his broom, "I've always admired your work. The way you put so much heart into everything you create - it's inspiring."

Holly felt a blush creep into her cheeks. "Thank you," she said softly, "that means a lot. I've always loved baking, ever since I was a little girl. There's something magical about creating something that brings joy to others."

Jingles nodded, his expression thoughtful. "I feel the same way about my inventions," he said. "Even when they don't quite turn out as planned, the process of creation - of dreaming something up and bringing it to life - it's exhilarating."

As they talked, the bakery slowly returned to its former glory, the glitter swept away and the surfaces wiped clean. But something had shifted between them, a new understanding forged in the midst of the unexpected.

Maybe perfection isn't everything, Holly mused, watching Jingles as he put away the cleaning supplies. *Maybe sometimes, the most beautiful things come from embracing the chaos.*

And as Jingles turned to her with a smile, his eyes filled with warmth and promise, Holly couldn't help but feel that the real magic of the season was just beginning to unfold.

Holly brushed a stray speck of glitter from her hair, her fingers coming away sparkling in the warm bakery light. She couldn't quite suppress the sigh that escaped her lips, a mixture of exasperation and reluctant amusement. *How did I get myself into this mess?* she wondered, her gaze drifting to the elf responsible for the chaos.

Jingles stood before her, his hat slightly askew and his cheeks flushed with embarrassment. "Holly, I'm so sorry," he said, his voice carrying a genuine note of apology. "I never meant for this to happen. I just wanted to help, but I guess I got a little carried away."

Despite her annoyance, Holly couldn't help but be charmed by the sincerity in his voice. There was something about Jingles that made it impossible to stay mad at him for long, even when he'd just covered her entire bakery in a layer of shimmering glitter.

"It's okay, Jingles," she found herself saying, her lips twitching into a small smile. "Accidents happen. And I have to admit, the bakery does look rather magical now, doesn't it?"

Jingles' face lit up at her words, his eyes sparkling with relief and gratitude. "It does indeed! But still, I feel terrible about the mess. Please, let me help you clean it up."

Holly hesitated for a moment, her perfectionist nature warring with the part of her that longed to spend more time in Jingles' presence. It would be faster with two, she reasoned, trying to ignore the flutter in her chest at the thought of working alongside him.

"Alright," she agreed, handing him a broom. "But try not to knock over any more glitter, okay? I think we've had enough magic for one day."

Jingles laughed, the sound as warm and inviting as a mug of hot cocoa on a cold winter's night. "I make no promises," he teased, "but I'll do my best."

As they set to work, sweeping up the glittering remnants of Jingles' mishap, Holly couldn't help but steal glances at the elf beside her. There was something about the way he moved, the energy and enthusiasm he brought to even the most mundane tasks, that made her heart beat just a little bit faster.

Stop it, she chided herself, focusing intently on the floor before her. *You barely know him. And besides, you have a bakery to run. There's no time for distractions, no matter how charming they may be.*

But even as she tried to push the thoughts away, Holly knew that something had shifted between them. The spark she'd felt when their eyes first met among the glittery chaos hadn't been imagined. And as they worked together, their conversation flowing as easily as the icing on her famous sugar cookies, she couldn't help but wonder where this unexpected connection might lead.

One step at a time, she reminded herself, sneaking another glance at Jingles as he hummed a cheerful tune under his breath. Let's get through this cleanup first. And then...who knows what the future might hold?

With a smile playing at the corners of her mouth, Holly turned her attention back to the task at hand, her heart feeling lighter than it had in years. Perhaps a little chaos wasn't such a bad thing after all, especially when it came in the form of a mischievous elf with a heart of gold.

Holly hesitated for a moment, her grip tightening on the broom handle as she considered Jingles' offer. Part of her wanted to refuse, to maintain the careful distance she'd cultivated over the years. But there was something about his earnest expression, the genuine remorse in his eyes, that made her pause.

"Alright," she said at last, a tentative smile tugging at her lips. "I suppose many hands make light work, as they say."

Jingles' face lit up with a grin that rivaled the twinkling lights strung throughout the bakery. "Exactly! And I promise, I'm much better at cleaning up messes than I am at making them. Usually."

He grabbed a dustpan and began sweeping the glitter into a neat pile, his movements surprisingly graceful for someone who had just caused such chaos. Holly watched him for a moment, a chuckle escaping her lips as she shook her head in amusement.

"I have to ask," she said, joining him in the cleanup efforts, "is it always this exciting in Santa's workshop?"

Jingles laughed, the sound as warm and inviting as a mug of hot cocoa on a cold winter's night. "Oh, you have no idea! Why, just last week, I accidentally set off a whole batch of rocket-powered reindeer toys. They were zooming around the workshop for hours!"

As they worked, trading stories and laughter, Holly felt herself relaxing in Jingles' presence. There was something about his easy charm, the way he found joy in even the most mundane tasks, that made her heart beat just a little bit faster.

"You know," she said, pausing to brush a stray lock of hair from her face, "I've always loved the magic of Christmas. It's what drew me to baking in the first place - the idea of creating something that could bring a smile to someone's face, even if just for a moment."

Jingles nodded, his expression softening with understanding. "That's the real magic, isn't it? The joy we can bring to others, the memories we create together."

His words struck a chord within Holly, and she found herself nodding in agreement. "Exactly. And that's why I pour my heart into every recipe, every design. Because I know that somewhere out there, someone will be enjoying a little piece of that magic."

As they continued to clean, their conversation flowed effortlessly from one topic to the next. Jingles regaled her with tales of his misadventures in the workshop, his eyes sparkling with mirth as he recounted the time he'd accidentally dyed a batch of teddy bears bright purple. In turn, Holly found herself sharing stories of her own baking mishaps, the laughter they shared easing the sting of past failures.

Before long, the bakery floor was sparkling once more, every last speck of glitter swept away. Holly looked around with a satisfied smile, her heart full of a warmth she hadn't felt in years.

"Thank you, Jingles," she said, turning to face him. "I couldn't have done this without you."

He grinned, giving her a playful wink. "Anytime, Holly. After all, what are friends for?"

Friends. The word hung in the air between them, a promise of something more than just a chance encounter. And as Holly watched Jingles depart with a cheerful wave, his bells jingling merrily, she knew that her life would never be quite the same again.

But perhaps, she thought, a smile playing at the corners of her mouth, that's not such a bad thing after all.

The tinkling of bells announced a new arrival, drawing Holly and Jingles' attention to the bakery door. Pepper Minthaven stepped inside, his green eyes twinkling with amusement as he took in the scene before him. A knowing smirk played on his lips, and he stroked his pointed beard thoughtfully.

"Well, well, well," Pepper chuckled, his voice warm and playful. "What do we have here? A couple of glitter-covered elves hard at work, I see."

Holly felt a blush creep into her cheeks, suddenly self-conscious of her disheveled appearance. She brushed a stray lock of hair from her face, leaving a trail of shimmering specks in its wake.

Jingles, on the other hand, seemed unfazed by Pepper's teasing. He grinned broadly, gesturing to the now-spotless bakery floor. "Just lending a helping hand, Pepper. You know me, always ready to jump in and save the day!"

Pepper raised an eyebrow, his expression a mix of amusement and skepticism. "Is that so? And here I thought you were more likely to cause the chaos than clean it up."

Holly couldn't help but laugh at the good-natured ribbing between the two friends. There was an ease to their banter that spoke of a long history together, and she found herself envying their camaraderie.

As if sensing her thoughts, Pepper turned his attention to Holly, his eyes softening with warmth. "You must be Holly Sugarplum. I've heard great things about your baking skills. Though I must say, I didn't expect to find you covered in glitter today."

Holly smiled ruefully, dusting off her apron. "It's been an... interesting morning, to say the least."

Pepper nodded, a mischievous glint in his eye. "Well, if you ever need a taste-tester for your creations, you know where to find me. I'm always happy to lend my expert opinion."

With a final wink and a cheerful wave, Pepper departed, leaving Holly and Jingles alone once more. The bakery seemed quieter in his absence, but the air still hummed with a newfound energy.

Holly turned to Jingles, a smile playing at the corners of her mouth. "Thank you again for your help, Jingles. I don't know what I would have done without you."

Jingles beamed, his blue eyes sparkling with warmth. "Anytime, Holly. I'm always happy to lend a hand, especially when it comes to spreading a little joy and laughter."

As they finished tidying up the last of the glitter, Holly couldn't help but marvel at the way their teamwork had transformed the bakery. The floors gleamed, the counters sparkled, and even the air seemed to shimmer with a newfound magic.

But it wasn't just the bakery that had changed. Holly could feel a subtle shift within herself, a warmth that had nothing to do with the ovens and everything to do with the elf beside her. Jingles' presence had brought a lightness to her heart, a sense of possibility that she hadn't felt in years.

Perhaps, she thought, sneaking a glance at Jingles as he put away the broom, there's more to this holiday season than just gingerbread and glitter. Perhaps there's a chance for something more, something unexpected and wonderful.

And as they stood together in the tidy bakery, the scent of cinnamon and sugar lingering in the air, Holly knew that whatever the future held, she was ready to embrace it with open arms and a heart full of hope.

Jingles turned to face Holly, his smile as bright as the North Star. "Well, I'd better be off. Lots of mischief to manage and joy to spread, you know." He winked playfully, the bells on his hat jingling with the movement.

Holly laughed, shaking her head in amusement. "I don't doubt it for a second. Just try not to cause too much chaos out there, okay?"

"No promises!" Jingles grinned, his eyes twinkling with mirth. "But I'll do my best to keep the glitter explosions to a minimum."

As he made his way towards the door, Holly felt a sudden pang of reluctance. She didn't want him to leave, not when she'd just begun to discover the magic he brought into her life.

"Jingles, wait!" she called out, surprising herself with the urgency in her voice.

He paused, turning back to face her with a curious tilt of his head. "Yes, Holly?"

She hesitated, searching for the right words. "I just wanted to say... thank you. For everything. You've made this day so much brighter than I could have imagined."

Jingles' expression softened, his smile gentler than before. "It was my pleasure, Holly. Truly. And who knows? Maybe we'll find ourselves in the midst of another glittery adventure soon enough."

With a final wink and a joyful jingle of his bells, Jingles slipped out the door, leaving Holly alone with her thoughts and the lingering warmth of his presence.

Another adventure, she mused, a smile playing at the corners of her lips. I think I'd like that very much.

And as she turned back to her gingerbread sketches, Holly couldn't help but feel a thrill of anticipation for what the future might hold. With Jingles by her side, anything seemed possible – even in a world as magical as the North Pole.

Chapter 4: The Runaway Candy Cane

The bakery door burst open, silver bells chiming merrily as Jingles bounded inside, his auburn curls bouncing beneath his lopsided hat. "Holly, I've got it! The most candy-tastic idea for our window display!"

Holly glanced up from the tray of cookies she was frosting, a smudge of green icing on her cheek. "Oh?" She arched an eyebrow, equal parts intrigued and wary. Jingles' ideas often walked the fine line between brilliance and disaster.

"Picture this," Jingles said, sweeping his arms wide. "A giant candy cane, taller than a polar bear, brighter than Rudolph's nose! It'll be a real treat for the eyes, the perfect way to spruce up the holiday season!"

Despite herself, Holly felt a grin tugging at the corners of her mouth. Jingles' enthusiasm was infectious, even if his plans sometimes led to sticky situations. Still, she hesitated, images of toppled displays and shattered sugar flashing through her mind.

"I don't know, Jingles," she said, setting down her piping bag. "A giant candy cane? Isn't that a bit...ambitious?" She tried to picture the logistics, the potential for chaos. Yet even as she voiced her doubts, a part of her was already imagining the awe on children's faces, the joy such a display could bring.

Jingles' eyes sparkled with mischief. "Ambitious? More like candy-licious!" He grinned, undeterred by her reservations. "Come on, Holly-day, where's your sense of adventure? Your dash of daring? This could be the sweetest thing since hot cocoa!"

Holly bit her lip, torn between caution and curiosity. Jingles had a way of making even the most outlandish ideas seem possible, his optimism as bright as the North Pole stars. And if she was honest with herself, the thought of creating something so unique, so eye-catching, sent a thrill of excitement through her.

She sighed, a smile playing at her lips. "Alright, you sugar-coated troublemaker. I'm in."

Jingles let out a whoop of delight, his hat bells jingling with glee. "Yes! This is going to be epic, Holly! A candy cane for the ages!"

As he launched into a flurry of pun-filled plans, Holly shook her head fondly, caught up in his exuberance despite her lingering reservations. She had a feeling this project would be anything but simple.

The North Pole Bakery buzzed with activity as Jingles and Holly gathered the ingredients for their ambitious candy cane project. Bags of sugar, peppermint extract, and food coloring lined the countertop, a vibrant array of ideas.

"Alright, my sweet sidekick," Jingles quipped, tying an apron around his waist. "Ready to rock this candy cane?"

Holly chuckled, her own apron already dusted with flour. "As ready as I'll ever be, you peppermint pixie."

They fell into a rhythm, Holly carefully measuring out the sugar while Jingles enthusiastically poured in the peppermint extract. The scent of sweet mint filled the air, a tangible reminder of the holiday magic they were creating.

"You know, Holly," Jingles mused, stirring the mixture with gusto, "this candy cane is going to be a real *treat* for the eyes!"

Holly groaned, even as a smile tugged at her lips. "Jingles, your puns are going to be the death of me."

"Oh, come on! My puns are *mint* to be!" He winked, his impish grin irresistible.

As they worked, the candy cane mixture began to take shape, the white sugar transforming into a glossy, peppermint-streaked confection. Jingles took the lead on stirring, his nimble fingers working the mixture with practiced ease.

Holly couldn't help but admire his dedication, the way he threw himself into every task with unbridled enthusiasm. It was one of the things she lov- liked about him, she corrected herself quickly, a blush warming her cheeks.

The sweet aroma of peppermint grew stronger, a delightful contrast to the usual scents of gingerbread and vanilla that permeated the bakery. Holly added a few drops of red food coloring, watching in satisfaction as the mixture swirled into the iconic candy cane stripes.

"Looking good, Holly!" Jingles praised, peering over her shoulder. "You've got a real talent for this!"

His nearness sent a flutter through her stomach, and she ducked her head to hide her pleased smile. "Well, I learned from the best."

As they poured the mixture onto the cooling table, Holly couldn't help but marvel at the vibrant colors, the glossy sheen of the candy. It was really happening - they were creating something extraordinary, together.

She glanced at Jingles, his face alight with joy and mischief, and felt a swell of affection in her chest. Maybe, just maybe, this candy cane adventure would be the start of something even sweeter.

As the candy cane mixture cooled on the table, Holly's brow furrowed, her keen baker's instincts alerting her that something wasn't quite right. The mixture seemed to be bubbling more vigorously than usual, tiny pockets of air forming and popping on the surface.

"Jingles, does this look... odd to you?" she asked, her voice tinged with concern.

Jingles leaned in, his eyes narrowing as he studied the mixture. "Hmm, it does seem a bit more lively than usual. But I'm sure it's just excited to become the world's greatest candy cane!"

Despite his reassuring words, Holly couldn't shake the feeling that something was amiss. She checked the temperature, her heart sinking as she realized it was several degrees higher than it should be.

"Oh no, I think we might have overheated the mixture," she fretted, her mind racing with potential solutions. "If we don't cool it down quickly, it could-"

Her words were cut off by a sudden eruption, the candy cane mixture surging upward like a sugary volcano. Jingles yelped in surprise, his hands darting out to try and contain the impending disaster.

"Quick, grab a spatula!" he cried, his movements a blur of frantic energy as he attempted to corral the runaway mixture.

Holly lunged for the nearest utensil, her fingers closing around a large metal spoon. She joined Jingles at the cooling table, her heart pounding as they fought to keep the candy cane from spilling onto the floor.

This can't be happening, she thought, a bead of sweat trickling down her temple. *We were so close to creating something magical, and now...*

But even as panic threatened to overwhelm her, Holly couldn't help but be impressed by Jingles' quick thinking. He worked tirelessly beside her, his brow furrowed in concentration as he wielded a spatula like a sugary sword.

"Don't worry, Holly," he panted, flashing her a reassuring grin. "We've got this under control. It's just a little Christmas chaos, that's all!"

His optimism was infectious, and Holly found herself smiling despite the sticky situation they'd found themselves in. Together, they managed to guide the errant mixture back into a semblance of control, their teamwork proving stronger than any sugary mishap.

As the candy cane slowly began to cool and harden, Holly let out a sigh of relief. "That was close," she breathed, wiping a smudge of sugar

from her cheek. "I thought for sure we were going to end up with a peppermint puddle."

Jingles chuckled, his eyes sparkling with mirth. "Nah, not on my watch. Besides, a little chaos just adds to the fun, don't you think?"

Holly shook her head, trying to hide the smile tugging at her lips. "You're incorrigible, you know that?"

"And you love it," Jingles teased, bumping his shoulder against hers.

As they stood there, surrounded by the sweet scent of peppermint and the glow of averted disaster, Holly couldn't help but think that maybe, just maybe, a little chaos wasn't so bad after all. Especially when it came with a side of Jingles' infectious laughter and unwavering support.

Holly reached for a towel to clean up the remaining sticky residue, her mind still reeling from the unexpected adventure. As she leaned across the counter, her foot caught on a stray mixing spoon that had fallen amidst the chaos. With a yelp of surprise, she felt herself losing balance, the towel slipping from her grasp.

Time seemed to slow as Holly braced herself for impact, but instead of the hard floor, she found herself cradled in Jingles' strong arms. He had moved with lightning speed, his reflexes honed from years of navigating the unpredictable world of Santa's workshop.

For a moment, they stood frozen, their faces mere inches apart. Holly's heart raced, though whether it was from the fall or the sudden proximity to Jingles, she couldn't be sure. His eyes, usually filled with mischief, now held a softness she'd never noticed before.

He smells like cinnamon and sugar, Holly thought, her mind momentarily drifting from the absurdity of their situation. *And his arms are so warm...*

Jingles, too, seemed lost in the moment, his gaze flickering to her lips before meeting her eyes once more. The air between them crackled with a newfound tension, the playful banter of earlier giving way to something deeper, more intimate.

Say something, Holly's mind screamed, but her voice seemed to have abandoned her. She was acutely aware of every point of contact between them, from the gentle pressure of his hands on her waist to the way his breath tickled her cheek.

The spell was broken by the sound of a timer going off in the background, startling them both back to reality. Jingles cleared his throat, a sheepish grin spreading across his face as he carefully set Holly back on her feet.

"Guess we got a little carried away there, huh?" he joked, running a hand through his curly hair. "Must be the sugar rush."

Holly laughed, hoping he wouldn't notice the blush staining her cheeks. "Yeah, I guess we did. Thanks for catching me, by the way. I seem to be making a habit of falling around you."

"Anytime, Holly," Jingles replied, his voice uncharacteristically soft. "I'll always be here to catch you."

As they turned their attention back to the now-cooled candy cane, Holly couldn't shake the feeling that something had shifted between them. The easy camaraderie of before had been replaced by a new awareness, a spark of possibility that both excited and terrified her.

Focus on the candy cane, she told herself, trying to ignore the way her skin still tingled where Jingles had touched her. *You've got a job to do, and there's no room for distractions. Even if those distractions have the most beautiful eyes you've ever seen...*

With a determined shake of her head, Holly grabbed the towel and set to work cleaning up the last of the mess, her heart still racing with the memory of Jingles' embrace. Little did she know, this was only the beginning of a journey that would change her life—and her heart—forever.

Jingles couldn't help but steal glances at Holly as they worked side by side, cleaning up the remnants of their candy cane mishap. His heart raced, echoing the rapid jingling of the bells on his hat. *Get it together, Jingles,* he chided himself silently. *You've known Holly for years. Why does this feel so different now?*

As they finished wiping down the last of the sticky surfaces, Holly turned to him with a smile that made his stomach flip. "Well, that was quite an adventure," she said, her eyes sparkling with amusement. "I never thought I'd see the day when Jingles Evergreen was at a loss for words."

Jingles grinned, finding his footing in their familiar banter. "What can I say? You have that effect on me, Holly Sugarplum."

The words slipped out before he could stop them, and he felt his cheeks burn beneath his perpetual rosy glow. *Smooth, Jingles. Real smooth.*

But Holly just laughed, a melodic sound that filled the bakery with warmth. "I never knew I had such power," she teased, bumping him playfully with her hip as she reached for a fresh baking sheet.

As they set to work shaping the now-cooled candy cane mixture into its final form, Jingles couldn't help but marvel at the easy rhythm they fell into. It was as if their brief moment of connection had forged a

new understanding between them, transforming their friendly camaraderie into something deeper, more meaningful.

Could this be the start of something special? he wondered, sneaking another glance at Holly as she carefully molded the candy cane's curve. *Or am I just letting my imagination run away with me again?*

Only time would tell, but one thing was certain—Jingles knew he would never look at Holly Sugarplum the same way again. And as they stepped back to admire their handiwork, the giant candy cane glittering in the bakery's twinkling lights, he couldn't help but feel that this was just the beginning of a truly magical adventure.

With the candy cane mishap behind them and the bakery restored to its usual pristine state, Holly and Jingles found themselves lingering, neither quite ready to let the moment pass. They moved about the space, putting away the last of the utensils and ingredients, their hands occasionally brushing against each other and sending sparks of electricity through their veins.

"You know," Jingles began, his voice uncharacteristically soft, "I never thought I'd find someone who could keep up with my crazy ideas."

Holly glanced up at him, a smile playing at the corners of her lips. "And I never thought I'd meet someone who could make even the biggest disaster feel like an adventure."

They shared a laugh, the sound mingling with the gentle hum of the ovens and the distant jingle of sleigh bells outside. In that moment, the bakery felt like a world all their own, a cozy haven where anything was possible.

As they made their way to the front of the shop, Jingles paused, his hand resting on the doorknob. "I don't know about you, but I'm not quite ready for this day to end."

Holly tilted her head, curiosity sparkling in her eyes. "What did you have in mind?"

A mischievous grin spread across Jingles' face. "Have you ever had a snowball fight in the middle of a sugar rush?"

Before Holly could respond, he pushed open the door and darted outside, scooping up a handful of snow and shaping it into a perfect sphere. Holly stood in the doorway, her laughter ringing out like Christmas bells as she watched him prance about, his red hat bobbing with each step.

"Oh, it's on, Jingles Evergreen!" she called, gathering her own handful of snow and joining him in the crisp, winter air.

They chased each other through the snow-covered streets of Frostyville, their laughter echoing off the candy cane lamp posts and gingerbread cottages. Snowballs flew back and forth, some finding their mark and others exploding in puffs of powdery white against the festive storefronts.

As they played, Holly couldn't help but marvel at the way Jingles made her feel—alive, carefree, and filled with a joy she hadn't known in years. And Jingles, for his part, found himself wondering how he'd ever managed to bring laughter to the North Pole without Holly by his side.

When at last they collapsed in a giggling heap, their cheeks flushed and their hearts full, Jingles reached out and brushed a stray snowflake from Holly's hair. "Today was the best day," he said softly, his eyes locking with hers.

"The best day so far," Holly corrected, her smile brighter than the North Star itself.

And as they lay there in the snow, their hands entwined and their hearts beating in sync, both Holly and Jingles knew that this was just the beginning of a story more magical than any candy cane or gingerbread house. It was the start of something truly special, a tale of love and laughter that would be told for many Christmases to come.

Chapter 5: Snowball Fight Shenanigans

The door to the bakery flew open, revealing a grinning Jingles who immediately scooped up a handful of snow. He quickly packed it into a perfectly round ball with his nimble fingers, the jingle bells on his red hat chiming happily as he worked. The nearby elves stopped what they were doing to watch him with interest.

"Hey everyone!" Jingles called out playfully, catching their attention. "Who's ready for a snowball fight? Last one to the town square is a stale candy cane!"

Laughter filled the crisp winter air as more and more elves gathered around Jingles, excitement shining in their eyes. Pepper Minthaven, his trusted partner in mischief, emerged from the workshop with a knowing smile on his face.

"I'm in, Jingles," Pepper said, his cheeks rosy from the cold. "But let's try not to cause too much chaos this time. We don't want a repeat of last year's incident with the reindeer."

Jingles chuckled, tossing the snowball back and forth between his hands. "Where's the fun in that, Pepper? A little chaos never hurt anyone!"

Cinnamon Sparklecake, her hair neatly braided under her baker's cap, stepped forward with a gentle smile. "I'm in too, but let's make sure everyone feels included. We're all friends here at the North Pole."

As more elves joined in on the fun and chatter filled the air, Jingles felt warmth spread through his chest. This was why he loved being an elf - bringing joy and laughter to those around him, even if it meant causing some well-intentioned mischief.

He looked around at his fellow elves with affection in his heart. But then his gaze fell upon the entrance to the bakery and he couldn't help but hope that Holly would join them today. He longed to see her emerald eyes light up and her reserved demeanor fade away in the midst of a snowball fight.

Shaking off the thought, Jingles rallied his fellow elves into a festive battle with a joyful whoop. Snowballs flew through the air and laughter filled the square as they all dodged and ducked with glee. Jingles scampered about, the bells on his hat jingling with each step, leading his comrades in the ultimate winter wonderland extravaganza. The town square transformed into a whirlwind of joy and camaraderie - a shining example of the magic that could happen when friends came together in the spirit of fun and togetherness.

Standing at the entrance of the bakery, Holly couldn't help but be torn between her daily routine and the snowball fight filled with laughter in front of her. She observed Jingles, his flushed cheeks displaying his excitement as he darted through a crowd of elves, dodging snowballs and launching them back with carefree abandon.

"Come on, Holly!" Jingles called out above all the commotion. "We need your expert aim on our team!"

A smile tugged at Holly's lips as she watched the inviting scene unfolding before her. Her reluctance was slowly melting away like snow under the warm glow of Jingles' invitation. She glanced down at her apron, covered in flour, a symbol of her dedication to her work and the walls she had built around her heart.

"I'm not sure, Jingles," she hesitated, "I have so much work to do and I'm not sure I'm cut out for this kind of thing."

But as she looked upon the joy on the faces of her fellow elves, their laughter ringing like silver bells in the crisp winter air, Holly felt a longing stir within her. When was the last time she allowed herself to let go and embrace the magic and wonder that filled every inch of Frostyville?

With a deep breath, Holly untied her apron and hung it on a nearby hook. She stepped out into the snow, hearing it crunch beneath her boots as she made her way towards the group of elves. A smile spread across Jingles' face as he saw her approaching, his eyes sparkling with warmth and encouragement.

"That's the spirit, Holly!" he cheered, tossing her a perfectly packed snowball. "Let's show them what the dynamic duo from North Pole Bakery can do!"

Holly caught the snowball and felt a surge of excitement rush through her. As she met Jingles' gaze, a tentative smile formed on her lips, and she could feel the walls around her heart beginning to crumble. Together, they turned to face their fellow elves, ready to embrace the magic of the moment and the joy of newfound connection.

As the snowball fight picked up with renewed energy, Holly found herself caught up in the laughter and playful banter. Her worries and self-doubt melted away like frost under the warmth of friendship and belonging.

The snowy field was alive with the sound of laughter and shouts, the air thick with the scent of pine and cinnamon. Jingles, his red hat a blur as he darted and weaved through the flurry of snowballs, seemed to embody the very spirit of Christmas itself. His eyes sparkled mischievously as he taunted his fellow elves, scooping up handfuls of snow and returning fire with expert precision.

Holly stood on the sidelines, hesitant at first to join in the chaotic game. But as she watched Jingles' infectious joy and skill, her trepidation melted away and she found herself caught up in the excitement. She ducked behind a bush, packing a perfect snowball between her mittened hands. With a deep breath, she popped up from her hiding spot and let the snowball fly.

To her surprise, it found its mark, hitting an elf square in the chest. The elf laughed good-naturedly, brushing off the snow and giving Holly a thumbs up. Encouraged by her success, Holly continued to participate in the snowball fight, growing more confident with each throw.

As she dodged and weaved through the chaos, Holly felt something stir within her - a sense of belonging and camaraderie that she had never experienced before. She couldn't help but smile as she caught Jingles' eye across the field, their unspoken understanding speaking volumes.

As the snow began to pile up and exhaustion set in for both sides, Holly found herself standing alongside Jingles. Their eyes met, their breath visible in the crisp winter air.

"You were amazing out there," Jingles said softly, admiration evident in his voice. "I knew you had a hidden talent for snowball fighting."

Holly blushed, feeling a warmth spread through her at his praise. "I surprised myself," she admitted. "But I guess with a little bit of magic and a friend like you, anything is possible."

Jingles reached out and brushed a snowflake from her hair, their eyes locked in a moment of understanding. In that moment, Holly felt something shift within her - a newfound confidence and sense of adventure that she never knew existed.

From a distance, Mrs. Claus watched the scene unfold, her eyes twinkling with a knowing warmth. She stood on the porch of her cozy cottage, her hands clasped in front of her, a soft smile playing on her lips.

The gentle glow of Christmas lights reflected off the snow, casting a magical hue over Frostyville.

Ah, young love, she thought, her heart swelling with joy as she observed Holly and Jingles lingering in the aftermath of the snowball fight. *Is there anything more magical, more precious?*

She had seen the connection between them growing over the past few weeks, had watched as they navigated their feelings, their uncertainties. Every stolen glance, every shared laugh had not escaped her notice. And now, seeing them together, so lost in each other's presence, Mrs. Claus knew that they had found something truly special.

They balance each other, she mused, her smile widening. *Holly's gentle warmth, Jingles' playful spirit. Together, they could accomplish anything.*

Her thoughts drifted back to her own early days with Santa, when they were just starting out. The rush of excitement, the tender moments, the sheer giddiness of discovering a kindred spirit—it was all so familiar. She and Kris had built a life of love and joy, and she could see the same potential in Holly and Jingles.

As if sensing her presence, Jingles glanced over his shoulder, catching Mrs. Claus' eye. She nodded slightly, a silent acknowledgment of the moment, of the magic that hung in the air. Jingles' face lit up with a grin, his eyes sparkling with mischief and joy.

He turned back to Holly, taking her hand in his. "Come on," he said, his voice filled with excitement. "Let's go make some more memories."

Holly laughed, the sound ringing out like silver bells. "Lead the way," she said, her heart soaring.

As they walked hand in hand, the snow falling softly around them, Mrs. Claus continued to watch with a contented sigh. *This,* she thought, *this is what the holiday spirit is all about. Love, joy, and the magic of new beginnings.*

She turned back to her cottage, her heart full of warmth and approval. The future was bright for Holly and Jingles, and Mrs. Claus knew that she would be there to guide them, to offer her wisdom and support, as they navigated the wonderful journey ahead.

Jingles and Holly made their way down the snowy lane, the sounds of the North Pole softly humming around them. Elves chatted merrily, and the distant clatter of toy-making filled the air with a rhythmic, comforting pulse.

"I can't feel my toes," Holly admitted with a giggle, her breath visible in the frosty air.

Jingles squeezed her hand. "We'll warm up soon. How about some hot cocoa at the bakery? We can taste test some of your new creations."

Holly's eyes sparkled at the suggestion. "That sounds perfect. I have a new peppermint bark cookie that I need an honest opinion on."

They rounded the corner, the bakery coming into view with its candy cane pillars and gumdrop roof. The warm glow from the windows beckoned them inside, promising a respite from the cold.

Holly paused for a moment, taking in the scene. "Jingles," she said softly, "thank you for today. I really needed it."

Jingles stopped and turned to her, his expression earnest. "Holly, you're not alone here. We're all in this together. And besides," he added with a wink, "I had a blast too."

With a spring in their step, they approached the bakery door. The scent of cinnamon and sugar wafted out, enveloping them in a delicious embrace as Holly opened the door.

"After you," Jingles said, holding the door for her.

Holly stepped inside, the warmth immediately soothing her cold cheeks. She turned to Jingles, who was still lingering in the doorway, the snowflakes catching in his hair and on his green elf tunic.

"Jingles," she called, making him look up. "I'm really glad you're my friend."

Jingles' face softened, and he stepped inside, letting the door close gently behind him. "Me too, Holly. Me too."

The bakery was quiet, a stark contrast to the earlier hustle and bustle. Holly moved behind the counter, retrieving a tray of cookies, while Jingles shrugged off his coat and rubbed his hands together to warm them.

"Sit," Holly instructed, pointing to a small table near the window. "I'll get the cocoa."

Jingles obeyed, watching as Holly expertly prepared two mugs of hot chocolate, complete with whipped cream and sprinkles. She brought them over, along with the tray of cookies, and sat down across from him.

"Cheers," Jingles said, raising his mug. Holly clinked hers against his, and they both took a deep, satisfying sip.

"So," Jingles said, eyeing the cookies. "Are you nervous about the bake-off tomorrow?"

Holly bit her lip, glancing at the cookies. "A little. Okay, a lot. What if I mess up again?"

Jingles reached across the table, taking her hand. "You won't. And even if you do, it's not the end of the world. Remember, it's all about the fun and the experience."

Holly squeezed his hand, taking comfort in his words. "You're right. I just need to relax and enjoy it."

They sat in companionable silence for a moment, watching the snow fall outside the window. The world seemed to slow, each snowflake a tiny moment of peace.

"These are amazing," Jingles said, breaking the silence as he took a bite of a cookie. "You have nothing to worry about."

Holly's face lit up with pride. "You really think so?"

"I know so," Jingles said, finishing the cookie in one last, satisfied bite.

The warmth of the bakery, the sweetness of the cocoa, and the comfort of Jingles' presence made Holly feel like everything would be okay. She was no longer an outsider looking in; she was part of something, part of a community that cared for her.

"Let's go," Jingles said, his voice gentle. "I have an idea for something fun."

Holly looked at him, curious. "What is it?"

Jingles stood, offering her his hand. "You'll see. Trust me."

Holly took his hand, rising from her seat. "I trust you, Jingles."

Chapter 6: The Gingerbread Challenge

Holly's heart plummeted as she read the message on her kitchen tablet screen. "Gingerbread order changed - must be gluten-free." Her mind reeled. Gluten-free? But her prized gingerbread recipe depended on the perfect balance of flours!

She gripped the edge of the flour-dusted counter, squeezing her eyes shut. A swell of panic rose in her chest. How could she possibly adapt the recipe in time? Everyone was counting on her gingerbread being the centerpiece of the North Pole Christmas Gala. If she failed...

Holly took a shaky breath, catching a glimpse of her reflection in the stainless steel mixing bowl. Doubt clouded her usually sparkling eyes. You're not good enough, whispered the voice in her head. You'll let them all down, just like before.

"No," Holly said aloud, her voice trembling slightly. "I can figure this out. I have to." She straightened her shoulders, determination pushing back against the fear.

But even as she reached for her recipe book, flipping to the dog-eared gingerbread page, the doubts continued their insidious chatter. What if the texture is all wrong? What if it tastes awful? You're no gluten-free baking expert!

Holly's perfectionism warred with her desperation. Part of her wanted to barricade herself in the kitchen, testing batch after batch until she got it right on her own. Asking for help felt like admitting defeat, showcasing her inadequacy to the whole North Pole.

She glanced around the cheery kitchen, with its candy cane tiles and gingerbread trim. This was her domain, her safe haven. The idea of inviting someone else into her struggle made her stomach churn.

But as the clock ticked on, each minute a precious resource slipping away, Holly knew she couldn't afford to let pride stand in her way. She needed help, a fresh perspective, someone to pull her out of her spiraling thoughts.

Her eyes fell on the framed photo beside the oven - her and Jingles, grinning in front of the North Pole Bakery sign on its opening day. Jingles... Of course. If anyone could help her salvage this gingerbread disaster, it was him.

Holly swallowed hard, her nerves jangling like sleigh bells. Asking for help still felt like leaping into the unknown. But with Christmas on the line and her reputation at stake, she knew it was a leap she had to take.

She wiped her hands on her apron, took a fortifying breath, and headed out of the kitchen, determination propelling her forward. It was time to find Jingles and face this gluten-free challenge head-on, perfectionism and fear of failure be damned. Christmas gingerbread depended on it.

Holly found Jingles in the bustling workshop, his nimble fingers repairing a delicate glass ornament. Glitter dusted his cheeks, and his tongue poked out in concentration. The sight of him, so absorbed in his task, made Holly's heart flutter like a swarm of butterflies.

"Jingles?" Her voice came out as a squeak. She cleared her throat, trying again. "Jingles, I need your help."

He glanced up, his blue eyes widening at the sight of her. "Holly! Of course, what's jingling your bells?"

She twisted her hands in her apron, the words sticking in her throat. "It's the gingerbread. For the Christmas festival. It... it needs to be gluten-free."

"Gluten-free gingerbread?" Jingles set down the ornament, giving her his full attention. "Why, that's as tricky as getting a reindeer to wear shoes!"

"I know." Holly's shoulders slumped. "I've tried everything, but I can't seem to get the recipe right. And with the festival so close..." She trailed off, blinking back the sting of tears.

In an instant, Jingles was at her side, his hand warm on her shoulder. "Hey, now. Don't let a little gluten get your tinsel in a tangle. We'll figure this out together!"

"You... you'll help me?" Hope bloomed in Holly's chest, fragile as a snowflake.

"Faster than you can say 'jingle bells'!" His grin was brighter than the star atop the Christmas tree. "Two heads are better than one, especially when one of them is topped with a jaunty elf hat."

Despite herself, Holly giggled. Jingles' enthusiasm was contagious, his optimism a balm to her frazzled nerves.

As they headed towards the kitchen, Jingles rubbed his hands together gleefully. "Gluten-free gingerbread, eh? Why, I bet we can make a batch so tasty, even Santa will be begging for seconds!"

"You think so?" Holly asked, daring to let herself believe.

"I know so! With your baking skills and my boundless optimism, we'll have this recipe jingled out in no time!" He winked, setting the bells on his hat jingling.

In the warmth of the kitchen, surrounded by the comforting scent of cinnamon and ginger, Holly felt her fears begin to melt away. With Jingles by her side, everything seemed possible. Even gluten-free gingerbread.

She tied on her apron, a newfound determination settling over her. "Alright, Jingles. Let's get baking!"

His laughter echoed through the kitchen, a merry sound that wrapped around Holly like a cozy scarf. Together, they dove into the challenge, ready to create a little gluten-free magic.

The North Pole Bakery was aglow with warm light, the ovens casting a golden hue across the flour-dusted counters. The air was thick with the comforting aroma of spices—cinnamon, ginger, and nutmeg—a fragrant promise of the sweet delights to come.

Holly and Jingles stood side by side, their elbows nearly touching as they surveyed the array of gluten-free flours before them. Rice flour, almond meal, coconut flour—each one a new frontier in their baking adventure.

Jingles reached for the almond meal, his eyes sparkling with mischief. "I've heard this one adds a nutty flavor. Shall we start with a dash of adventure?"

Holly nodded, a smile tugging at her lips. "A dash of adventure and a pinch of hope, I think."

They fell into a rhythm, measuring and mixing, their movements a choreographed dance of culinary creation. The kitchen filled with the sound of their laughter, punctuated by the clatter of bowls and the whir of the mixer.

As Holly reached for the rice flour, her hand accidentally knocked over the bag. A cloud of white powder exploded around them, dusting their hair and clothes with a fine layer of gluten-free snow.

For a moment, they stared at each other, wide-eyed and silent. Then, Jingles let out a snort of laughter, and the tension shattered like a sugar cookie.

"Well, don't you look positively frosted!" he chuckled, brushing a smudge of flour from Holly's nose.

She giggled, feeling the weight of her worries lift with each peal of laughter. "You're one to talk! You look like you've been caught in a blizzard!"

They brushed themselves off, grinning like children caught in a snowball fight. The mishap seemed to break the ice, their earlier nervousness melting away like snowflakes on a warm tongue.

As they returned to their baking, the air hummed with a new energy—a sense of camaraderie and possibility. The challenge of the gluten-free gingerbread no longer seemed insurmountable. With Jingles by her side, Holly felt like she could conquer anything, one recipe at a time.

Holly carefully measured out the almond flour, her brow furrowed in concentration. Jingles stood beside her, whisking the wet ingredients together with gusto.

"You know," he said, his eyes twinkling with mischief, "I once tried to make a gingerbread house entirely out of candy canes. It was a sticky situation, to say the least!"

Holly laughed, shaking her head. "Why does that not surprise me? I can just picture you, surrounded by a peppermint disaster."

"Hey, it wasn't a total loss! The reindeer loved it. I think Blitzen even got a cavity that year."

Their laughter mingled with the warm scent of ginger and cinnamon, filling the kitchen with the essence of the holidays. Holly felt herself relaxing into the easy banter, her earlier tension fading like a distant memory.

They poured the batter into the waiting pans, smoothing the tops with practiced movements. Holly slid the trays into the oven, a hopeful smile playing on her lips.

"Now, we wait," she said, setting the timer.

Jingles rubbed his hands together gleefully. "The anticipation is half the fun! It's like waiting for Santa to arrive on Christmas Eve."

As the minutes ticked by, they tidied the kitchen, their movements falling into a comfortable rhythm. Holly found herself sneaking glances at Jingles, admiring the way his eyes crinkled when he smiled, the dimple that appeared in his left cheek when he laughed.

The timer dinged, startling her from her thoughts. She pulled the trays from the oven, her heart sinking as she saw the flat, dense squares of gingerbread.

"Oh no," she whispered, poking at the unyielding surface. "They didn't rise at all. I must have messed up the ratios."

Disappointment welled up inside her, hot and prickly. She blinked back the sudden sting of tears, frustrated with herself for failing yet again.

Jingles placed a gentle hand on her shoulder, his voice soft with understanding. "Hey, it's okay. We'll figure it out."

He studied the gingerbread for a moment, his forehead creased in thought. Then, his face lit up with a grin.

"I've got it! We can crumble these up and use them as a base for a gingerbread trifle! Layers of custard, whipped cream, and gingerbread crumbs—it'll be a new holiday favorite!"

Holly stared at him, amazed by his ability to find the silver lining in any situation. His optimism was infectious, chasing away the shadows of her self-doubt.

"Jingles, you're a genius," she said, a slow smile spreading across her face. "Let's do it."

They set to work, crumbling the gingerbread into a large bowl. As they layered the components together, Holly felt a renewed sense of determination. With Jingles by her side, she knew they could create something wonderful, even from the most unexpected of circumstances.

As they worked side by side, assembling the gingerbread trifle, Holly found herself opening up to Jingles in a way she hadn't with anyone else.

"You know," she began, her voice soft and tinged with sadness, "I've always been so afraid of failing. When I was younger, I entered a big baking competition. I spent weeks perfecting my recipe, but on the day of the event, everything went wrong. My cake collapsed, and I was so embarrassed."

Jingles listened intently, his eyes full of empathy. "That must have been really tough," he said, gently squeezing her hand. "But look at you now—you're one of the most talented bakers in all of Frostyville!"

Holly felt a warmth bloom in her chest at his words. "Thank you, Jingles. It's just... sometimes I worry that I'm not good enough, that I'll let everyone down."

He shook his head, his expression serious. "Holly, you could never let anyone down. Your dedication and passion shine through in everything you do. And even when things don't go as planned, you never give up. That's what makes you so amazing."

His sincerity touched her deeply, and she felt a lump form in her throat. "I... I don't know what to say," she whispered, blinking back tears.

Jingles smiled softly, his eyes twinkling with understanding. "You don't have to say anything. Just know that

I believe in you, and I'll always be here to support you, no matter what."

They worked in comfortable silence for a while, the air between them filled with a new depth of connection. As Holly added the final layer of whipped cream to the trifle, Jingles stepped back to admire their creation.

"Holly, look at this! It's incredible!" he exclaimed, his face splitting into a wide grin.

She stood beside him, taking in the sight of the beautiful dessert they had made together. Layers of golden gingerbread crumbs, creamy custard, and fluffy whipped cream, all topped with a sprinkle of cinnamon and a glittery sugar star.

"We did it," she breathed, a sense of pride and accomplishment swelling in her chest. "Jingles, we actually did it!"

In a burst of excitement, she threw her arms around him, hugging him tightly. Jingles laughed, spinning her around in a circle as the bells on his hat jingled merrily.

As he set her down, their eyes met, and for a moment, the world seemed to still. Holly felt a flutter in her stomach, a warmth spreading through her as she realized just how much Jingles meant to her.

"Thank you," she whispered, her voice filled with emotion. "For everything."

Jingles smiled, his eyes soft and full of something that made Holly's heart skip a beat. "Anytime, Holly. Anytime."

And as they stood there, surrounded by the warmth and sweetness of the North Pole Bakery, Holly knew that with Jingles by her side, anything was possible.

Holly and Jingles settled into a comfortable silence, perched on stools at the bakery's worn wooden counter. Steam curled invitingly from their mugs of hot cocoa, the rich aroma mingling with the lingering scents of ginger and cinnamon.

Holly cradled her mug, savoring the warmth that seeped into her hands. She glanced around the kitchen, taking in the dusting of flour on the countertops, the scattered mixing bowls, and the tray of perfectly golden gingerbread cooling on the rack.

"I can't believe we pulled it off," she mused, a note of wonder in her voice. "Jingles, I couldn't have done this without you."

Jingles grinned, his blue eyes sparkling with mischief and affection. "That's what friends are for, Holly. Besides, I knew you had it in you all along."

Holly ducked her head, a blush creeping up her cheeks. "I'm not so sure about that. I was ready to give up, but you..." She met his gaze, her heart swelling with gratitude. "You believed in me, even when I didn't believe in myself."

Jingles reached out, his hand resting gently on hers. "That's because I see how amazing you are, Holly. You pour your heart into everything you do. That's a rare and special gift."

Holly's breath caught in her throat, the sincerity in his words warming her from the inside out. She laced her fingers through his, marveling at how natural it felt. "I'm lucky to have you in my life, Jingles."

They sipped their cocoa in companionable silence, the quiet broken only by the occasional clink of a mug on the counter. As the minutes ticked by, Holly found herself leaning closer to Jingles, drawn to his comforting presence.

Eventually, Jingles set his mug aside, a mischievous glint in his eye. "Well, this kitchen isn't going to clean itself!"

Holly laughed, the sound bright and carefree. "I suppose we should get started, then."

They fell into an easy rhythm, washing dishes and wiping down surfaces. Jingles hummed a festive tune as he worked, his cheerful energy infectious. Holly found herself joining in, their voices blending in harmony as they tidied the bakery.

As Holly placed the last mixing bowl on the shelf, she stepped back, surveying their handiwork with satisfaction. The kitchen gleamed, every surface spotless and ready for the next baking adventure.

Jingles draped an arm around her shoulders, pulling her close. "We make a pretty good team, don't we?"

Holly leaned into his embrace, a contented sigh escaping her lips. "The best."

Chapter 7: Recipe Rivalry

The warm, spicy scent of cinnamon filled the bustling North Pole Bakery as Holly Sugarplum carefully measured out a precise cup of rice flour, her brow furrowed in concentration. Beside her, Jingles Evergreen laughed merrily, tossing a puff of gluten-free flour into the air and watching it drift down around them like fresh snowfall.

"Oopsie daisy!" Jingles giggled, brushing the dusting of flour from Holly's nose with a playful smile. "I think we might need to add a pinch more magic to this batch, don't you?"

Holly couldn't help but laugh, feeling her cheeks flush a soft rose. "I think your boundless cheer is magic enough, Jingles." She paused, glancing at the recipe card once more. "I just hope this new gluten-free gingerbread will impress our distinguished guest. It has to be perfect."

The jingle of bells announced a new arrival, and they turned to see Frosty McFrosterson stride into the bakery, his snowy mustache twitching above a frown. He surveyed the scene of spilled flour and baking ingredients, crossing his arms over his broad chest.

"What's all this fuss about? Hmph!" Frosty grumbled, his warm eyes betraying a hint of curiosity beneath his gruff demeanor. "Why are you messing around with some newfangled recipe? The traditional gingerbread has always been a huge success!"

Holly's heart raced, a flicker of self-doubt clouding her usual confidence. She took a deep breath and met Frosty's gaze. "We're creating a gluten-free version to accommodate our guest's dietary needs. It's important that everyone feels included in the North Pole's holiday celebration."

"Bah humbug!" Frosty harrumphed, eyeing the mixing bowl skeptically. "Gluten-free, smuten-free! Back in my day, we never had to worry about such nonsense."

Jingles bounced on his toes, his infectious smile never waning. "But just imagine the joy on their face when they bite into a gingerbread cookie made especially for them! It'll be a Christmas miracle!"

As Frosty and Jingles bantered back and forth, Holly's mind raced with the recipe's details—the perfect flour ratio, the ideal blend of spices, the precise baking time. She had to get this right, not just for the guest, but for herself. To prove that she could adapt and create something wonderful despite the challenges.

Frosty's brusque voice broke through her thoughts. "Well, I suppose we'll just have to wait and see about that! I expect nothing short of perfection, understand? This new recipe of yours better live up to the North Pole's standards!"

With that, Frosty spun around and marched out, leaving a trail of snowy footprints behind him. Holly and Jingles exchanged worried glances, feeling the weight of the task ahead of them. But as Jingles reached out to give Holly's hand a reassuring squeeze, she felt a spark of determination ignite within her. Together, they would create a gluten-free

Christmas on Peppermint Lane

gingerbread masterpiece—and perhaps discover a little more magic along the way.

Holly's hands hesitated above the mixing bowl, Frosty's skeptical words still lingering in the air like a stubborn chill. She took a deep breath, her voice steady despite the flicker of self-doubt in her eyes. "It's our duty to accommodate the visiting dignitary's specific dietary needs. Everyone deserves a little holiday magic, even if they can't have gluten."

Jingles, sensing the tension in Holly's shoulders, bounded over with his usual cheerful jingle. "Absolutely! And with Holly's baking skills and my unwavering enthusiasm, we'll create a gluten-free gingerbread that will melt even Frosty's frosty heart!" He punctuated his statement with a infectious laugh, filling the bustling bakery with joy.

A smile tugged at Holly's lips at Jingles' unyielding optimism. It was like a warm light leading her through the fog of her own doubts. She reached for the almond flour, feeling Jingles' fingers brush against hers as he handed her the measuring cup. There was a small spark that seemed to pass between them, and for a moment, it felt like it was just the two of them in the midst of all the chaos.

Side by side, Holly and Jingles worked on their dough, each ingredient added with more confidence than before. Jingles' presence was a constant comfort, his playful jokes and genuine encouragement soothing Holly's frazzled nerves. Together, they created a mixture that smelled of spices and promises, its scent floating through the air like an irresistible invitation.

As the first batch went into the oven, Holly stepped back and wiped a dusting of flour from her cheek. Jingles beamed at her, his eyes sparkling mischievously and with something deeper that made Holly's heart flutter like a butterfly covered in sugar. "You've got a little something..." he whispered, reaching out to gently brush away a stray strand of hair from her face.

Holly's breath caught in her throat, the simple gesture sending shivers down her spine. In that moment, surrounded by the warmth of the ovens and the sweetness of their creation, anything felt possible. Even a gluten-free gingerbread miracle that could win over even the grumpiest of elves.

As the timer rang, signaling the first batch was ready, Holly and Jingles shared a knowing look filled with anticipation, their hands clasping together in silent determination. Whatever obstacles they may face, they would tackle them together—one whisk, one laugh, and one sprinkle of magic at a time.

A warm, comforting aroma filled the kitchen as Holly pulled the tray of freshly baked gingerbread out of the oven. She placed them on a cooling rack, eyeing each cookie with a critical gaze.

Jingles complimented her on the delicious-looking cookies, but Holly's thoughts were consumed by the looming challenge set by Frosty - to create a gluten-free gingerbread recipe. Doubts crept into her mind, but Jingles reassured her that she was the most talented baker in the North Pole and he believed in her abilities.

Their moment was interrupted by a loud noise from across the kitchen, and they both stepped back, breaking the tension between them. As they continued to bake together, their teamwork and chemistry was evident, creating a sense of magic in the kitchen.

With each successful batch, Holly's confidence grew, and doubts faded away. Jingles' presence provided comfort and encouragement, making her feel like she wasn't alone in this challenge.

As they finished the last batch of cookies and stood back to admire their work, Holly felt a sense of pride and accomplishment. They had successfully created a gluten-free gingerbread that looked and smelled just as amazing as the traditional recipe.

They each took a bite of their creation, marveling at the flavors dancing on their tongues.

Holly and Jingles worked together to clean and organize the bakery, moving in perfect unison. As they wiped down counters and put away ingredients, they chatted easily, occasionally joking around and playfully tapping each other's flour-dusted noses.

"You know," Jingles said, his tone becoming more serious, "I've always admired your dedication to baking. The way you pour your heart into every recipe and every little detail is truly inspiring."

Holly blushed and smiled shyly. "Thank you, Jingles. That means a lot coming from you." She bit her lip, a hint of doubt crossing her face. "I just hope it's enough to impress Frosty and the important visitor."

Jingles stepped closer, gently placing his hand on her shoulder. "Holly, you've got this. We've got this. And even if things don't go perfectly, it doesn't change the fact that you're an amazing baker and an even better friend."

Holly felt a warmth spread through her chest at his words, unrelated to the lingering heat from the oven. She met his gaze, gratitude shining in her eyes along with another feeling she had been too scared to acknowledge before.

"I couldn't do this without you, Jingles. Your support, your laughter, your unwavering belief in me—it's what keeps me going even when I doubt myself."

Jingles grinned, reaching up to tuck a strand of hair behind her ear. "That's what partners are for, right? To lift each other up and make the impossible seem possible."

As they stood there, something between them seemed to shift, the air suddenly charged with a new electricity. Holly's breath caught in her throat as Jingles leaned in closer, making his intentions clear.

Just as their lips were about to meet, the doorbell chimed happily as someone entered the bakery. They quickly pulled apart, their cheeks flushed and hearts racing, as a group of elves bustled in, talking excitedly about the upcoming taste test.

Holly and Jingles shared a knowing look, silently acknowledging their promise to explore this new feeling later. For now, they had a challenge to face and a mission to lead: the gluten-free gingerbread revolution.

With a determined smile and a nod, they turned to greet their fellow elves, ready to take on the world one cookie at a time.

The elves, blissfully unaware of the tender moment they had disrupted, swarmed around Holly and Jingles with a flurry of excitement. "Is it true?" one elf exclaimed, her eyes sparkling with curiosity. "Are you really creating a gluten-free gingerbread recipe for the visiting dignitary?"

Holly nodded, slipping back into her professional demeanor with practiced ease. "We are, and we're putting our hearts into making it the best gingerbread anyone has ever tasted, gluten-free or not."

Jingles, his mischievous grin firmly in place, added, "And we'll prove it in the blind taste test. Frosty won't know what hit him when he bites into these!"

A chorus of cheers and applause erupted from the gathered elves, their enthusiasm and faith in Holly and Jingles' abilities shining through. As the group began to disperse, returning to their own holiday tasks, Holly turned to Jingles, her eyes alight with renewed determination.

"Let's get back to work," she said, rolling up her sleeves with purpose. "We have a recipe to perfect and a taste test to win."

Jingles nodded, his resolve matching hers. "Lead the way, partner. I'll be right beside you, every step of the way."

They plunged back into their work with a focused intensity, the earlier tension between them morphing into a united sense of purpose. They moved around each other with the fluidity of a well-rehearsed dance, their contrasting styles blending harmoniously.

Holly's meticulous nature ensured that every ingredient was measured with exacting precision, while Jingles' creative spontaneity introduced unexpected, delightful twists to the mix. Together, they were an unstoppable force, their combined passion for baking and their growing connection driving them forward.

As the hours slipped by, the once-bustling bakery settled into a gentle hum. Holly and Jingles found themselves lost in their work, their conversation flowing as smoothly as melted butter. They shared stories from their childhoods, their aspirations, and even their fears, the bond between them growing deeper with each revelation.

"Remember when we first tried making peppermint bark?" Jingles reminisced, laughing at the memory. "We ended up with more chocolate on us than in the bark!"

Holly giggled, her eyes crinkling at the corners. "That was a disaster, but also so much fun. We've come a long way since then."

"Indeed we have," Jingles said, his tone turning more thoughtful. "And we've faced every challenge together."

As the latest batch of gluten-free gingerbread emerged from the oven, filling the air with its warm, spicy fragrance, Holly and Jingles paused to admire their work. The cookies were a testament to their dedication and teamwork, each one a golden-brown promise of deliciousness.

Holly looked at Jingles, a mixture of pride and affection in her eyes. "We really did it, didn't we?"

Jingles' face softened, his usual playful demeanor giving way to something more tender. "Yeah, we did. And it's been amazing."

The timer chimed, signaling that the latest batch of gluten-free gingerbread was ready. Holly, her hair dusted with flour and her cheeks flushed from the heat of the oven, carefully removed the tray, the warm, spicy aroma enveloping her senses.

Holly and Jingles stood side by side, admiring their handiwork as the last batch of gluten-free gingerbread cookies cooled on the wire rack. The bakery was filled with the warmth of the ovens and the sweet scent of cinnamon and ginger.

Despite their successful recipe, Holly couldn't shake her self-doubt. "Jingles," she whispered, gazing at the cookies, "what if Frosty is right? What if our cookies aren't up to par?"

Jingles turned towards her, his blue eyes softening with understanding. "Holly, you're the most talented baker in all of Frostyville. If anyone can make a gluten-free gingerbread cookie that will impress Frosty, it's you."

Holly sighed, feeling weighed down by her worries. "But what if I disappoint everyone? The visiting dignitary, North Pole Bakery, you..."

Jingles reached out and took Holly's flour-covered hands in his own. "You could never let me down, Holly. We're a team, remember? We support each other no matter what."

The warmth of his touch sent a flutter through Holly's stomach, drawing her closer to his positive energy. "I don't know what I would do without you, Jingles."

A playful smirk tugged at the corners of Jingles' mouth. "Well for starters, you'd probably have less kitchen mishaps to clean up."

Despite the tension in the air, Holly couldn't help but laugh along with the jingling of bells on Jingles' hat. "That's true. But I'd also have less laughter in my life."

As their laughter faded, Holly found herself gazing at Jingles, noticing how the firelight made his cheeks rosy and the glint of affection in his eyes. In that moment, she realized her feelings for him had evolved into something deeper than friendship - a tender seed of love had blossomed in her heart.

But before she could find the words to express her newfound emotions, the timer on the oven beeped, signaling that the last batch of cookies was done.

"Time to get back to work," Jingles joked, reluctantly letting go of Holly's hands. "We have to show Frosty what we're capable of."

The warm light of the fire illuminated Holly and Jingles as they stood together, their eyes conveying a shared understanding. The flurry of flour and sugar coated them both, giving them a snow-kissed appearance that added to the charm of their Christmas bakery.

Chapter 8: Mistletoe Mishap

The smell of fresh gingerbread enveloped the cozy North Pole Bakery as Holly and Jingles worked together, gathering ingredients for their special gluten-free recipe. Jingles hummed happily while he measured out ingredients and Holly reached for jars on high shelves.

"Could you pass me the molasses, Jingles?" Holly asked, a twinkle in her eye as she reached for some cinnamon on the top shelf.

Jingles sprang into action, his silver bells jingling as he retrieved the jar. "Here you go, one jar of molasses!" He grinned, handing it to her.

As they both leaned in to reach for the same spice, they suddenly realized they were standing inches apart with a sprig of mistletoe hovering over them. They froze, eyes wide with surprise.

"Oh! I-I didn't realize..." Holly stuttered, her cheeks turning pink at their close proximity. She couldn't help but notice how Jingles' blue eyes sparkled in the warm light of the bakery.

Jingles chuckled nervously, mirroring Holly's blush. "Well, this is unexpected," he joked, trying to ease the tension.

They took a step back, laughing off their awkward moment. Holly's heart raced and she scolded herself for getting so flustered. 'It's just mistletoe, stay focused on the baking,' she thought determinedly as she reached for the cinnamon again.

"So, about that recipe," Holly started, redirecting their conversation to safer ground. "I was thinking we could add some nutmeg to give it a little extra holiday twist."

Jingles eagerly agreed, his familiar grin returning. "Great idea, Holly! Your recipes are always amazing." He winked playfully and Holly felt a flutter in her stomach.

As they continued working on their gingerbread, the memory of the mistletoe hung in the air as a reminder of the growing connection between them. The bakery was filled with a sense of possibility, the scent of gingerbread now intertwined with the promise of something more.

Holly carefully measured out the flour, her hands staying steady despite the fluttering butterflies in her stomach. Passing the bowl to Jingles, their fingertips brushed briefly during the exchange, sending a jolt of electricity through Holly's body. She quickly withdrew her hand, hoping Jingles hadn't noticed her reaction.

"Be careful there, Holly," Jingles teased with a twinkle in his eye. "We don't want to spill any of this precious flour."

Holly laughed, her voice sounding a bit too high-pitched even to her own ears. "Right, can't have that." She focused on the remaining ingredients, trying to ignore the lingering tingling sensation where they had touched.

Jingles couldn't resist making a playful comment as he added his own ingredients. "You know, I'm starting to think this bakery is a minefield of mistletoe. We'll have to be careful not to find ourselves in another... 'situation.'" He wiggled his eyebrows mischievously, earning a genuine laugh from Holly.

"Stop it," she playfully scolded, swatting at him with a dish towel. "We have gingerbread to make and I won't tolerate any more distractions."

But deep down, Holly knew it was a losing battle. The more time she spent with Jingles, the harder it became to resist his infectious energy and kind heart. 'Focus, Holly,' she reminded herself sternly. 'The gingerbread competition is what matters now.'

With renewed determination, Holly guided Jingles through the next steps of the recipe, their banter flowing effortlessly as they worked together. The comforting aroma of gingerbread filled the bakery, a testament to their teamwork and shared passion for baking.

As they waited for the gingerbread to finish baking, Holly and Jingles found themselves leaning against the counter side by side, almost touching shoulders as they admired their creation. The mistletoe hung above them, a silent reminder of the unspoken spark between them, but for now, they were content to simply enjoy their friendship and the joy of working together.

The bakery door chimed merrily as Sugar Snowbelle strolled in. "Well, hello my little baking elves!" she exclaimed, her voice radiating warmth like a mug of hot cocoa. "I couldn't resist stopping by to see how our favorite duo is doing."

Sugar's eyes twinkled with mischief as she looked around the bakery, pausing at the sight of mistletoe hanging above Holly and Jingles. "Isn't that just lovely? It adds such a festive touch to the place, don't you think?"

Holly felt her cheeks heat up, a sure sign of her growing feelings for Jingles. She tried to focus on wiping down the counter, ignoring the knowing look in Sugar's eyes. "It's definitely... noticeable," she managed to say with a slightly higher pitch.

Jingles flashed a charming grin at Sugar. "It's been keeping us on our toes, that's for sure. We've had a few close calls already."

Sugar clapped her hands in delight, her silver hair shining under the bakery lights. "Oh, how delightful! Mistletoe has a way of bringing two hearts together." She gave Holly a playful wink before announcing that she had other festivities to attend to and left the bakery in a flurry of glittering snowflakes.

As the door closed behind her, Holly and Jingles exchanged a knowing look, their laughter breaking out like flour dust in the air.

"She's not exactly subtle, is she?" Jingles chuckled, shaking his head in amusement.

Holly grinned, feeling relieved as tension dissipated. "About as subtle as a reindeer in a china shop. But that's just Sugar - always trying to spread cheer."

Jingles stepped closer, his hand brushing against Holly's as he reached for a spatula. "Well, we can't disappoint her now. But let's focus on perfecting this gingerbread first. We wouldn't want to let our matchmaker down."

Holly's heart skipped a beat at his touch, but she nodded determinedly. "Agreed. The gingerbread competition is our top priority. As for everything else... we'll just have to see where the mistletoe takes us."

With a shared smile and a renewed sense of camaraderie, Holly and Jingles dove back into their baking, their laughter and playful banter filling the air like the sweet scent of gingerbread. And if their hands brushed a little more often than necessary, well, that was just the magic of the mistletoe in action.

Working side by side, Holly was fascinated by the way their talents complemented each other. Jingles' imaginative ideas and unique combinations of flavors were enhanced by her precise measurements and technical skills, resulting in perfectly crafted batches every time.

"What do you think about adding a hint of cardamom to the mix?" Jingles suggested with a glint of excitement in his eyes. "It'll give the cookies an extra layer of flavor."

Holly considered the suggestion, a slow smile spreading across her face. "That's brilliant, Jingles! And maybe for some of the cookies, we could use star-shaped cutters to make them even more festive."

Jingles grinned, dimples appearing on his cheeks. "I love the way your mind works, Holly. Together, we'll create the most exquisite gingerbread cookies that Frostyville has ever seen!"

As they continued working together, their conversation flowed effortlessly, intertwined with playful banter and shared grins. Holly found herself relishing in Jingle's company and enthusiasm filling the kitchen.

It's just a friendly competition, she reminded herself, trying to ignore the butterflies in her stomach whenever their hands touched. We're just collaborating to make the ultimate gingerbread.

But as they both reached for the same mixing bowl, their fingers accidentally touched and sent a jolt of electricity through Holly. They both froze, wide-eyed, as they realized they were standing under another sprig of mistletoe.

Holly's breath hitched in her throat, her heart racing as she met Jingle's gaze. In that moment, it felt like it was just the two of them, surrounded by the warm scent of gingerbread and the soft glow of the kitchen lights.

Jingles cleared his throat and spoke with a slightly raspy voice. "Holly, I..."

But before he could finish his sentence, the oven timer went off and broke the spell. Holly stepped back, her cheeks flushed, and busied herself with removing the tray of perfectly baked cookies.

Focus, she scolded herself, trying to ignore the lingering tingling sensation where their fingers had briefly touched. The competition is all that matters. Everything else can wait.

But as they resumed their baking, sneaking glances at each other from time to time, Holly couldn't help but wonder if maybe the true magic of the holiday season wasn't in the gingerbread after all, but in the unexpected connection growing between them.

"Could you pass me the nutmeg, please?" she asked, her voice a little too bright. "And then we'll need to mix the dry ingredients together before we add the wet ones."

Jingles handed her the nutmeg, his fingers brushing against hers in the process. Holly's heart skipped a beat, and she nearly dropped the jar.

"Careful there," Jingles said with a grin, his blue eyes twinkling. "We don't want to lose any of that precious spice."

Holly laughed, the sound a little too high-pitched to her own ears. "Right, of course. I'm just a little... distracted today, I guess."

She turned back to the mixing bowl, her cheeks burning. Get it together, Holly. You're acting like a lovesick teenager.

But as she measured out the flour and sugar, her mind kept wandering back to Jingles. The way his smile lit up his whole face, the infectious sound of his laughter, the gentle warmth of his hands...

"Hey," Jingles said softly, breaking into her thoughts. "You okay?"

Holly looked up, startled to find him standing so close. "Y-yeah, I'm fine. Just... thinking about the competition, that's all."

Jingles placed a hand on her shoulder, his touch sending a jolt of electricity through her. "We've got this, Holly. With your baking skills and my creativity, we'll make the best gluten-free gingerbread this town has ever seen."

His words were meant to be reassuring, but all Holly could focus on was the warmth of his hand, the sincerity in his eyes. Her heart raced, her palms suddenly clammy.

"Thanks, Jingles," she managed, her voice barely above a whisper. "I... I couldn't do this without you."

The words hung in the air between them, heavy with unspoken meaning. For a moment, they simply stared at each other, the rest of the world fading away.

Then Jingles smiled, his eyes crinkling at the corners. "We make a pretty good team, don't we?"

Holly nodded, a genuine smile spreading across her face. "The best."

As they returned to their baking, their movements perfectly in sync, Holly felt a new sense of determination wash over her. Maybe there was something special happening between her and Jingles, but for now, they had a competition to win.

Holly and Jingles worked in comfortable silence, their hands moving with practiced precision as they rolled out the gingerbread dough and cut out festive shapes. The scent of cinnamon and ginger filled the air, mingling with the undercurrent of excitement that seemed to crackle between them.

As Holly reached for the icing, her hand brushed against Jingles', and she felt a familiar flutter in her stomach. She glanced up at him, a shy smile playing on her lips. "Sorry, I didn't mean to..."

"No worries," Jingles grinned, his eyes twinkling with mischief. "I think we've established that personal space isn't really a thing in this bakery."

Holly laughed, the sound echoing through the cozy kitchen. "I guess you're right. Between the mistletoe and the close quarters, it's a wonder we haven't..."

She trailed off, her cheeks flushing pink as she realized what she'd been about to say. Jingles raised an eyebrow, his smile turning sly. "Haven't what, Holly?"

"N-nothing," she stammered, busying herself with piping intricate designs onto a gingerbread reindeer. "I just meant... we've been spending a lot of time together, and..."

"And it's been pretty great, hasn't it?" Jingles finished, his voice soft and sincere. Holly looked up at him, her heart skipping a beat at the tenderness in his gaze.

"Yeah," she breathed, setting down the icing. "It really has."

They worked in silence for a few more minutes, their hands moving in perfect harmony as they decorated the cookies. Holly marveled at how easy it was, how natural it felt to be here with Jingles, creating something beautiful together.

As they placed the last cookie on the tray, Jingles let out a triumphant whoop. "We did it! Holly, these look amazing!"

Holly beamed, pride swelling in her chest. "They really do, don't they? I can't believe we actually pulled it off."

Jingles reached out and took her hand, his fingers lacing through hers. "I never doubted us for a second."

Holly looked down at their intertwined hands, a warm feeling spreading through her. She knew she should probably pull away, keep things professional, but she couldn't bring herself to let go.

Suddenly, a glint of green caught her eye, and she glanced up to see a sprig of mistletoe hanging directly above them. Her eyes widened, her heart racing as she realized what it meant.

Jingles followed her gaze, his own eyes sparkling with amusement. "Well, would you look at that? Seems like the mistletoe has struck again."

Holly laughed nervously, her free hand fluttering to her hair. "I guess it has. You know, we really should talk to Sugar about her decorating choices."

Jingles chuckled, his thumb tracing circles on the back of her hand. "Maybe later. But for now..."

He leaned in closer, his breath warm on her cheek. Holly's eyes fluttered shut, her lips parting slightly in anticipation. But instead of a kiss, she felt Jingles press something into her hand.

She opened her eyes to see a perfectly decorated gingerbread heart, with the words "Team Holly & Jingles" written in elegant script.

"For luck," Jingles winked, straightening up. "Not that we need it."

Holly grinned, her heart swelling with affection. "No, we definitely don't."

The gingerbread cookies lay before them, each one a perfect golden brown, decorated with intricate designs in shimmering icing. The sweet aroma of cinnamon and ginger filled the air, a testament to their baking prowess.

"We make a pretty good team, don't we?" Jingles grinned, nudging Holly with his elbow.

She laughed, the sound like tinkling bells in the cozy bakery. "We do indeed. Who would've thought that the North Pole's most notorious troublemaker would turn out to be such a baking maestro?"

Jingles placed a hand over his heart, feigning offense. "You wound me, Holly! I'll have you know that causing mischief and creating culinary masterpieces are not mutually exclusive talents."

Holly shook her head, smiling fondly at his antics. *He really is something special,* she thought to herself. *Beneath all that playful energy lies a heart of pure gold.*

"Well, maestro," she said aloud, "I think it's safe to say we're ready for the gingerbread challenge. These cookies are going to knock everyone's Christmas stockings off!"

Jingles' eyes sparkled with excitement. "You're right! And you know what? I think we should celebrate our impending victory."

He reached behind him, producing a small sprig of mistletoe seemingly out of thin air. With a mischievous grin, he held it above their heads.

"What do you say, Holly? Care to seal our partnership with a little holiday tradition?"

Holly's cheeks flushed as red as Santa's suit, her heart hammering in her chest. *Is this really happening?*

She looked into Jingles' eyes, seeing the warmth and affection shining there. In that moment, all her doubts and insecurities melted away like snow in the sun.

"I thought you'd never ask," she whispered, leaning in closer.

Their lips met in a gentle kiss, sweet and tender as a sugar cookie. Holly felt a warmth spreading through her, like sipping hot cocoa on a cold winter's night.

As they pulled apart, Jingles rested his forehead against hers, his voice soft and sincere. "Holly, I know we agreed to focus on the gingerbread challenge, but I can't deny what I feel for you. You're the cinnamon to my sugar, the icing on my cookie."

Holly giggled, her heart soaring with joy. "And you're the sprinkles to my cupcake, Jingles. I never thought I'd find someone who understands me like you do."

They stood there for a moment, lost in each other's eyes, the rest of the world fading away. The gingerbread challenge, the mistletoe mishaps, even the bustling activity of the North Pole seemed distant and unimportant.

All that mattered was the love blossoming between them, as sweet and magical as the spirit of Christmas itself.

As they stepped out of the bakery, hand in hand, the festive chaos of Frostyville swirled around them like a whirlwind of holiday cheer. Elves hurried to and fro, carrying armfuls of glittering decorations and singing merry tunes. The air was filled with the scent of pine needles and freshly baked cookies, a reminder of the magic that permeated every corner of the North Pole.

Holly and Jingles walked through the bustling streets, their steps falling into a synchronized rhythm. They exchanged glances, their eyes sparkling with the shared secret of their newfound connection. The challenges that lay ahead seemed less daunting now that they had each other to lean on.

"You know," Jingles said, a playful grin tugging at the corners of his mouth, "I have a feeling our gingerbread creation is going to be the talk of the town. With your baking skills and my creative flair, we'll be unstoppable!"

Holly laughed, the sound ringing out like sleigh bells in the crisp winter air. "I don't doubt that for a second, Jingles. But let's not forget the real prize - spending more time together in the kitchen."

"I couldn't agree more," Jingles replied, giving her hand a gentle squeeze. "And who knows, maybe we'll find a few more sprigs of mistletoe along the way."

As they turned the corner, they were greeted by the sight of the grand Christmas tree at the center of Frostyville, its twinkling lights casting a warm glow over the snow-covered square. Holly felt a sense of excitement bubbling up inside her.

And so, with hearts full of love and minds brimming with ideas, Holly and Jingles set off to navigate the delightful chaos of Frostyville, their partnership a shining beacon of hope and joy amidst the festive frenzy.

Chapter 9: The Taste Test

Santa's eyes twinkled with merriment as he declared, "The winner of this year's Frostyville Gingerbread Competition is... Holly Sugarplum and Jingles Evergreen, with their delightfully innovative gluten-free gingerbread!"

The hall erupted in a chorus of cheers and applause, the sound reverberating off the walls and filling the air with electric joy. Holly stood frozen, her eyes wide with disbelief as the reality of their victory slowly sank in. She could hardly process the enormity of what Santa had just announced. This was more than a win; it was a validation of all their hard work and a dream come true.

Jingles let out a whoop of delight, his infectious laughter mingling with the crowd's exuberant response. He bounced on his toes, the bells on his hat and shoes creating a symphony of jingles. He turned to Holly, his smile brighter than the North Star. "We did it, Holly! Our gingerbread won!" His excitement was palpable, his joy uncontainable.

Holly blinked, a slow smile spreading across her face as the initial shock gave way to pure, unadulterated happiness. "We won," she repeated, her voice barely audible above the din. "Jingles, we actually won!" Her eyes sparkled with tears of joy, her heart swelling to a size she didn't think possible.

The crowd surged forward, friends and fellow bakers eager to congratulate the victorious duo. The warmth and camaraderie of the townsfolk washed over them like a tidal wave. Mrs. Claus enveloped Holly in a warm hug, her eyes shining with pride. "Your gingerbread was simply divine, my dear. You've truly outdone yourself this year."

Holly returned the embrace, her heart swelling with gratitude. "Thank you, Mrs. Claus. Your words mean the world to me." She remembered all the past competitions where she had come close but never quite clinched the title. This moment was sweeter than she had ever imagined.

As the celebratory atmosphere swirled around them, Holly found herself pulled into a whirlwind of hugs, handshakes, and heartfelt compliments. She basked in the glow of their shared achievement, her earlier doubts and insecurities melting away like snow in the warm embrace of Frostyville's love and support. Each kind word and gesture was like a sprinkle of sugar on her already overfilled heart.

Jingles remained by her side, his hand never leaving hers as they navigated the sea of well-wishers. His presence was a constant reminder of the incredible journey they had embarked upon together, the challenges they had overcome, and the love they had discovered along the way. Every squeeze of his hand was a silent "we did it," every glance a shared memory of their baking adventures.

In that moment, surrounded by the joy and laughter of their cherished community, Holly realized that their victory was about more than just a gingerbread competition. It was a testament to the power of friendship, the magic of the holiday spirit, and the unbreakable bond she and Jingles had forged.

This was their story, a tale of two hearts coming together over a mixing bowl and a common goal.

As the celebrations continued, Holly's smile grew more radiant with each passing second. She had found not only success in her craft but also the greatest gift of all - the love and support of those who mattered most. With Jingles by her side and the warmth of Frostyville in her heart, she knew that anything was possible. Their future was as bright as the fairy lights that adorned the town square.

Amidst the joyous chaos of the celebration, Holly's gaze locked with Jingles'. In that charged moment, the world seemed to fall away, the cheers of the crowd fading into a distant hum. His twinkling blue eyes, usually alight with mischief, now held a tender intensity that made her heart skip a beat. She could almost see the words forming in his mind, the confession she had been waiting for.

Jingles leaned in, his voice low and warm. "Holly, I..."

The distance between them narrowed, the air electric with anticipation. Holly's breath caught in her throat as Jingles' lips drew closer to hers, the promise of a kiss hanging sweetly in the space between them. She closed her eyes, ready to surrender to the moment.

Just as their lips were about to meet, a renewed eruption of applause jolted them back to reality. The crowd, caught up in their own elation, remained oblivious to the intimate moment they had inadvertently interrupted. Their cheers and claps created a cacophony of holiday spirit that echoed through the hall.

Holly and Jingles shared a look of surprised amusement, their laughter mingling with the joyful din. The interruption, though untimely, could not diminish the affection that shone in their eyes. It was a silent acknowledgment of the deep connection they had forged, a promise of something more to come. They knew that their time would come, and when it did, it would be perfect.

We'll have our moment, Holly thought, her heart swelling with a mixture of relief and anticipation. *And when we do, it will be even sweeter for the wait.*

Hand in hand, Holly and Jingles stepped off the stage, their fingers interlaced in a display of unity and partnership. As they made their way through the throng of well-wishers, Holly marveled at the journey that had brought them to this point. What had begun as a simple collaboration had blossomed into something far more profound - a bond built on shared passions, mutual respect, and the magic of the holiday season.

Their victory in the gingerbread competition was not just a testament to their culinary skills, but to the strength of their teamwork and the depth of their growing love. Each bite of their gingerbread was a piece of their hearts, a symbol of the love and effort they had poured into every batch.

As the celebrations continued around them, Holly and Jingles exchanged glances filled with warmth and promise. Whatever the future held, they would face it together, their hearts united by the sweetness of their love and the joy of their shared triumph. Each step they took was a step into a future they were excited to build together.

Just then, a reporter from the Frostyville Gazette burst through the crowd, her notepad and pen at the ready. "Holly! Jingles! Can we get a statement from the winners?"

Chapter 10: Ice Skating Under the Stars

Jingles' eyes danced with excitement as he turned to Pepper. "This is going to be the most magical evening ever! Holly won't know what hit her when she sees the winter wonderland we've created."

Pepper chuckled, shaking his head. "I'm sure it will be unforgettable, Jingles. Just try not to get too carried away, like last time with the runaway reindeer."

"That was one time!" Jingles protested, but a grin tugged at his lips. "Now come on, we've got a frozen lake to decorate!"

The two elves set to work, stringing twinkling lights around the perimeter of the shimmering ice. Jingles hummed merrily as he looped the glowing strands through the bare branches of the surrounding trees, while Pepper meticulously arranged a cozy hot chocolate station nearby. The aroma of rich cocoa mingled with the crisp winter air.

As Pepper ensured each mug was perfectly aligned, Jingles added his signature touch of whimsy—a sprinkle of shimmering glitter over the marshmallows. "There! Now it's perfect."

Just then, a bundled-up figure approached the lake, her breath visible in the frosty air. Holly's eyes widened as she took in the enchanting scene, the shimmering lights reflecting off the ice like a thousand stars. "Oh, Jingles," she breathed. "It's beautiful."

Jingles bounded over to her, his silver bells jingling with each step. With a playful bow, he presented her with a pair of ice skates. "For you, m'lady."

Holly hesitated, biting her lip. "I don't know, Jingles. It's been years since I've skated. What if I fall?"

Jingles gave her a warm, reassuring smile. "Don't worry, Holly. I'll be right here beside you."

With a gentle nudge, he led her to a nearby bench. As Holly laced up her skates, her fingers fumbled slightly, betraying her nerves. 'I can't believe I'm doing this,' she thought, her heart fluttering. 'What if I make a fool of myself in front of Jingles?'

Noticing her apprehension, Jingles leaned in conspiratorially. "Don't tell anyone, but I once accidentally skated right into a snowman. Took me days to get the carrot out of my ear!"

Despite herself, Holly laughed, the tension easing from her shoulders. "I'll try to avoid any rogue snowmen, then."

Hand in hand, they stepped onto the ice. Holly wobbled, her free arm windmilling as she sought balance. Jingles remained steady beside her, offering his support. "I've got you," he murmured.

Slowly, tentatively, Holly began to glide forward. With each stroke, her movements grew more fluid, more confident. Jingles matched her pace, his infectious energy lifting her spirits.

"You're doing great, Holly!" he cheered. "See? You're a natural!"

As they skated side by side, Holly felt a warmth blossom in her chest that had nothing to do with the exertion. Maybe, just maybe, with Jingles by her side, she could face anything—even her own self-doubts.

The frozen lake sparkled under the twinkling lights, a mesmerizing canvas of glittering stars reflected on the ice. The soft scrape of their skates whispered through the crisp air, a soothing rhythm that seemed to weave a spell of enchantment around Jingles and Holly.

Hand in hand, they glided across the ice, their movements synchronized in a dance of growing connection. Jingles' bells jingled merrily with each stroke, a festive accompaniment to their shared laughter. In a moment of playful inspiration, he began to serenade Holly with a spirited, if slightly off-key, rendition of "Jingle Bells."

"Dashing through the snow, on a one-horse open sleigh," he crooned, his voice carrying across the lake. "O'er the fields we go, laughing all the way!"

Holly's laughter rang out, pure and joyful, her earlier nervousness melting away in the warmth of the moment. She joined in, her sweet voice harmonizing with his. "Bells on bobtails ring, making spirits bright. What fun it is to ride and sing a sleighing song tonight!"

As they sang, Holly's initial clumsiness faded, replaced by a blossoming confidence and newfound sense of freedom. The worries that had weighed on her seemed to drift away, carried off by the gentle breeze that played with the wisps of her hair.

Emboldened by the magic of the evening, Jingles attempted a fancy spin, his arms outstretched with theatrical flair. But as he twirled, his skate caught on a stray pine cone hidden beneath the snow. With a yelp of surprise, he stumbled, arms pinwheeling as he fought to regain his balance.

Quick as a flash, Holly reached out and caught him, her hands grasping his waist to steady him. For a breathless moment, they stood frozen, their faces inches apart. Jingles' eyes sparkled with mirth, his cheeks flushed from more than just the cold.

"My hero," he quipped, his voice soft and teasing.

Holly ducked her head, a rosy blush blooming on her cheeks. "I couldn't let you fall," she murmured. "Not after you've been here to catch me."

Their laughter echoed across the lake, a symphony of shared joy and deepening connection. As they resumed their skating, snowflakes began to drift down from the star-strewn sky, dusting the scene in a veil of enchantment.

Jingles and Holly paused to admire the view, their breath mingling in the frosty air. The snowflakes caught in Holly's eyelashes, tiny diamonds glittering against her rosy cheeks. Jingles reached out, his mittened hand gently brushing a snowflake from her nose.

In that quiet moment, as they stood hand in hand amid the falling snow, everything else seemed to fade away. The worries, the self-doubts, the uncertainties—all melted like snowflakes on a warm hearth. What remained was the magic of the evening, the connection they had forged, and the promise of something wonderful blossoming between them.

As the snowfall thickened, Jingles reluctantly guided Holly toward the edge of the lake. "I think it's time for a hot chocolate break," he suggested, his hand finding hers as they glided to a stop.

Holly nodded, her cheeks flushed from the cold and the exhilaration of the evening. "That sounds perfect."

They made their way to the cozy hot chocolate station, where wisps of steam curled invitingly from the waiting mugs. Jingles carefully handed one to Holly, his fingers brushing against hers in the process. The rich aroma of chocolate and cinnamon enveloped them, chasing away the chill.

Holly cradled the mug in her hands, savoring the warmth that seeped through her mittens. She watched as Jingles added a generous swirl of whipped cream to his own mug, a mischievous glint in his eye. He finds joy in the little things, she mused, a smile tugging at her lips. It's one of the things I lo-- like about him.

Jingles caught her gaze over the rim of his mug, his eyes crinkling with warmth. "Penny for your thoughts?" he asked, his voice soft and inviting.

Holly ducked her head, suddenly shy. "I was just thinking about how much I've enjoyed this evening," she admitted. "How much I enjoy spending time with you."

Jingles' smile widened, his cheeks dimpling with pleasure. "I feel the same way, Holly," he confessed. "Being with you... it feels like magic."

They sipped their hot chocolate in companionable silence, the twinkling lights casting a soft glow over their faces. As they finished their drinks, Jingles set his mug aside and turned to face Holly fully.

"Holly," he began, his voice uncharacteristically serious. "I..."

But before he could continue, Holly set down her own mug and reached for his hands. "Jingles," she breathed, her heart racing in her chest. "You don't have to say anything. I... I feel it too."

And then, as naturally as snowflakes falling from the sky, they leaned in, their lips meeting in a tender kiss. The world around them faded away, leaving only the two of them, lost in a moment of perfect magic.

When they finally pulled apart, Jingles rested his forehead against Holly's, a soft laugh escaping his lips. "Wow," he whispered, his voice filled with wonder.

Holly giggled, her eyes sparkling with joy. "Wow indeed."

They stood there, gazing at each other, wrapped in the warmth of one another as the snow continued to fall around them. Jingles tilted Holly's chin with his finger. "I don't know what my life would be like without you." he said as his lips met with hers.

Chapter 11: Blizzard Warning

Jingles' melodic laughter reverberated through the bustling North Pole Bakery as he twirled Holly in his arms, her apron flaring out like the skirt of a ballerina. Cinnamon, nutmeg, and freshly baked gingerbread suffused the air, the scents of holiday magic. Holly giggled, her cheeks flushed with joy and exertion as she steadied herself against Jingles' chest.

"You're incorrigible," she chided playfully, her eyes sparkling up at him. "We're supposed to be working on the gingerbread housing development project, not waltzing through the kitchen!"

Jingles grinned impishly, the silver bells on his crimson hat jingling as he leaned in close. "Ah, but all work and no play makes for a very dull North Pole indeed! Besides," he added, his voice dropping to a conspiratorial whisper, "I find I'm far more creative with my beautiful muse by my side."

Holly shook her head fondly, a smile playing at the corners of her lips. She knew she ought to focus - the gingerbread housing was her most ambitious undertaking yet, a chance to prove her skill to all of Frostyville. But with Jingles' infectious enthusiasm and the love shining in his eyes, she found her perfectionist drive momentarily derailed.

Just a few more minutes, she told herself, leaning up on tiptoe to brush a feather-light kiss across Jingles' cheek. *Then it's back to-*

The bakery door burst open with a sudden, icy gust, startling the couple apart. Tinsel, the excitable elf who served as Frostyville's town crier, tumbled inside, his emerald coattails flapping. "Urgent news!" he cried, his normally exuberant voice edged with uncharacteristic tension. "A severe blizzard approaches! All elves are advised to seek shelter and prepare for power disruptions!"

A hush fell over the bakery as the gathered elves exchanged worried glances, the previously festive atmosphere chilling like a forgotten cup of cocoa. Holly felt her stomach drop, her gaze darting to the meticulously drafted gingerbread blueprints scattered across the floury workbench. A blizzard? Now? But the delicate icing work required precision temperature control, and if the power were to fail...

She swallowed hard, her smile fading as the potential ramifications sunk in. Months of planning, countless hours poring over recipes and sketches - all potentially undone by a twist of cruel, wintry fate. Holly's hands trembled as she reached for the blueprints, her mind awhirl with contingencies and backup plans, each more desperate than the last.

No, she thought fiercely, her perfectionist nature surging to the forefront. I won't let one storm jeopardize everything. There has to be a way. There just has to be.

But as the wind howled outside the frosted windows, rattling the candy cane frames, Holly couldn't quite quell the sinking feeling that her gingerbread dreams were about to crumble like so many stale cookies. She turned to Jingles, her brow furrowed with worry, wondering if even his boundless optimism could find a silver lining in this ominous turn of events.

As if on cue, the bakery door burst open, a gust of frigid air heralding the arrival of Frosty McFrosterson. His gruff voice cut through the anxious chatter, his bushy eyebrows knitted together in a stern expression. "Listen up, everyone," he barked, his eyes sweeping the room. "This blizzard's no joke. We're talking gale-force winds, whiteout conditions, the whole shebang. And if the power goes out..." He let the implication hang in the air, heavy as a fruitcake.

Holly's heart sank further, her gaze once again drawn to the gingerbread house plans. Temperature control was crucial for the intricate icing work - even a slight fluctuation could spell disaster. She could practically feel the seconds ticking away, her carefully crafted timeline crumbling like a stale gingerbread wall.

Frosty's gaze landed on Holly, his expression softening slightly. "I know you've got your heart set on this project, Miss Sugarplum, but we've got to be realistic here. If the power goes out, there's no telling when we'll get it back."

Holly nodded, her throat tight. She knew Frosty was right, but the thought of abandoning her vision, her chance to prove herself, left a bitter taste in her mouth. Her perfectionist nature warred with the looming threat of the storm, each vying for dominance in her whirling thoughts.

Jingles, ever the optimist, piped up from beside her. "Now, hold on just a minute," he said, his blue eyes twinkling with determination. "What about moving the project to Santa's workshop? They've got those backup generators, don't they? We could keep right on schedule, blizzard or no blizzard!"

Holly's heart leaped at the suggestion, a flicker of hope rekindled. Santa's workshop... of course! With their state-of-the-art facilities and failsafe power systems, it could be the perfect solution. But just as quickly, doubt crept in, her protective instincts over the secret recipe rearing their head.

The workshop is always bustling with activity, she thought, her brow furrowing. *Can I really risk exposing the recipe to so many eyes? What if someone tries to steal it, or worse, what if they think it's not good enough?*

She looked to Jingles, torn between gratitude for his quick thinking and hesitation at the potential risks. His enthusiasm was infectious, but could it really outweigh her deep-seated fears?

As the wind continued to rattle the windows, a constant reminder of the impending storm, Holly knew she had to make a decision - and fast. The fate of her gingerbread dreams hung in the balance, and every moment of indecision brought them closer to crumbling entirely.

Holly took a deep breath, her fingers nervously twisting the edges of her flour-dusted apron. "I don't know, Jingles," she said, her voice trembling slightly. "Moving the project to Santa's workshop... it's a big risk. What if something goes wrong? What if the recipe gets out, or someone thinks it's not good enough?"

Jingles' smile softened, his eyes filled with understanding. He reached out, gently taking Holly's hand in his own. "Holly, my dear," he said, his voice warm and reassuring, "You've got to have faith in yourself, and in your recipe. It's not just good enough - it's extraordinary! And as for the risk..."

He paused, a mischievous glint in his eye. "Well, we'll just have to be extra sneaky, won't we? Operation Gingerbread Relocation, commence!" He gave her a playful wink, eliciting a reluctant smile from Holly.

For a moment, the gravity of the situation seemed to fade away, replaced by the comforting familiarity of their banter. *How does he always know just what to say?* Holly wondered, her heart swelling with affection.

But the moment was short-lived, as another gust of wind rattled the windows, sending a shiver down Holly's spine. She sighed, the weight of responsibility settling heavily on her shoulders once more.

"It's not just about the recipe, Jingles," she confessed, her voice barely above a whisper. "It's... it's about me. What if I can't do this? What if I let everyone down, like I have before? I don't think I could bear it..."

Jingles' expression softened, his hand gently squeezing hers. "Holly, listen to me," he said, his voice filled with conviction. "You are the most talented, passionate, and determined elf I know. You pour your heart into everything you do, and it shows in every delicious creation that comes out of this bakery."

He smiled, his eyes shining with unwavering loyalty. "We're in this together, remember? You and me, against the world - or at least, against this blizzard. And with your skills and my dashing good looks, there's nothing we can't handle!"

Despite herself, Holly couldn't help but laugh, the sound a welcome respite from the tension that had settled over the bakery. *Maybe he's right,* she thought, a flicker of hope reigniting in her chest. *Maybe, just maybe, we can pull this off after all.*

She took a deep breath, squaring her shoulders with newfound determination. "Alright, Jingles," she said, a small smile tugging at the corners of her mouth. "Operation Gingerbread Relocation it is. But we're going to need a foolproof plan - and a whole lot of luck."

Jingles grinned, his bells jingling merrily as he bounced on the balls of his feet. "That's the spirit!" he exclaimed, his enthusiasm infectious. "Now, let's get cracking - we've got a gingerbread house to save, and a blizzard to beat!"

As they huddled together over Holly's plans, their heads bent in concentration, the world outside seemed to fade away. In that moment, it was just the two of them, united in their determination to make the impossible possible - and to prove, once and for all, that with a little bit of magic and a whole lot of heart, anything was possible in the North Pole.

Holly's gaze lingered on the intricate gingerbread house plans spread out before her, the delicate lines and carefully sketched details a testament to her unwavering dedication. The weight of the decision pressed heavily upon her shoulders, the tension between her desire for perfection and the looming threat of the blizzard an almost tangible presence in the room.

Can I really do this? she wondered, her fingers tracing the edges of the parchment. *Can I risk everything I've worked so hard for, all for the sake of a single project?*

Jingles placed a gentle hand on her shoulder, his touch a reassuring anchor amidst the swirling chaos of her thoughts. "Holly," he said softly, his voice filled with unwavering conviction, "I know this isn't an easy choice. But I also know that if anyone can make this work, it's you."

Holly looked up at him, her eyes searching his for any hint of doubt or uncertainty. But all she found was a steadfast belief in her abilities, a faith that burned brighter than the twinkling lights strung throughout the bakery.

"You really think so?" she asked, her voice barely above a whisper.

Jingles smiled, his eyes crinkling at the corners. "I know so," he replied, giving her shoulder a gentle squeeze. "You're Holly Sugarplum, the most talented baker in all of Frostyville. If anyone can create a gingerbread masterpiece in the face of a blizzard, it's you."

As if on cue, a sudden gust of wind rattled the bakery's windows, the howling sound a stark reminder of the impending storm. Holly flinched, her gaze darting to the frosted panes as a flurry of snowflakes swirled past, their delicate forms a fleeting dance against the darkening sky.

Time's running out, she realized, a sense of urgency rising within her. *If we're going to do this, we need to act now.*

With a deep breath and a determined nod, Holly turned back to Jingles, her decision made. "Alright," she said, her voice steady despite the butterflies in her stomach. "Let's do this. Let's move the gingerbread house to Santa's workshop."

Jingles grinned, his enthusiasm contagious. "That's my girl!" he exclaimed, pulling her into a quick hug. "I knew you had it in you."

While they gathered the necessary supplies, the wind outside continued to howl, a constant reminder of the blizzard that lay ahead.

Chapter 12: Power Struggle

Holly's hands trembled as she piped delicate swirls of royal icing along the gingerbread roof's steep slope, each breath measured and careful. The rich aroma of freshly baked spices—ginger, cinnamon, and clove—wrapped around her like a familiar blanket, usually bringing comfort but now only heightening her anxiety. Outside, the wind howled with increasing fury, rattling the frost-kissed windows of the North Pole Bakery with an ominous persistence.

She glanced across the elaborate gingerbread house at Jingles, who braced the other side with steady hands dusted in powdered sugar. His emerald eyes caught hers, warm with encouragement despite the tension evident in his furrowed brow. The tiny bells sewn into his hat jingled softly with each careful movement, their gentle chiming a counterpoint to the storm's growing rage.

"Just... a little... more," Holly whispered through clenched teeth, willing her hands to stay steady. The structure before them represented more than just gingerbread and royal icing—it was her chance to prove herself worthy of Frostyville's trust, to show that a summer-born elf could master the delicate art of holiday baking. The sweet, spicy scent of fresh gingerbread mingled with the metallic tang of approaching snow, creating an atmosphere thick with possibility and dread.

Jingles offered her that trademark grin of his, though she noticed how it wavered slightly at the edges. "We've got this, Holly! Together, we can weather any storm." The forced cheer in his voice couldn't quite mask the concern underneath, but his unwavering faith in her made something warm flutter in her chest despite her fears.

The warmth was short-lived. The bakery lights flickered ominously, casting dancing shadows across their careful work. The electric oven behind them beeped erratically, its digital display flashing random numbers like a countdown to disaster. Holly's heart leaped into her throat, the taste of fear bitter on her tongue.

"Jingles," she breathed, her voice barely audible above the wind's mournful song, "what's happening?"

He glanced around the bakery, his usual mischievous expression replaced by something more serious. The cheerful holiday decorations—twinkling lights, shimmering tinsel, and glittering snowflakes—suddenly seemed to mock their predicament. "Don't worry, Holly. It's just a power fluctuation. Nothing we can't handle." The slight tremor in his voice betrayed his own uncertainty.

Holly's mind raced faster than a reindeer on Christmas Eve, her thoughts spiraling into darker territory with each flicker of the lights. The cool air of the bakery seemed to grow colder, raising goosebumps along her arms. She'd worked so hard to make this gingerbread house perfect—every angle precise, every decoration placed with mathematical accuracy. The thought of it crumbling now, when she was so close to proving herself, made her stomach twist into pretzel knots.

"We need to stabilize the foundation," she declared, forcing strength into her voice even as her hands shook. The piping bag felt slippery in her grip as she reached for the base of the house. The sweet scent of the royal icing reminded her of childhood dreams and current fears, all mixed together in a complex recipe of emotion.

Jingles nodded, his nimble fingers already working to secure the roof. The bells on his hat created a soothing rhythm as he moved, a familiar sound that usually brought her comfort. "I've got your back, Holly. We're a team, remember?" His words carried the weight of months of shared laughter, quiet moments, and growing connection.

As they worked in tandem, Holly couldn't help but steal glances at her partner. Jingles had been a constant source of both joy and distraction since she'd arrived at the North Pole Bakery, his infectious laughter and creative solutions brightening even the most stressful moments. Now, watching him work with such focused compassion, she felt something shift in her heart—a recognition of something deeper than mere relationship.

The lights flickered again, more insistently this time. The air crackled with electricity and tension, making Holly's pointed ears twitch. Her fingers flew as she piped, desperate to keep their creation standing. She could feel Jingles' gaze on her, sense his own determination to see this through. The scent of ozone mixed with gingerbread, creating an oddly apocalyptic holiday atmosphere.

"Almost there," Holly whispered, more to herself than to Jingles. She refused to let her doubts win, refused to let this setback define her. With Jingles by her side, she felt a flicker of hope amidst the chaos. The sweet taste of possibility lingered on her tongue, mingling with the lingering flavor of the candy canes she'd been nibbling on earlier for courage.

But fate had other plans. A sudden, violent power surge sent a shock through the bakery, plunging everything into darkness. The abrupt silence felt deafening, broken only by the sickening crack of breaking gingerbread. Holly's heart stopped, her breath caught in her throat as she watched in horror as their creation began to collapse.

Time seemed to slow as the walls crumbled, each piece falling with terrible precision. The sound of breaking gingerbread and shattering candy echoed in her ears like breaking dreams. The once-proud structure transformed into a twisted heap of candy canes, fractured gingerbread, and smeared icing before her eyes. The sight was a physical blow, sending her stumbling backward as the weight of failure pressed down on her shoulders.

The piping bag slipped from her nerveless fingers, landing with a soft thud on the flour-dusted floor. The sweet scent of destruction rose around her—sugar and spice and everything she'd worked so hard to achieve, all reduced to crumbs.

"No, no, no," Holly whispered, her voice raw with emotion. She couldn't tear her eyes away from the ruined gingerbread house, couldn't escape the suffocating feeling of failure that threatened to consume her. The taste of defeat was bitter in her mouth, sharp and acrid like burnt sugar.

Jingles' hand on her shoulder startled her back to the present, his touch warm and steady despite everything. "Holly, it's okay. We can fix this." His voice was gentle but carried an undercurrent of strength that made her want to believe him.

She turned to face him, tears stinging her eyes like winter wind. The darkness of the bakery seemed to press in around them, broken only by the faint glow of emergency lights and the occasional flash of lightning outside. "How, Jingles? Look at it. It's ruined. I've ruined everything." The words tasted bitter on her tongue, but she couldn't hold them back. The pressure, the expectations, the fear of letting everyone down—it all came crashing down upon her like the gingerbread walls.

But as she looked into Jingles' eyes, she saw something that made her pause. There was no judgment there, no disappointment. Only a steadfast belief in her, a faith that seemed to glow from within like a Christmas star. His gaze held hers, unwavering, and Holly felt something shift inside her—a spark of strength igniting in her core.

"We'll rebuild it, together," Jingles said, his hand squeezing her shoulder. The familiar jingling of his hat bells seemed to take on a different melody now, one of hope. "You're Holly Sugarplum, the most talented baker in all of Frostyville. This gingerbread house won't define you. Your resilience will."

Holly drew in a shaky breath, letting Jingles' words wash over her like warm cocoa on a cold night. The sweet, spicy scent of the bakery surrounded them, no longer overwhelming but comforting—a reminder of countless successes and failures, all part of her journey. He was right. She had faced challenges before, had poured her heart and soul into her craft. This setback, while devastating, was not the end.

Slowly, Holly nodded, his strength settling over her like a dusting of fresh snow. "Okay," she said, her voice growing stronger with each word. "Let's try this again." She reached up to squeeze his hand on her shoulder, feeling the warmth of his skin against hers, the slight tremor in his fingers that matched her own.

As they turned to face the ruined gingerbread house, Holly felt the change within herself solidify. The doubts and fears were still there, like shadows at the edge of candlelight, but they were tempered by a growing sense of confidence and resilience. With Jingles' support and her own unwavering passion, she knew they could create something even more magical from the ruins.

The blizzard continued to rage outside, but inside the bakery, Holly and Jingles stood united, ready to rebuild not just the gingerbread house, but also the faith in themselves and each other. The air around them seemed to crackle with the sweet promise of something new and wonderful taking shape. A stronger united front not just as lovers, but something more.

Holly surveyed the remnants of their creation, her mind already whirring with fresh ideas. The foundation remained intact, and several walls still stood proud—a testament to their initial craftsmanship. It wasn't a complete loss. She could work with this. She would work with this.

"Jingles," she said, her voice steady despite the lingering tremors in her hands, "can you gather the salvageable pieces?" She met his gaze. "I'll start mixing a new batch of gingerbread to rebuild the damaged sections."

His face lit up like a Christmas tree, that infectious enthusiasm she'd come to rely on returning full force. "On it!" he replied, already moving. She watched as he carefully picked through the rubble, his movements precise and gentle, treating each broken piece with respect—as if they were precious memories rather than failures.

Holly turned to her workstation, finding comfort in the familiar motions of measuring and mixing. The rhythmic sifting of flour created a soft percussion, accompanied by the clinking of measuring spoons and the whisper of sugar falling like snow. Each ingredient added its voice to the symphony of creation—the sharp snap of ginger, the warm embrace of cinnamon, the deep richness of molasses.

As she worked, Holly felt the tension in her shoulders beginning to ease. The sweet, spicy aroma of fresh gingerbread batter filled the air. She poured the mixture onto the baking sheet with steady hands, her movements sure and confident once more.

While the gingerbread baked, filling the bakery with its intoxicating scent, Holly turned her attention to the decorations. She sorted through their supplies with fresh eyes—candy canes gleaming like striped promises, gumdrops glowing like tiny jewels, chocolate buttons waiting to become stepping stones on a new path.

"I've got an idea," Jingles announced, practically bouncing on his toes. The bells on his hat created a cheerful melody that matched the growing lightness in Holly's heart. "What if we add a candy cane archway at the entrance? It'll be like walking into a winter wonderland!"

Holly smiled warm and genuine. She looked at Jingles—really looked at him—and saw not just the cheerful elf who brought laughter to her days, but someone who understood her on a deeper level, who could help her find joy in the midst of chaos.

"I love it," she said softly, meaning more than just the archway. "And we can use the chocolate buttons to create a path leading up to the door." Her creative spirit sparked to life, dancing like sugar crystals in sunlight.

They worked together in perfect harmony, their movements synchronized as if they'd been partners for centuries rather than months. Holly's precision complemented Jingles' creativity, each bringing out the best in the other. The sweet scent of success began to replace the bitter tang of failure.

As the final piece of the roof settled into place, Holly stepped back to admire their handiwork. The gingerbread house stood proud and tall, more beautiful than its predecessor. The candy cane archway gleamed with invitation, and the chocolate button path wound its way to the entrance like a story waiting to be told. Every imperfection, every slightly asymmetrical decoration, spoke of resilience and growth.

"It's even better than before," Jingles whispered, his eyes shining with something that made Holly's heart skip a beat. The emergency lights had come back on, casting a soft glow that made everything seem magical and new.

Holly nodded, emotion making her throat tight. "We did it," she said softly, the words carrying the weight of all they'd overcome. "Together."

She felt Jingles' hand find hers, their fingers intertwining naturally, like pieces of a puzzle finally finding their match. A spark of electricity that had nothing to do with power surges danced between them. In that moment, Holly understood that this gingerbread house represented more than just a baking project. It was a symbol of their resilience, their connection, and the magic that could happen when two hearts found each other amidst the chaos of life.

As the blizzard quieted outside, its fury spent, Holly and Jingles stood hand in hand in their bakery. The air was sweet with success and warmth with shared understanding and growing love. They had weathered the storm together, emerging stronger and more united than ever before.

The North Pole Bakery glowed a bit brighter, and as Holly looked at their creation—and at Jingles—she knew that sometimes the most beautiful things could rise from destruction, and the sweetest victories came not from perfection, but from the courage to try again, together.

Chapter 13: The Icing on the Cake

The morning light filtered weakly through the bakery windows, casting pale shadows across the floor where Holly stood frozen, her hands pressed against her mouth in horror. Before her, the gingerbread house—their second attempt at creating the perfect centerpiece for Frostyville's holiday display—lay in ruins. The humidity from the previous night's blizzard had proven too much for the delicate structure, leaving rivers of red and green icing pooled beneath what remained of the collapsed walls.

"No," Holly whispered, her voice cracking. "No, no, no. Not again."

She reached out with trembling fingers toward the wreckage, watching as another piece of gingerbread slid free, splattering into the mess below. The sound echoed in the empty bakery like a gunshot, and something inside Holly finally snapped.

"I'm done," she said, her words sharp enough to cut. "I can't—I can't do this anymore." Her shoulders began to shake as she backed away from the destruction, nearly stumbling over her own feet in her haste to escape the sight.

Holly turned and ran, her footsteps thundering across the wooden floor as she fled toward the storage room. The heavy door slammed behind her with enough force to rattle the jars on the shelves, and she collapsed against it, sliding down until she hit the floor. The familiar scent of flour and sugar that usually brought her comfort now seemed to mock her failures.

"Why?" she sobbed, drawing her knees to her chest. "Why does everything I touch fall apart?"

The tears came freely now, hot and bitter, soaking into the fabric of her apron. Every ounce of disappointment, every moment of self-doubt she'd been holding back crashed over her like a wave, leaving her gasping for breath in its wake.

The gentle creak of the door several minutes later barely registered through her grief. It wasn't until she heard the soft jingle of bells that she looked up, finding Jingles hovering uncertainly in the doorway, his face etched with concern.

"Holly," he said softly, taking a tentative step forward. "I just saw what happened. I'm so sorry—"

"Don't," Holly cut him off, her voice raw. She pushed herself to her feet, anger suddenly blazing through her grief like wildfire. "Don't you dare say you're sorry. This is your fault!"

Jingles flinched as if she'd struck him. "My fault? Holly, I—"

"Yes, your fault!" The words poured out of her like poison. "You're the one who convinced me to try again after the first one fell. You're the one who said it would work this time. You and your endless optimism, always pushing me to do more, to try harder, when maybe I should have just accepted that I'm not good enough!"

"That's not true," Jingles protested, reaching for her. "Holly, you're one of the most talented—"

"Get out," Holly said, her voice dropping to a dangerous whisper. "Just get out, Jingles. Get out of this room, get out of the bakery, get out of my life. I can't do this anymore. I can't handle your constant hovering, your eternal cheerfulness when everything is falling apart. Just go!"

The silence that followed her outburst was deafening. Jingles stood there, his hand still outstretched, looking as if she'd shattered something precious. Slowly, he lowered his arm, and Holly watched as the light in his eyes dimmed, like stars going out one by one.

"If... if that's what you want," he said quietly, his voice thick with emotion. "I'm sorry I've caused you so much pain, Holly. Truly, I am."

He turned away, his shoulders hunched as if bearing an invisible weight. The bells that usually chimed so merrily with his movement now seemed to toll like funeral bells as he walked away. At the doorway, he paused for just a moment, as if hoping she might call him back.

Holly said nothing, her anger already cooling into something worse—a hollow ache that threatened to consume her from the inside out. The soft click of the door closing behind Jingles echoed with a terrible finality.

Hours later, as evening settled over Frostyville like a heavy blanket, Jingles stood alone on the train platform. A single bag sat at his feet, containing what little he'd chosen to take with him. Snow had begun to fall again, thick flakes catching in his hair and on his coat, but he barely noticed the cold.

His gaze remained fixed on the bakery's distant rooftop, barely visible through the swirling snow. The warm glow of its windows, once so inviting, now seemed to mock him with memories of what he was leaving behind. As the distant whistle of the approaching train pierced the winter air, Jingles closed his eyes, letting the tears he'd been holding back finally fall.

The bells on his coat jingled softly in the wind, a lonely sound in the gathering dark.

Chapter 14: The Christmas Eve Miracle

The streets of Frostyville had never seemed so quiet. Where festive carols once filled the air, now only the soft whisper of falling snow could be heard. The destruction of the gingerbread house had cast a shadow over the town that even the twinkling Christmas lights couldn't fully brighten. In her cottage, Holly sat surrounded by perfectly organized baking supplies, each measuring spoon and pastry tube exactly where it should be – yet nothing felt right anymore.

Santa found her there, gently knocking on her door with the kind of patience that comes from centuries of understanding human hearts. "You know," he said, settling into her grandmother's old rocking chair, "some of my favorite Christmas memories started with things going completely wrong."

Holly looked up, her eyes red-rimmed but curious. "Even you make mistakes, Santa?"

His belly shook with a gentle laugh. "Oh, Holly. The year I delivered presents in a thunderstorm, or when the reindeer got tangled in the Northern Lights – those aren't mistakes. They're the moments that make magic real. Just like Jingles and his wonderful chaos."

The mention of his name made her heart ache. "But the gingerbread house—"

"Was never about perfection," Santa interrupted softly. "It was about bringing people together. And look what Jingles did – he brought more joy to this town in a few weeks than all the perfect frosting roses in the world could manage."

Through her window, Holly could see movement in the town square. Curious, she moved closer, Santa joining her with a knowing smile. There, in the gently falling snow, the entire town had gathered. Elves and townspeople alike were working together, carrying armfuls of gingerbread panels and buckets of icing. They were rebuilding the house.

Mrs. Peppermint, the town's oldest resident, was directing traffic with her candy cane cane, while young elves darted between adults' legs with bags of candies and sprinkles. Even grumpy Mr. Icicle, who hadn't participated in a town event since the Great Blizzard of '82, was carefully placing gumdrops along a roof panel.

"They're doing it all wrong," Holly whispered, but there was no judgment in her voice – only wonder. The walls weren't perfectly aligned, the frosting dripped in places, and someone had clearly let the kindergarten class decorate one entire side with what appeared to be a rainbow explosion of candies.

It was beautiful.

Holly's feet were moving before she realized it, Santa's warm chuckle following her out the door. The townspeople looked up as she approached, their faces showing not judgment but joy. Little Timmy, face covered in frosting, ran up to her with a candy cane. "We're fixing it, Miss Holly! We remembered how you said the secret ingredient is love!"

That's when she saw it – the magic she'd been missing all along. It wasn't in the perfectly piped borders or the mathematically precise angles. It was in the smudged fingerprints of children helping to hold panels steady, in the slightly crooked windows that somehow made the house look like it was winking at passersby, in the way the whole town had come together.

"Jingles," she breathed, suddenly realizing what she needed to do. "Has anyone seen Jingles?"

"He's heading to the Santa Express," called out an elf. "Said something about giving Frostyville back its perfect Christmas."

Holly's heart leaped into her throat. Without a word, she turned and ran, her boots slipping on the icy streets. She could hear the train whistle in the distance, its mournful sound echoing off the snow-covered buildings. Twice she nearly fell, but she didn't slow down. She couldn't.

The platform was empty except for one figure, his familiar mismatched socks visible beneath his coat. "Jingles!" she called out, her voice carrying on the winter wind.

He turned, suitcase in hand, his usually bright eyes dim with sadness. "Holly? What are you doing here?"

She stopped in front of him, breathing hard, snowflakes catching in her eyelashes. "Making the biggest mistake of my life," she said, "by letting you leave."

"But the gingerbread house—"

"Is perfect," she interrupted, taking his hand. "Not because of straight lines or proper proportions, but because it's filled with love and laughter and yes, a little bit of chaos. Your chaos."

Reaching into her pocket, Holly pulled out a handful of the magical edible glitter that had started everything. "You know what I realized? Life isn't about following recipes exactly. It's about adding your own ingredients." She blew the glitter into the air, where it caught the light and danced around them like stars.

"The town is rebuilding the house right now, and it's wonderfully, perfectly imperfect. Just like us." Holly took a deep breath, her heart racing but her voice steady. "Which is why I have a very important question to ask you."

Jingles' eyes widened as Holly dropped to one knee, pulling out a ring she had hastily crafted from twisted candy cane strips. "Jingles Merryweather, you turned my perfectly ordered world upside down, and it's the best thing that ever happened to me. Will you marry me and keep adding your sprinkle of chaos to my life forever?"

For a moment, the only sound was the distant whistle of the Santa Express and the soft falling of snow. Then Jingles broke into the brightest smile Holly had ever seen, pulling her up into his arms. "Only if you promise to never make anything perfect again," he whispered against her hair.

"I promise to make everything perfectly imperfect with you," she replied, laughing through happy tears.

The entire town had followed Holly to the station, and their cheers echoed through the winter air. Santa stepped forward, his eyes twinkling brighter than ever. "Well," he announced, "I believe we have a wedding to plan – and a gingerbread house to finish decorating!"

As Holly and Jingles walked hand in hand back to the town square, the magical glitter still swirling around them, the gingerbread house came into view. It wasn't the architectural masterpiece Holly had originally planned. Instead, it was something far better – a true reflection of Frostyville's heart, with all its quirks and imperfections.

The elves had strung lights everywhere, their warm glow reflecting off the snow and turning the entire square into a magical wonderland. Mrs. Peppermint was already discussing wedding cake flavors with the other townspeople, while Mr.

Icicle, now completely caught up in the spirit, was teaching young elves how to make snow angels.

Holly looked at the beautiful chaos around her, then at Jingles, who was attempting to juggle candy canes and failing magnificently. This was her perfect moment – not because everything was flawless, but because it was real, and wonderful, and filled with love.

"You know," Santa said, appearing beside them with two mugs of hot chocolate, topped with imperfectly swirled whipped cream, "sometimes the best gifts come wrapped in unexpected packages. And sometimes the most perfect love stories are the ones that don't follow the recipe at all."

As the snow continued to fall gently over Frostyville, Holly and Jingles shared their first kiss as an engaged couple in front of the beautifully imperfect gingerbread house, while the magical glitter swirled around them like a thousand twinkling stars. The town had never looked more festive, more alive, or more perfect in its own wonderfully chaotic way.

And if you looked very closely at the gingerbread house, you might notice that the slightly crooked heart-shaped window in the center seemed to beat with its own magical rhythm, a reminder that true love, like the best Christmas memories, doesn't need to be perfect to be absolutely right.

Chapter 15: Mistletoe and Memories

The crowd gathered in Frostyville's town square, a sea of colorful hats and scarves bobbing with excitement. Breaths mingled in the crisp air, rising like wisps of smoke from chimneys. Elves chattered animatedly as they jostled for prime viewing spots along the parade route, their pointy-toed shoes crunching in the fresh snow. Children perched on parents' shoulders, eyes wide with anticipation. The square practically vibrated with festive energy.

Near the towering gingerbread house, Holly Sugarplum and Jingles Evergreen made last-minute adjustments, their gloved hands brushing as they straightened peppermint sticks and adjusted gumdrop trim. Holly's heart fluttered at the contact, and she glanced up to find Jingles smiling at her, his blue eyes twinkling.

"We make quite the team, don't we, Holls?" He winked, bells jingling merrily on his hat.

Holly flushed, ducking her head to hide a smile. "I couldn't have done it without you, Jingles. Your creativity never ceases to amaze me."

Jingles puffed out his chest. "Well, I am known for my brilliant ideas! Like the time I tried to make reindeer fly with rocket boosters..."

Holly giggled, remembering the chaos that had ensued. "Maybe we should stick to gingerbread engineering for now."

They shared a laugh, the sweet sound mingling with the festive din. Holly marveled at how comfortable she felt with Jingles, despite her usual reserved nature. His lighthearted presence put her at ease, making her believe anything was possible.

A hush fell over the gathered crowd as Santa Claus himself stepped onto the stage, his majestic presence commanding immediate attention. The very air seemed to shimmer with anticipation, the only sound the crisp crunch of snow beneath his polished boots. His cheeks, rosy as holly berries, dimpled as he smiled benevolently at the sea of upturned faces.

"Ho ho ho!" His rich baritone carried across the square, instantly igniting a spark of childlike wonder in every heart. "What a magnificent sight to behold! The spirit of the season is truly alive in Frostyville tonight."

Santa's eyes twinkled as he continued, "Each year, I am astounded by the creativity and dedication of our little community. The gingerbread houses lining the square are a testament to the talent and heart that resides within each and every one of you."

His voice grew somber. "But tonight, we celebrate a gingerbread house like no other. A confectionery marvel born of unexpected partnership, of a love for the craft that transcended all obstacles."

Holly's pulse quickened as Santa's gazed at Holly Sugarplum and Jingles Evergreen. He declared, "your tireless efforts and unwavering dedication have not gone unnoticed.

The gingerbread house you've created together is a shining example of what can be accomplished when we open our hearts to the magic of the season, and to each other."

With a grand flourish, Santa unveiled their creation. The gingerbread house shimmered beneath the lights, the edible glitter casting a magical glow. The intricate lattice work of the candy cane fence gleamed in shades of red and white, while the walls were adorned with delicate icing filigrees that seemed to come alive in the twinkling light. Gumdrop accents added whimsical pops of color, and the roof, dusted with powdered sugar, looked as though it had been kissed by a gentle snowfall.

In the gingerbread garden, miniature marzipan elves frolicked, their tiny features alight with joy. A spun sugar replica of Santa's sleigh seemed poised to take flight, the intricately sculpted reindeer straining forward with lifelike eagerness.

As the crowd's wonder turned to thunderous applause, even gruff old Frosty McFrosterson was moved to tears. "Well, I'll be a candy cane's stripes," he muttered, his voice thick with emotion. "In all my years, I've never seen anything quite like this."

Santa placed a gentle hand on Frosty's shoulder. "It's truly remarkable, isn't it, old friend?"

As the celebration continued, a gentle snowfall descended upon the town square, the delicate flakes dancing in the air. Jingles turned to Holly, his eyes sparkling with adoration. "Holly, I couldn't have done this without you," he said softly. "You've been my rock through this entire journey, and I've come to realize that my feelings for you have grown deeper than I ever thought possible."

Holly's heart skipped a beat as she met his gaze. "Jingles, I feel the same way. Being with you has been the most incredible experience of my life.

Standing beneath a sprig of mistletoe that had seemingly appeared out of nowhere, Santa gave a wink and looked above. "You may now kiss her." The crowd erupted in renewed cheers. The scene was one of pure enchantment, a moment frozen in time that would be forever etched in the memories of all who witnessed it.

As the last of the townsfolk made their way home, Holly and Jingles remained in the square, their silhouettes illuminated by the soft glow of the Christmas lights. They stood there, lost in the promise of their newfound love, knowing that this was just the first chapter in a tale as enchanting as the spirit of Christmas itself.

Chapter 16: Sweet Celebrations

Holly's fingers intertwined with Jingles' as they wove through the cheerful crowd, the glow of lanterns and crackle of marching bands fading behind them. She glanced over at Jingles, his bright eyes twinkling with mischief and barely-contained excitement. A warm flutter danced in her chest. Being with him made her feel alive in a way baking never could.

They slipped behind a row of festively adorned cottages, seeking a moment of solitude amidst the revelry. The jubilant noise of the parade became a distant hum as they reached a secluded spot—a small gazebo dusted with fresh snow and illuminated by soft, twinkling fairy lights. Holly's breath caught at the enchanting sight.

"Jingles, it's beautiful," she whispered, her words forming puffs of mist in the crisp air.

He squeezed her hand. "Not as beautiful as you, Holly-berry."

She ducked her head as a blush warmed her cheeks, still not used to his earnest compliments. The gentle crunch of snow underfoot and the stillness of their shared moment enveloped them like a cozy blanket.

Jingles led her up the gazebo steps, the bells on his hat jingling merrily. He turned to face her, taking both her hands in his. His gaze held hers, simultaneously playful and sincere.

"Holly, I...I've been wanting to tell you something. Being with you, it's like...like all the joy of Christmas morning, but every single day." He paused, uncharacteristically nervous. "What I'm trying to say is..."

Holly's heart raced, a swirl of hope and trepidation rising within her. Could this charming, wonderful elf truly feel the same way she did? After guarding her heart for so long, she hardly dared to believe it.

Snowflakes drifted lazily around the gazebo, catching the glow of the fairy lights like falling stardust. In that perfect, frozen moment, the rest of Frostyville faded away, and it was just the two of them, hearts laid bare under the magic of the North Pole night.

Holly's breath visible in the crisp night air as she reached into her bag, her fingers trembling with anticipation. She retrieved a carefully wrapped package, the shimmering paper reflecting the twinkling fairy lights that illuminated the snow-dusted gazebo.

This is it, she thought, her heart pounding. The perfect gift to show Jingles how much he means to me.

With a shy smile, Holly held out the present to Jingles. "I made this for you. I hope you like it."

Jingles' eyes sparkled with delight as he accepted the gift. "For me? Oh Holly, you shouldn't have!"

He tore open the wrapping paper with barely-contained excitement. As the custom apron unfolded, his eyes widened in awe. The deep red fabric was embroidered with intricate gold snowflakes that glittered in the soft light. Pockets of various sizes adorned the front, perfectly designed to hold Jingles' mischievous tools and gadgets.

"Holly, this is... it's magnificent!" Jingles ran his hands over the apron, marveling at every thoughtful detail. "The craftsmanship, the design - I can tell you put your whole heart into making this."

A rosy blush bloomed on Holly's cheeks, her eyes shining with joy at Jingles' reaction. "I wanted it to be special, just like you. Every stitch is filled with my gratitude for all the laughter and light you bring to Frostyville... and to my life."

Jingles looked up from the apron, his gaze meeting Holly's. In that moment, the rest of the world seemed to fade away, leaving only the two of them in their enchanted bubble. The gentle snowfall swirled around the gazebo, dusting their hair and clothes with glittering flakes.

How did I get so lucky? Jingles thought, his heart swelling with affection. To have someone like Holly, who sees past my mishaps and loves me for who I am.*

"I don't know what to say," Jingles murmured, his voice thick with emotion. "No one has ever given me such a meaningful gift before. Thank you, Holly. I'll treasure this always."

He stepped forward, closing the distance between them. As he wrapped his arms around Holly in a warm embrace, the bells on his hat jingled merrily, their cheerful sound mingling with the distant music of the parade. Holly melted into his hug, savoring the feeling of being cherished and understood.

In that perfect moment, amidst the twinkling lights and falling snow, Holly and Jingles knew they had found something truly special - a love that could weather any storm and fill even the coldest winter night with warmth and joy.

A mischievous twinkle danced in Jingles' eyes as he reluctantly pulled back from the embrace. "Now, it's my turn," he said, his voice brimming with excitement. With a flourish, he produced a small, velvet-lined box from the depths of his pocket. The box seemed to shimmer under the soft glow of the fairy lights, hinting at the treasure within.

Holly's eyes widened, her breath catching in her throat as Jingles gently placed the box in her hands. Her fingers trembled slightly as she lifted the lid, revealing a delicate sugar sculpture nestled inside. The intricate creation depicted Holly and Jingles ice skating hand in hand beneath a crescent moon, their expressions captured in perfect detail. Every swirl and curve of the sculpture radiated with the love and care Jingles had poured into it.

"Oh, Jingles," Holly whispered, her voice barely audible above the soft whisper of the falling snow. "It's... it's breathtaking."

Jingles watched as Holly's fingers hovered reverently over the sculpture, tracing the delicate contours with a feather-light touch. The awe in her eyes sent a warm flutter through his chest, and he found himself falling even more deeply in love with her in that moment.

"How did you manage this?" Holly asked, finally tearing her gaze away from the sculpture to meet Jingles' eyes. "The detail, the artistry... it's unlike anything I've ever seen."

Jingles grinned, a hint of pride mingling with the affection in his expression. "Well, you know me," he said with a playful wink. "I've got a few tricks up my sleeve. But really, it was a labor of love. I wanted to create something that would capture the magic of our time together."

Holly's heart swelled with emotion, and she felt tears prickling at the corners of her eyes. *How did I get so lucky?* she thought, echoing Jingles' earlier sentiment. *To have found someone who sees the world with such wonder and creates beauty in everything he touches.*

"It's perfect," Holly said, her voice thick with feeling. "Just like you."

Jingles' cheeks flushed a deeper shade of red, and he ducked his head bashfully. "I'm far from perfect," he mumbled, his bells jingling softly as he shifted his weight. "But with you by my side, I feel like I can be the best version of myself."

Holly reached out, gently tilting Jingles' chin up until their eyes met once more. "That's all I could ever ask for," she whispered, her thumb brushing tenderly across his cheek. "You, just as you are."

As they stood there, lost in each other's gaze, the world around them seemed to shimmer with a magic all its own. The snowflakes danced in the air, the fairy lights twinkled, and the distant sounds of the parade faded into a soft, joyful hum. In that perfect moment, Holly and Jingles knew that they had found something rare and precious - a love that could turn even the simplest of moments into an enchanted memory.

Their conversation turned heartfelt as they shared their dreams, their words weaving a tapestry of hope in the stillness of the gazebo. Holly's eyes sparkled with excitement as she spoke of expanding her bakery, her hands gesturing animatedly.

"I've always dreamed of creating a cozy little haven where people can gather and enjoy the simple pleasures in life," she said, her voice warm with passion. "A place where the aroma of freshly baked treats fills the air and laughter echoes off the walls."

Jingles listened intently, his heart swelling with admiration for Holly's vision. "That sounds incredible," he said, his own excitement building. "And I know just how to add a touch of elf magic to make it even more special."

His eyes twinkled with mischief as he described his ideas, from enchanted gingerbread houses that never crumble to hot cocoa that always stays at the perfect temperature. Holly's laughter mingled with his own as they traded ideas back and forth, their enthusiasm growing with each passing moment.

This is what it's all about, Jingles thought, his heart full to bursting. Sharing our passions, supporting each other's dreams, and creating something beautiful together.

As their conversation wound down, a comfortable silence settled over them. They gazed at each other, their unspoken feelings hanging in the air, the quiet moment heavy with the promise of something more. Snowflakes drifted lazily around them, their breaths mingling in the stillness.

Jingles reached out, gently taking Holly's hands in his own. Her skin was soft and warm against his, and he marveled at how perfectly they fit together. Like two pieces of a puzzle, he mused, destined to interlock.

Holly's heart raced at Jingles' touch, a pleasant shiver running down her spine that had nothing to do with the cold. She stepped closer, drawn to his warmth and the irresistible pull of his presence. In that moment, the rest of the world fell away, and all that mattered was the two of them, standing together in their own little wonderland.

Is this what falling in love feels like? Holly wondered, her pulse quickening as she lost herself in Jingles' eyes. Like everything suddenly makes sense, and the world is brighter and more beautiful than ever before?

Around them, Frostyville glowed with the magic of the season, the distant sounds of the parade a joyful soundtrack to their own private fairy tale. As the snowflakes continued to fall, Holly and Jingles stood hand in hand, their hearts full of love and their minds brimming with dreams of a future together.

The melodic jingling of Santa's sleigh bells broke the spell, drawing Holly and Jingles' attention skyward. They watched in awe as the sleigh streaked across the starlit expanse, leaving a faint glittering trail in its wake. The magic of the moment seemed to permeate the air, filling them both with a sense of wonder and possibility.

Jingles turned to face Holly, his eyes shining with the reflection of the stars above and the depth of his emotions. He took her hands in his, marveling at the way they fit together so perfectly, as if they were always meant to be. His voice was soft but sure as he spoke, the words pouring out like a long-held secret finally set free.

"Holly," he began, his tone filled with warmth and sincerity, "I know I'm not perfect. I'm clumsy and I make mistakes, but there's one thing I know for certain: I want to be there for you, always. I promise to take care of you, to make you laugh when you're sad, and to be your partner in all of life's adventures."

Holly's breath caught in her throat as she listened to Jingles' heartfelt confession. She searched his face, finding nothing but honesty and love in his expressive features. Her own emotions swelled within her chest, threatening to overflow.

"Jingles," she whispered, her voice trembling with the weight of her feelings, "I... I don't know what to say. No one has ever made me feel the way you do. You make me believe in myself, in magic, in the possibility of something truly special."

She squeezed his hands, her heart racing as she took a leap of faith. "I want to be there for you, too. Through all the chaos and the laughter, the ups and the downs. I want to be your partner, in every sense of the word."

Jingles' face lit up with pure joy, his signature grin stretching from ear to ear. He pulled Holly closer, wrapping her in an embrace that felt like coming home. The warmth of their bodies contrasted with the cool winter air, creating a cocoon of perfect contentment.

As they held each other close, the snow continued to fall around them, blanketing Frostyville in a layer of pure white magic. The distant sounds of the parade faded into the background, replaced by the beating of their hearts and the whispered promises of a future filled with love and laughter.

For Holly and Jingles, this moment marked the beginning of a new chapter - one written in the language of love and sealed with the magic of the North Pole. They knew that whatever challenges lay ahead, they would face them together, hand in hand, ready to embrace the endless possibilities that stretched out before them like a glittering horizon.

In the enchanting glow of the fairy lights, Holly gazed into Jingles' eyes, her heart swelling with the depth of her emotions. Her voice, soft and tender, carried the weight of her feelings as she spoke. "Jingles, I never thought I could find someone who understands me so completely, who accepts me for all that I am. You've brought so much joy and laughter into my life, and I can't imagine a future without you by my side."

Jingles' eyes sparkled with adoration as he listened to Holly's heartfelt words. His fingers gently caressed her cheek, wiping away a stray tear of happiness that had escaped. "My darling Holly," he whispered, his voice filled with reverence, "you are the sweetest confection in all of Frostyville, and I am so lucky to have found you. Your love is the greatest gift I could ever receive."

As they held each other close, the snowflakes danced around them, seemingly in tune with the rhythm of their hearts. The world beyond the gazebo faded away, leaving only the two of them in this perfect, timeless moment. Holly's fingers traced the intricate embroidery on Jingles' apron, the one she had lovingly crafted for him, while Jingles' hand rested on the small of her back, holding her close as if she were the most precious treasure in all the North Pole.

This is where I belong, Holly thought, wrapped in the arms of the one who makes my heart sing. With Jingles by my side, I know that anything is possible.

The snowfall around them seemed to slow, each flake drifting lazily through the air, as if even nature itself was pausing to witness the beauty of their love. In this frozen moment, Holly and Jingles were the very embodiment of the magic and wonder that filled the streets of Frostyville.

As they leaned in closer, their foreheads touching, Jingles whispered, "I love you, Holly Sugarplum, with every fiber of my being. You are the star that guides me home, the sweetness that fills my days, and the love that warms my heart."

Holly's reply was a soft, contented sigh, her eyes fluttering closed as she savored the warmth of Jingles' words. In this perfect, crystalline moment, their love was a beacon of hope and joy, a testament to the power of two hearts united in the magic of the holiday season.

As their lips met in a tender, sweet kiss, the world around them seemed to fade away, leaving only the two of them in this enchanted bubble of love and magic. The snow glistened on their lashes, each flake a tiny diamond that sparkled in the soft light of the gazebo. For a heartbeat, time itself seemed to pause, as if the universe was holding its breath, honoring the beauty and purity of their love.

In this moment, Holly and Jingles were not just two elves in love; they were the embodiment of the very spirit of Christmas - the joy, the wonder, and the magic that filled the air of Frostyville. Their kiss was a promise, an unspoken vow to cherish and support each other through all the adventures that lay ahead.

As the kiss deepened, Holly felt a warmth spreading through her body, a sensation that had nothing to do with the layers of her festive attire. It was the warmth of love, of belonging, of knowing that she had found her true home in the arms of this wonderful, mischievous elf who had captured her heart so completely.

When they finally pulled apart, breathless and giddy, Jingles rested his forehead against Holly's, his eyes shining with adoration. "I never knew love could feel like this," he whispered, his voice rough with emotion. "You've brought a magic into my life that I never knew existed, Holly. You've made me believe in the impossible."

Holly smiled, her eyes brimming with happy tears. "You are my impossible, Jingles," she replied softly, her fingers tracing the curve of his cheek. "You are the miracle that I never saw coming, the love that I never knew I needed. With you by my side, I feel like I can conquer anything."

As they stood there, lost in each other's eyes, the world around them slowly came back into focus. The distant cheer of the parade, the golden glow of Frostyville's lights, and the shimmering snowflakes that blanketed the streets - all of it seemed to be infused with a new magic, a magic born of the love that Holly and Jingles shared.

It was as if their love had cast a spell over the entire town, transforming it into a place of pure enchantment. The twinkling lights seemed brighter, the laughter of the elves merrier, and the snow itself seemed to sparkle with an extra touch of wonder. In this moment, Frostyville was not just a place; it was a testament to the power of love, a reminder that even in the darkest of times, hope and joy could be found in the hearts of those who believed.

As the enchanting world of Frostyville enveloped them in its magical embrace, Holly and Jingles stood hand in hand, their hearts beating as one. The distant echoes of the parade faded into the background, replaced by the gentle whisper of falling snow and the soft glow of twinkling lights. In this perfect moment, time seemed to stand still, suspending them in a bubble of pure love and endless possibility.

Holly's eyes sparkled with the reflection of a thousand stars as she gazed up at Jingles, her smile radiant and filled with hope. "Can you believe it?" she whispered, her voice trembling with barely contained excitement. "Everything we've dreamed of, everything we've worked for... it's all coming true."

Jingles squeezed her hand, his own grin stretching from pointed ear to pointed ear. "And there's no one I'd rather share this adventure with than you, my sweet Holly," he declared, his tone brimming with adoration. "Together, we'll make Frostyville the most magical place in all the realms."

As they stood there, surrounded by the glittering beauty of their snow-dusted world, Holly's mind raced with visions of the future. She pictured her bakery, expanded and thriving, filled with the warm scent of cinnamon and the joyful laughter of satisfied customers. She imagined Jingles by her side, his mischievous spirit and creative genius infusing every corner of Frostyville with an extra touch of elfin magic.

"I can see it all so clearly," Holly murmured, her eyes misty with emotion. "Our lives intertwined, our dreams woven together like the most intricate sugar sculpture. And through it all, our love will be the guiding star, leading us forward."

Jingles brought her hand to his lips, pressing a gentle kiss against her knuckles. "Our love will be the stuff of legends," he proclaimed, his voice ringing with unshakable conviction. "A tale whispered by the snowflakes and sung by the winter winds. Holly and Jingles, the unstoppable duo who brought joy and wonder to the world."

With their gazes locked on the horizon, Holly and Jingles took their first steps forward, their hearts filled with love, laughter, and the unshakable belief in the endless possibilities that lay ahead. The future stretched out before them like a blank canvas, ready to be painted with the vibrant colors of their shared dreams and the unbreakable bond of their love.

As they walked hand in hand, the snow crunching beneath their feet and the fairy lights twinkling above, Holly and Jingles knew that no matter what challenges or adventures lay ahead, they would face them together. For in each other, they had found not just love, but a home—a place where their hearts could forever reside in the warm embrace of eternal magic and unending joy.

Chapter 17: New Year, New Beginnings

Holly stood at the front of the Frostyville bakery kitchen, a dusting of flour on her red apron, as a dozen young elves looked up at her with bright, eager eyes. She took a deep breath, feeling a newfound sense of confidence rising within her.

"Good morning, everyone!" Holly said, her voice warm and steady. "Today, we're going to learn how to make Santa's favorite treat - peppermint bark cookies!"

The elves cheered and clapped, their pointed ears wiggling with excitement. Holly smiled, her earlier nerves melting away. She glanced over at Jingles, who gave her an encouraging wink as he bustled around the kitchen.

Jingles juggled candy canes and bars of white chocolate, his silver bells jingling merrily. "Hey Holly, what did the peppermint say to the chocolate?" He grinned mischievously. "Let's stick together!"

The elves erupted into giggles as Jingles pretended to get tangled in a strand of red and white ribbons. Holly shook her head, trying to hide her own amused smile.

Jingles always knew how to lighten the mood and get everyone laughing, she thought. His playful energy was infectious, setting the perfect tone for a fun baking lesson.

"Alright, settle down now," Holly called out, still smiling. "Jingles, why don't you help me pass out the ingredients?"

"Aye aye, Captain Sugarplum!" Jingles saluted, making the elves laugh again as he grabbed trays of peppermint and chocolate.

As the two of them moved around the kitchen, their hands brushed as they reached for the same spatula. Holly felt a spark of warmth at Jingles' touch. She met his twinkling blue eyes and they shared a brief, knowing glance before turning back to the eager young elves.

Holly's heart fluttered, a blush rising to her cheeks that had nothing to do with the heat of the ovens. Working alongside Jingles filled her with a joy she'd never known - like baking the most delectable treat, laughing and covered in flour and frosting. She'd spent so long keeping others at a careful distance, but with Jingles, she felt herself opening up, bit by bit.

As she began demonstrating how to melt the chocolate, Holly let herself get swept up in the magic of baking with friends, old and new. The Frostyville kitchen seemed to glow with the warmth of camaraderie and holiday spirit. With Jingles by her side and a kitchen full of laughter, Holly had never felt more at home.

Holly guided the elves through melting the chocolate, her movements precise and confident. "Stir gently, and keep an eye on the heat," she instructed, moving between the workstations with a patient smile. "If the chocolate gets too hot, it can seize up and become grainy."

As she helped a particularly tiny elf adjust the temperature on their stovetop, Holly caught sight of Jingles from the corner of her eye. He was animatedly demonstrating how to crush candy canes, his cheerful voice carrying across the kitchen

Holly carefully measured out the sugar, her steady hand pouring the sparkling crystals into the mixing bowl. "The key is precision," she said, her voice warm and encouraging as she turned to the eager faces of the young elves gathered around the work table. "Too much or too little can throw off the entire recipe."

The elves nodded, their eyes wide with rapt attention. Holly smiled, a rush of confidence flowing through her as she guided them through the next steps. Her movements were fluid and graceful, the result of countless hours spent perfecting her craft in the cozy kitchen of the North Pole Bakery.

As she demonstrated how to cream the butter and sugar together until light and fluffy, Holly paused to offer gentle corrections and praise to the elves as they followed along. "Wonderful job, Tinsel! Your mixture is the perfect consistency. And Snowflake, try folding the flour in gently, like this."

Holly marveled at the patience and dedication of her students. Their enthusiasm was contagious, filling the kitchen with an air of joyful determination. For a moment, she allowed herself to bask in the warmth of their shared passion, the doubts that often plagued her momentarily melting away.

Suddenly, Jingles bounded over to the table, his bells jingling merrily with each step. "Mind if I add a little extra sparkle to the recipe?" he asked with a mischievous grin.

Holly hesitated, her perfectionist nature warring with the excitement shining in Jingles' eyes. "I suppose a little creativity couldn't hurt," she conceded, stepping aside to let him take the reins.

Jingles rubbed his hands together gleefully. "Alright, my little sugar plums, let's have some fun!" He reached for a jar of shimmering sprinkles, sprinkling a generous amount into each elf's mixing bowl. "Don't be afraid to experiment! That's how we create the most magical treats."

The elves giggled as they stirred the colorful sprinkles into their dough, their faces alight with joy and wonder. Holly watched as Jingles moved among them, offering encouragement and playful quips that kept the atmosphere light and engaging.

As the lesson progressed, Holly found herself drawn to Jingles' infectious enthusiasm. His approach was so different from her own careful precision, yet she couldn't deny the value of his spontaneity and creativity. Together, they made a perfect team - a balance of structure and whimsy that brought out the best in their students and each other.

Holly's heart swelled with a newfound appreciation for Jingles as she watched him guide the elves in shaping the dough into whimsical designs. Perhaps there was room in her world for a little more chaos and a lot more joy. With Jingles by her side, anything seemed possible - even finding the courage to open her heart once more.

The kitchen erupted into a flurry of activity as the young elves eagerly followed Jingles' lead, their tiny hands shaping the dough into a variety of imaginative creations. Laughter filled the air, mingling with the sweet scent of vanilla and cinnamon. Holly watched in amusement as Jingles encouraged the elves to add their own unique flair to each treat, his eyes sparkling with mischief.

Suddenly, a puff of flour exploded from one of the mixing bowls, covering a group of elves in a fine white powder. Giggles turned into full-blown laughter as the elves playfully tossed flour at one another, creating a delightful mess of sticky dough and cloudy flour.

Holly's eyes widened, a mixture of concern and amusement playing across her face. "Oh my goodness, look at this delicious disaster!" She glanced at Jingles, who was grinning from ear to ear.

"Isn't it wonderful?" Jingles chuckled, brushing a dusting of flour from his hat. "Nothing brings more joy than a little bit of chaos in the kitchen!"

Together, Holly and Jingles waded into the fray, helping the elves regain control of their baking stations. They wiped floury cheeks, untangled sticky fingers, and rearranged wayward sprinkles, their movements perfectly synchronized as they worked side by side.

As the chaos subsided, a sense of camaraderie filled the kitchen. The elves beamed with pride as they presented their unique creations, each one a delightful reflection of their individual personalities.

Holly and Jingles stepped back to admire their students' work, their shoulders brushing lightly against one another. In that quiet moment, Holly felt a surge of respect and appreciation for Jingles' unconventional approach.

"You know," she said softly, "I never thought I'd say this, but a little chaos can be a good thing."

Jingles turned to her, his eyes crinkling with warmth. "And a little structure can be pretty magical too." He reached out, gently brushing a streak of flour from her cheek.

Holly's heart fluttered at his touch, a blush rising to her cheeks. As they turned their attention back to the elves, preparing the next batch of treats, Holly couldn't help but marvel at the way their strengths complemented each other. Together, they were creating something truly special - not just in the kitchen, but in the unspoken connection growing between them.

As the class continued, Holly found herself lost in thought, her hands moving on autopilot as she helped the elves shape dough into festive designs. She marveled at how far she had come, not just in her baking skills, but in her confidence as a teacher and a friend.

"I never thought I'd find such joy in teaching," she mused silently, a soft smile playing on her lips. "And I certainly never expected to find a partner like Jingles."

Her gaze drifted to the lively elf, his laughter ringing out as he guided a young student through a particularly tricky technique. Jingles' unwavering support and infectious enthusiasm had been a constant source of strength, helping her navigate the challenges and embrace the unexpected delights of their shared adventure.

"Thank you," she whispered, the words meant for Jingles' ears alone, even though he was too far away to hear.

As if sensing her thoughts, Jingles glanced up, his eyes meeting hers across the bustling kitchen. A moment of understanding passed between them, a silent acknowledgment of the bond they had forged through flour-dusted aprons and sugar-sprinkled laughter.

With a wink and a grin, Jingles excused himself from the class, his mind already whirring with new ideas for Santa's workshop. He made his way to a quiet corner of the kitchen, where a small workbench stood cluttered with sketches and prototypes.

Settling into his chair, Jingles began to tinker, his hands moving with practiced ease as he brought his visions to life. Bits of metal, wood, and glittering gears came together beneath his fingertips, each creation a testament to his boundless imagination.

"What if we could make a toy that changes color with the seasons?" he murmured to himself, his brow furrowed in concentration. "Or a teddy bear that gives warm hugs on the coldest winter nights?"

As he worked, the world around him seemed to fade away, replaced by a kaleidoscope of possibilities. Sketches spilled across the workbench, each one a window into a child's wildest dreams. Jingles lost himself in the joy of creation, his love for his craft evident in every carefully placed piece and every delighted smile.

From across the kitchen, Holly watched him work, her heart swelling with affection. In Jingles, she saw a kindred spirit - someone who poured their heart into everything they did, whether it was baking the perfect cookie or dreaming up the most wondrous toy. Together, they were weaving a little bit of magic into the very fabric of Frostyville, one laugh, one lesson, and one creation at a time.

The sweet aroma of freshly baked cookies mingled with the lively chatter of the young elves as they gathered around the decorating station. Holly and Jingles stood side by side, their aprons a mirror of their personalities - Holly's pristine and precise, Jingles' a colorful canvas of frosting splatters and sprinkles.

"Alright, my little sugar plums," Holly began, her voice warm with encouragement, "it's time to let your creativity shine! Remember, there's no right or wrong way to decorate a cookie."

Jingles grinned, his eyes sparkling with mischief. "Just don't forget to taste your creations along the way! After all, a baker's secret weapon is a well-trained sweet tooth."

The elves giggled, their tiny hands already reaching for the array of frostings, sprinkles, and candies laid out before them. As they set to work, Holly moved among them, offering gentle guidance and praise.

"Ooh, I love how you've combined those colors, Tinsel! And look at that intricate design, Snowflake - you've got a real talent for detail!"

Beside her, Jingles took a more playful approach, encouraging the elves to think outside the box. "Why not try something a little different, Twinkle? What if we added some crushed candy canes for a little extra crunch?"

As the elves experimented, their creations began to take shape - some precise and elegant, others a joyful explosion of color and texture. Holly and Jingles worked in tandem, their contrasting styles complementing each other perfectly.

"I never would have thought to use jimmies as a border," Holly mused, admiring one of Jingles' more unorthodox designs. "It's like a little fence of happiness!"

Jingles laughed, his cheeks dimpling with delight. "And your snowflake design is so delicate, it looks like it might melt right off the cookie! You've got a real gift for making things beautiful, Holly."

As their eyes met, a spark of something deeper passed between them - a recognition of the special connection they shared. In that moment, the world seemed to narrow to just the two of them, the laughter and chatter of the elves fading into the background.

"I couldn't do this without you, Jingles," Holly said softly, her voice filled with genuine affection. "You bring so much joy and laughter to everything you do. It's like you sprinkle a little bit of magic into every moment."

Jingles reached out, his hand brushing against hers in a gesture that felt both natural and electrifying. "We make a pretty good team, don't we? The perfect recipe for spreading holiday cheer."

As they turned back to the elves, their hearts felt lighter, their smiles brighter. Together, they had created something truly special - not just delicious treats, but a sense of belonging and happiness that would linger long after the last cookie crumb was gone.

As the baking class concluded, Holly and Jingles moved in harmony, their actions coordinated as if they'd been working together for years. They gathered mixing bowls and spatulas, their hands brushing against each other as they reached for the same utensil. A warm flush crept up Holly's neck, and she glanced at Jingles, a smile playing at the corners of her lips.

Jingles grinned back, his eyes twinkling with mischief. "You wash, I dry?" he offered, holding up a dish towel.

Holly nodded, her heart fluttering at the easy companionship they'd fallen into. As they stood side by side at the sink, their elbows bumping playfully, she marveled at how natural it felt to work alongside him. The kitchen filled with the sound of running water and the soft clink of dishes, a soothing melody that spoke of comfort and familiarity.

"You know," Jingles said, his voice taking on a more serious tone, "I've never met anyone quite like you, Holly. You've got this way of making everything brighter, just by being you."

Holly ducked her head, a pleased blush coloring her cheeks. "I could say the same about you, Jingles. You have a gift for bringing laughter and joy to every situation."

They finished their tasks in comfortable silence, the air between them charged with a new understanding. As they stepped outside into the crisp Frostyville air, the festive lights twinkling around them, Holly felt a sense of contentment settle deep in her bones.

"Today was magical," she said, her breath forming tiny clouds in the chill. "Seeing the elves so excited about baking, watching them create something beautiful... it reminded me of why I love what I do."

Jingles nodded, his gaze soft as he looked at her. "You're a natural teacher, Holly. Those elves adore you, and it's easy to see why."

They walked side by side, their shoulders brushing, as they made their way through the snow-covered streets. Around them, the village bustled with activity, elves hurrying to and fro with armfuls of presents and garlands. The scent of cinnamon and pine filled the air, a reminder of the magic that permeated every corner of Frostyville.

"I never thought I'd find a place where I truly belonged," Holly confessed, her voice barely above a whisper. "But being here, with you... it feels like home."

Jingles reached for her hand, his fingers lacing with hers in a gesture that felt both daring and inevitable. "I know exactly what you mean," he said, his voice rough with emotion. "It's like we were meant to find each other, to create this magic together."

As they stood hand in hand, the future stretched out before them, filled with endless possibilities. Whatever challenges lay ahead, Holly knew that with Jingles by her side, anything was possible. Together, they could create a love story as sweet and enduring as the magic of Christmas itself.

Holly's heart raced as Jingles's hand held hers, the warmth of his touch sending a shiver down her spine despite the chilly air. She turned to face him, her eyes searching his, and found a depth of emotion that took her breath away. In that moment, the rest of the world seemed to fall away, leaving only the two of them, lost in a connection that felt both thrilling and inevitable.

Could this really be happening? Holly wondered, her thoughts a whirlwind of hope and uncertainty. After all this time, after all the heartbreak and disappointment, could I finally have found someone who understands me, who sees me for who I truly am?

Jingles lifted his free hand, gently brushing a stray lock of hair from Holly's face. His touch was feather-light, yet it ignited a spark within her, a longing for something she'd never dared to dream of before.

"Holly," he whispered, his voice rough with emotion, "I... I know this might seem sudden, but I can't help feeling that this, what we have... it's something special. Something rare and precious."

Holly swallowed hard, her heart pounding in her chest. "I feel it too," she confessed, her voice trembling slightly. "It's like... like magic. Like something out of a fairy tale."

Jingles smiled, his eyes crinkling at the corners in a way that made Holly's stomach flutter. "Well, we are in the North Pole," he teased gently. "If there's anywhere that fairy tales can come true, it's here."

Holly laughed softly, the sound mingling with the jingling of bells in the distance. "I suppose you're right," she agreed, her eyes sparkling with a newfound joy. "And maybe... maybe it's time for me to start believing in magic again. In the possibility of something wonderful."

As they stood there, hand in hand, the snow falling softly around them, Holly felt a sense of peace and rightness settle over her. Whatever the future held, whatever challenges lay ahead, she knew that with Jingles by her side, she could face anything. Together, they would write their own fairy tale, one filled with laughter and love and all the magic of the holiday season.

Chapter 18: Happily Ever After in Frostyville

The warm glow of the oven illuminated Holly's face as she peered through the glass, watching the cookies rise to perfection. A smile played at her lips, the sweet aroma of buttery dough and spices enveloping her senses. With a soft chime, the timer announced the cookies' readiness.

Holly slipped on her festive oven mitts, their cheerful design a gift from Jingles last Christmas. She carefully extracted the tray, the heat radiating against her cheeks as she inhaled deeply. The scent of pine from the garland draped across the mantle mingled with the freshly baked treats, creating a symphony of holiday cheer.

She set the tray on the cooling rack, each cookie a tiny masterpiece waiting to be adorned. With a steady hand, Holly reached for the piping bag filled with delicate icing, the color a perfect match to the shimmering edible glitter she had mixed herself. She began to decorate, each swirl and flourish an expression of her love for the craft.

As she worked, her thoughts drifted to Jingles, his infectious laughter echoing in her mind. She imagined his reaction to the cookies, his blue eyes sparkling with delight as he sampled her latest creations. A warmth spread through her chest, a feeling that had nothing to do with the heat of the kitchen.

Holly stepped back, tilting her head as she inspected the tray with a critical eye. Each cookie was a work of art, the icing glistening in the soft light of the cottage. She adjusted a sprinkle here, a dollop of icing there, her perfectionism guiding every movement.

The sound of jingling bells announced Jingles' arrival, his cheery whistle preceding his entrance. Holly turned, a smile already tugging at her lips as she watched him bound into the kitchen, his red hat slightly askew on his auburn curls.

"Mmm, smells like Christmas in here!" he exclaimed, his eyes widening as he caught sight of the cookies. "Holly, you've outdone yourself again!"

A blush crept into her cheeks at the compliment. "They're for the bakery," she explained, her voice warm with pride. "I wanted to try something new with the glitter."

Jingles leaned in, his nose nearly touching a particularly sparkly gingerbread man. "They're almost too pretty to eat. Almost." He grinned, mischief dancing in his eyes.

Holly laughed, the sound mingling with the soft chime of Jingles' bells. "I'm sure you'll manage," she teased, gently swatting his hand away as he reached for a cookie.

As they bantered, the worries of the day melted away, replaced by the comfort of their easy companionship. Holly marveled at the way Jingles could brighten even the gloomiest of moods, his presence as warm and inviting as the glow of the fireplace.

Together, they packed the cookies into festive tins, their laughter punctuating the comfortable silence. With each brush of their hands, each shared smile, Holly felt the love between them grow, as strong and steady as the North Star.

As they prepared to head to the bakery, Holly paused, her hand resting on Jingles' arm. "Thank you," she said softly, her eyes meeting his. "For everything."

Jingles' expression softened, his smile tender. "Anytime, Holly," he replied, his voice low. "I'll always be here for you."

With a final check of the cookie tins, they stepped out into the crisp North Pole air, ready to share their creations with the world. The future stretched before them, as bright and full of promise as the shimmering glitter on Holly's cookies. Whatever lay ahead, they would face it together, their love a guiding light through any storm.

The walk to the North Pole Bakery was a familiar one, the path worn smooth by countless trips over the years. Holly and Jingles strolled hand in hand, the cookie tins balanced precariously in their free arms. The air was crisp and cold, the scent of pine and cinnamon wafting from the nearby shops.

As they approached the bakery, Holly's steps slowed, a flicker of uncertainty crossing her features. "Do you think they'll like the new designs?" she asked, her voice barely audible above the rustling of the wind.

Jingles squeezed her hand, his smile reassuring. "They'll love them," he declared, his voice ringing with confidence. "You've outdone yourself this time, Holly. These cookies are nothing short of magical."

Holly's cheeks flushed with pleasure, the praise warming her from the inside out. "I couldn't have done it without you," she replied, her eyes sparkling with affection. "Your ideas for the candy cane accents? Pure genius."

Jingles grinned, his bells jingling merrily as he bounced on his toes. "We make a pretty great team, don't we?"

"The best," Holly agreed, her heart swelling with love and gratitude.

As they stepped into the bakery, the familiar scents of sugar and spice enveloped them, the warmth a welcome respite from the chill outside. The shop was already bustling with activity, elves darting to and fro as they prepared for the day ahead.

Holly and Jingles made their way to the kitchen, the cookie tins balanced carefully in their arms. As they set them down on the counter, a chorus of excited murmurs rippled through the gathered elves.

"Are those the new designs?" one elf asked, her eyes wide with anticipation.

"They're stunning!" another exclaimed, reaching for a tin with eager hands.

Holly stood back, her heart racing as she watched her creations being admired and appreciated. Jingles slipped an arm around her waist, his presence a steady comfort at her side.

"You see?" he murmured, his breath warm against her ear. "I told you they'd love them."

Holly leaned into his embrace, a smile playing at the corners of her lips. "Thank you," she whispered, her voice thick with emotion. "For believing in me, even when I didn't believe in myself."

Jingles pressed a gentle kiss to her temple, his love for her shining in his eyes. "Always," he promised, his voice low and fervent.

As the elves bustled around them, exclaiming over the intricately decorated cookies, Holly and Jingles shared a moment of quiet contentment. The future stretched before them, as bright and full of promise as the shimmering glitter on Holly's creations.

And as they stood there, surrounded by the warmth and love of their community, Holly knew that whatever challenges lay ahead, they would face them together. With Jingles by her side, anything was possible.

The scene faded, the bakery dissolving into a shimmering haze of sugar and spice. But the love between Holly and Jingles remained, a constant light guiding them forward into a future filled with joy, laughter, and endless possibilities.

Jingles sighed dramatically, leaning against the counter, his bells jingling with the movement. His mischievous grin faded into an exaggerated pout as he watched Holly expertly arrange the gingerbread cookies on the tray. "You're too good at resisting my charm. It's almost unfair."

Holly chuckled, her eyes sparkling with amusement as she set the tray aside. She brushed a stray lock of hair from her face, leaving a smudge of flour on her cheek. "And you're too good at trying to distract me." She pointed towards the small office at the back of the bakery. "Go check on the delivery list while I finish packing these up."

Jingles pushed himself off the counter, his pout transforming into a playful smirk. "As you wish, my dear." He bowed with a flourish, his hat slipping slightly to the side. "But don't think I won't be back to steal a taste of your delectable creations."

As he sauntered towards the office, Holly shook her head, a fond smile tugging at her lips. Jingles' antics never failed to lift her spirits, even on the busiest of days. She turned her attention back to the cookies, her hands moving with practiced precision as she nestled each one into its designated spot.

The scent of ginger and cinnamon enveloped her, and Holly allowed herself a moment to appreciate the magic of her craft. Each cookie was a work of art, a tangible expression of the love and care she poured into every batch. It was in these quiet moments, surrounded by the fruits of her labor, that Holly felt truly at peace.

Her mind wandered to the upcoming Christmas Eve celebration, and the flutter of nerves in her stomach intensified. She knew that her creations would be the centerpiece of the festivities, and the thought of disappointing her friends and neighbors made her heart clench. But as she glanced towards the office, catching a glimpse of Jingles' red hat bobbing as he searched for the delivery list, a wave of calm washed over her.

With Jingles by her side, Holly knew that she could face anything. His unwavering support and infectious enthusiasm had become her anchor in a world that often felt uncertain. Together, they had weathered storms both literal and figurative, their love growing stronger with each challenge they faced.

As if sensing her thoughts, Jingles poked his head out of the office, his eyes twinkling with mirth. "Found the list!" He waved a piece of parchment triumphantly. "And I only knocked over one stack of papers in the process."

Holly laughed, the sound ringing through the bakery like the chime of silver bells. "A new record, I'm sure." She placed the last cookie on the tray, stepping back to admire her handiwork.

Jingles joined her, his arm slipping around her waist as he surveyed the glistening array of gingerbread. "They're perfect," he murmured, his voice filled with genuine awe. "Just like you."

Holly leaned into his embrace, her heart swelling with love and gratitude. In that moment, surrounded by the warmth of the bakery and the steadfast presence of her true love, Holly knew that no matter what the future held, they would face it together.

And as the scene faded, the promise of a lifetime of love and laughter lingered in the air, as sweet and enchanting as the scent of freshly baked gingerbread.

With a contented sigh, Holly gathered the trays of cookies, her steps light as she carried them to the display case. The bakery was a hive of activity, with elves bustling to and fro, their arms laden with freshly baked treats and their faces bright with excitement.

As Holly arranged the cookies, her mind wandered to the upcoming wedding. In just a few short days, she and Jingles would exchange vows beneath the twinkling lights of the North Pole, surrounded by the love and support of their friends and family.

"Penny for your thoughts?" Jingles asked, his voice breaking through her reverie.

Holly glanced up, a soft smile playing at the corners of her mouth. "Just thinking about our wedding," she admitted, a faint blush coloring her cheeks. "I can't believe it's almost here."

Jingles grinned, his eyes sparkling with mischief. "Well, believe it, because I've got big plans for our honeymoon. Think glitter, think adventure, think—"

"Chaos?" Holly finished, arching an eyebrow.

"I prefer to call it 'spontaneous fun,'" Jingles countered, his laughter infectious.

As they bantered back and forth, the bakery continued to buzz with life around them. Elves chattered and laughed, their voices mingling with the clatter of baking sheets and the hiss of the espresso machine.

Holly paused, taking a moment to drink in the scene. This bakery, with its cozy atmosphere and delectable treats, had become more than just a workplace. It was a testament to the love and dedication she and Jingles had poured into every aspect of their lives together.

"You know," she said softly, her gaze meeting Jingles', "I used to dream about having a place like this. Somewhere that felt like home, where people could come and find a little bit of joy in their day."

Jingles pulled her close, his embrace warm and reassuring. "And now you have it," he murmured, pressing a kiss to her temple. "We both do."

In that moment, Holly felt a surge of emotion, her heart so full it threatened to burst. She had found her place in the world, and it was right here, in the arms of the elf who had stolen her heart and filled her life with love and laughter.

As the scene drew to a close, the bakery continued to thrive, a symbol of the enduring love and partnership between Holly and Jingles. And though the future held untold adventures and challenges, they knew that together, they could weather any storm and emerge stronger than ever.

Holly and Jingles stepped back from their display, admiring the intricate details of the gingerbread houses. The tiny candy cane fence posts added a charming touch, their red and white stripes standing out against the shimmering backdrop of edible glitter.

"I think we've outdone ourselves this time," Holly said, her voice tinged with pride. She reached out to straighten a slightly crooked gumdrop, her fingers brushing against Jingles' as he did the same.

The brief touch sent a spark of electricity through her, a reminder of the connection they shared. She glanced up at him, her cheeks flushing slightly as she met his gaze.

Jingles grinned, his eyes crinkling at the corners. "We make a pretty great team, don't we?"

Holly nodded, her heart swelling with affection. "The best."

As they stepped back to allow customers to admire their creations, Holly couldn't help but reflect on how far they'd come. When she'd first arrived in Frostyville, she'd been unsure of her place, her confidence shaken by past disappointments. But Jingles had believed in her from the start, his unwavering support and infectious enthusiasm helping her to rediscover her passion for baking.

Together, they'd built something truly special. The North Pole Bakery wasn't just a business; it was a reflection of their shared love for spreading joy through their creations. Every glittering cookie and intricately decorated cake was a testament to their partnership, both in and out of the kitchen.

As the day wore on, Holly and Jingles worked seamlessly together, their movements perfectly synchronized as they filled orders and greeted customers. The bakery was alive with the buzz of conversation and the sweet scent of freshly baked treats, a warm haven against the chill of the North Pole winter.

In a rare moment of quiet, Holly found herself watching Jingles as he carefully piped icing onto a batch of sugar cookies. His brow was furrowed in concentration, his tongue poking out slightly as he focused on creating the perfect design.

The sight filled her with a rush of tenderness, her heart aching with the depth of her love for him. In Jingles, she'd found not just a partner, but a soulmate – someone who understood her completely and loved her unconditionally.

As if sensing her gaze, Jingles looked up, his eyes meeting hers across the kitchen. The corners of his mouth lifted in a soft smile, his expression one of pure adoration.

"What are you thinking about?" he asked, setting down the piping bag and making his way over to her.

Holly shook her head, a smile playing at her own lips. "Just how lucky I am," she said quietly, reaching out to take his hand in hers. "To have you, and this place, and everything we've built together."

Jingles brought her hand to his lips, pressing a gentle kiss to her knuckles. "I'm the lucky one," he murmured, his eyes shining with emotion. "You've brought so much light into my life, Holly. I can't imagine a future without you in it."

The words hung in the air between them, a promise of forever. And as they stood there, hand in hand, Holly knew that whatever challenges lay ahead, they would face them together.

For now, though, there were cookies to bake and customers to serve. With a final squeeze of Jingles' hand, Holly turned back to her work, her heart full and her spirit buoyed by the love that surrounded her.

The North Pole Bakery continued to thrive, a beacon of warmth and sweetness in the heart of Frostyville. And at its center, Holly and Jingles stood side by side, their love a shining example of the magic that could happen when two hearts found their perfect match.

As the scene drew to a close, there was a sense of contentment and hope in the air, a promise of even brighter days to come. For Holly and Jingles, this was just the beginning of their happily ever after – a love story as sweet and enduring as the treats they crafted with such care and devotion.

And though the future was uncertain, one thing was clear: together, they could weather any storm and emerge stronger than ever, their love a guiding light in the enchanting world of Frostyville.

Holly tilted her head, studying the gingerbread house Jingles held with a critical eye. "It's charming," she admitted, her lips curving into a thoughtful smile, "but we'll need to make sure the overall design stays balanced. Too much whimsy and it'll look cluttered."

Jingles' eyes sparkled with mirth as he set the prototype down on the counter. "Ah, balance. Your favorite word," he teased, nudging her playfully with his elbow. "Where would we be without your eye for structure?"

Holly felt a blush creep into her cheeks, warmth spreading through her chest at the playful banter that had become so familiar between them. She turned to face him, her hands finding their way to his chest, fingertips tracing the intricate patterns of his festive sweater. "Probably buried under a pile of candy canes and gumdrops," she replied, her tone light and teasing.

Jingles chuckled, the sound sending a pleasant shiver down Holly's spine. "And what a delicious way to go that would be," he quipped, his arms encircling her waist, drawing her closer.

For a moment, the world around them faded away, the bustling activity of the bakery reduced to a distant hum. Holly gazed up at Jingles, marveling at the way his eyes seemed to hold an entire universe within their depths. In them, she saw a future filled with laughter, love, and endless possibilities.

"I love you," she whispered, the words slipping out with the ease of a long-held truth.

Jingles' expression softened, his smile turning tender. "And I love you, my sweet Holly," he murmured, leaning down to capture her lips in a gentle kiss.

As they parted, Holly felt a renewed sense of purpose and determination. Together, they would create a bakery that not only delighted the senses but also warmed the hearts of all who entered. With Jingles by her side, she knew that anything was possible.

"Now," she said, a mischievous glint in her eye, "let's see about those candy cane fence posts. I think we can make them work, but we'll need to get creative with the placement."

Jingles grinned, his enthusiasm infectious. "Lead the way, my love. Together, we'll make this the most magical gingerbread house Frostyville has ever seen."

And so, they set to work, their laughter and love infusing every detail of their creations. As the sun began to set outside the bakery windows, casting a golden glow over the snow-covered streets, Holly and Jingles stood back to admire their handiwork.

The gingerbread house was a masterpiece, a perfect balance of whimsy and structure, just like the love they shared. And as they closed up the bakery for the night, hand in hand, Holly knew that this was just the beginning of a lifetime filled with sweet moments and endless love.

As the days passed, Holly and Jingles found themselves immersed in the joyful chaos of wedding planning. Between taste-testing cakes, selecting the perfect shade of glittery gold for the decorations, and finalizing the guest list, they barely had a moment to breathe. Yet, amidst the whirlwind of preparations, their love only grew stronger.

One particularly hectic afternoon, as they sat huddled over a seating chart, Jingles suddenly looked up, his eyes sparkling with an idea. "Holly," he said, his voice filled with excitement, "what if we create a special wedding favor for our guests? Something that represents our love story?"

Holly tilted her head, intrigued. "What did you have in mind?"

Jingles grinned, pulling out a sketch he'd been working on. "Picture this: a miniature gingerbread house, complete with a tiny version of us standing outside, surrounded by glittering snow. We could package them in clear boxes, tied with a gold ribbon and a tag that tells our story."

As Holly studied the sketch, her heart swelled with love and admiration for the elf beside her. "Jingles, it's perfect," she breathed, tracing a finger over the delicate lines. "It's like giving each of our guests a little piece of our happily ever after."

Jingles beamed, his cheeks flushed with pride. "Exactly! And we can make them together, just like everything else we do."

Over the next few weeks, the couple poured their hearts into creating the perfect wedding favors. They spent long hours in the bakery, meticulously crafting each tiny gingerbread house, their laughter and love infusing every detail. And as the pile of completed favors grew, so did their excitement for the future they were building together.

On the eve of their wedding, as the first flakes of snow began to fall over Frostyville, Holly and Jingles stood hand in hand, gazing out at the twinkling lights that adorned the town square. The air was filled with the scent of cinnamon and pine, and the soft strains of Christmas carols drifted on the breeze.

"I can't believe it's finally here," Holly whispered, leaning her head against Jingles' shoulder. "Tomorrow, we'll be husband and wife."

Jingles pressed a kiss to her forehead, his voice soft and filled with emotion. "I've waited my whole life for this moment, Holly. To find someone who understands me, who loves me for all that I am, and who makes every day feel like Christmas morning."

Holly turned to face him, her eyes shining with tears of joy. "You are my everything, Jingles. My partner, my best friend, my soulmate. I can't wait to spend forever with you."

As the clock struck midnight, signaling the start of their wedding day, Jingles pulled Holly close, his lips finding hers in a kiss that held the promise of a lifetime of love and laughter. And as the snow continued to fall, blanketing Frostyville in a shimmering cloak of white, Holly and Jingles knew that their story was only just beginning.

For theirs was a love that could weather any storm, a love that burned brighter than the stars in the sky. A love that would be remembered long after the last cookie had been eaten and the last glittery snowflake had fallen. A love that would inspire generations to come, a testament to the magic that can happen when two hearts find their perfect match.

And so, as the sun began to rise over the North Pole, casting a golden glow over the snow-covered landscape, Holly and Jingles prepared to embark on their greatest adventure yet. Hand in hand, heart to heart, they stepped forward into their happily ever after, ready to face whatever the future might bring, together.

As the first rays of sunlight filtered through the frosted windows of the North Pole Bakery, Holly and Jingles stood together, their hands intertwined, gazing at the sparkling display of gingerbread houses and glittery treats they had created. The bakery had become more than just a place of work; it was a testament to their love, their partnership, and the magic they had woven together.

Holly's heart swelled with a mix of emotions as she realized that this would be their last day in the bakery before the wedding. Excitement, nervousness, and an overwhelming sense of love all vied for dominance within her. She turned to Jingles, her eyes shining with unshed tears.

"I can't believe this is really happening," she whispered, her voice trembling slightly. "Tomorrow, we'll be married. It feels like a dream."

Jingles smiled softly, his hand reaching up to cup her cheek. "A dream come true," he murmured, his thumb gently wiping away a tear that had escaped down her cheek. "And I get to spend the rest of my life making all your dreams a reality."

Holly leaned into his touch, her heart so full it felt ready to burst. "You already have," she told him, her voice filled with conviction. "You've given me more than I ever thought possible. Love, laughter, and a lifetime of adventures to look forward to."

Jingles pulled her into his arms, holding her close as he rested his chin atop her head. "And you've given me a home," he replied softly, his voice thick with emotion. "A place to belong, and a love that I never knew could exist."

They stood there for a long moment, content in each other's embrace, as the world around them seemed to fade away. The bakery, with its twinkling lights and sugary scents, became a cocoon of warmth and love, a safe haven from the outside world.

Finally, Holly pulled back, her eyes sparkling with a mixture of tears and laughter. "We should probably finish up here," she said, gesturing to the few remaining tasks that needed to be completed before they could close up the bakery. "After all, we have a big day tomorrow."

Jingles grinned, his trademark mischief returning to his eyes. "I don't know," he teased, his fingers dancing along her sides in a playful tickle. "I think the bride and groom are entitled to a little break, don't you?"

Holly laughed, squirming away from his touch. "Jingles!" she protested, though her smile never wavered. "We have responsibilities!"

"And we also have each other," Jingles countered, pulling her back into his arms and pressing a quick kiss to her lips. "The rest can wait."

And as they lost themselves in each other's embrace once more, the world around them seemed to shimmer with the promise of all the tomorrows yet to come. A future filled with love, laughter, and the kind of magic that can only be found in the warmth of a shared heart.

For Holly and Jingles, this was just the beginning of their happily ever after. And as the snow continued to fall outside, blanketing the world in a shimmering cloak of white, they knew that no matter what the future might bring, they would face it together. Always.

Holly drew comfort from Jingles' embrace, his arms providing a sanctuary from her worries. Yet, a flicker of doubt persisted, nagging at the edges of her mind. She pulled back slightly, her eyes searching his. "I want to believe that, Jingles. I do. But what if the storm is a sign that we're not meant to be together?"

Jingles cupped her face in his hands, his touch gentle and reassuring. "Holly, my love, the only sign I need is the love I see in your eyes every day. The way your smile lights up my world. The way your laughter fills my heart with joy."

He leaned forward, resting his forehead against hers. "We've weathered so many storms together, both literal and figurative. This is just one more adventure for us to tackle, hand in hand."

Holly closed her eyes, letting his words wash over her like a soothing balm. In the depths of her heart, she knew he was right. Their love had been forged in the crucible of shared challenges and triumphs, each one strengthening the bond between them.

She thought back to the day they'd first met, when a flour-dusted collision in the bakery had sent them both tumbling to the ground in a tangled heap of limbs and laughter. Even then, amidst the chaos and the spilled sugar, she'd felt the first stirrings of something special between them.

And now, standing here in his arms on the eve of their wedding, she marveled at how far they'd come. Two hearts, once adrift in a sea of uncertainty, now anchored together by a love that knew no bounds.

Holly opened her eyes, a smile playing at the corners of her mouth. "You're right," she murmured, her fingers tracing the curve of his cheek. "No

Holly gazed out the frost-covered window, her breath creating fleeting patterns against the glass. Beyond the cozy confines of the bakery, heavy snowflakes swirled in an intricate dance, blanketing the streets of Frostyville in a shimmering cloak of white. The mesmerizing sight filled her with a sense of wonder, but a flicker of doubt crept into her heart.

Jingles stepped behind her, wrapping his arms around her waist and resting his chin on her shoulder. "Penny for your thoughts, my sweet Holly berry," he murmured, his warm breath tickling her ear.

She leaned back into his embrace, drawing comfort from his solid presence. "It's just... everything seems so perfect. The bakery, our wedding plans, this magical moment right here." She turned to face him, her eyes searching his. "But what if it's too perfect? What if something goes wrong?"

Jingles tilted his head, his lips quirking into a lopsided smile that never failed to melt her heart. "You mean like a rogue reindeer crashing the ceremony or a gingerbread man uprising?" he teased, his eyes sparkling with mirth.

Despite the worry gnawing at her, Holly couldn't help but chuckle. Jingles had a way of turning even the most daunting scenarios into opportunities for laughter. "I'm serious," she insisted, though her tone softened. "What if the snowstorm ruins everything? We've put so much into planning this day, and I just want it to be..."

"Perfect?" Jingles finished for her, his expression tender. He cupped her face in his hands, his thumbs gently caressing her cheekbones. "Holly, my love, don't you see? It already is perfect, because it's you and me."

Holly felt her heart swell, a warmth spreading through her chest that had nothing to do with the crackling fireplace nearby. "You always know what to say," she murmured, leaning into his touch.

"That's because I know you," Jingles replied, his voice low and earnest. "I know your heart, your dreams, your fears. And I promise you, no matter what happens, our love will make it magical."

Holly's eyes glistened with unshed tears, her worries melting away like snowflakes on a warm windowpane. "But what if the snowstorm does ruin the ceremony?" she whispered, giving voice to the lingering fear.

Jingles pressed a gentle kiss to her temple, his lips soft and reassuring. "Then we'll get married in the middle of the storm," he declared, his tone filled with unwavering conviction. "We'll exchange our vows amidst the swirling snowflakes, and it will be a moment etched in the tapestry of Frostyville's history. A love so strong, even the fiercest blizzard couldn't stop it."

Holly closed her eyes, imagining the scene he painted. She could see them standing hand in hand, their faces flushed with joy and exhilaration as the wind whipped around them, their voices rising above the howling gusts as they pledged their hearts to each other. It was a vision of raw, unbridled love, a testament to the unbreakable bond they shared.

When she opened her eyes, Jingles was gazing at her with an intensity that stole her breath. In his eyes, she saw a reflection of her own love, a love that had taken root in the depths of her soul and blossomed into something extraordinary.

"You're right," she breathed, a smile blossoming on her lips. "No matter what, as long as we're together, it will be magical."

Jingles grinned, his face alight with the infectious joy that had drawn her to him from the very beginning. "That's the spirit! Now, what do you say we add a little extra sparkle to those wedding favors? I have an idea involving edible glitter and tiny candy canes that just might be crazy enough to work."

Holly laughed, shaking her head in fond exasperation. "Lead the way, my mischievous elf. With you by my side, I'm ready for anything."

Hand in hand, they turned back to the task at hand, their hearts lighter and their love stronger than ever. The snowstorm outside continued to rage, but within the warmth of the bakery, Holly and Jingles knew they had everything they needed to weather any storm, as long as they had each other.

Before Holly could respond, the bell above the door jingled, announcing a customer. A cheerful woman stepped inside, her eyes lighting up at the display. "This is incredible! I've never seen anything like it," she exclaimed, gesturing to the glittering treats.

Holly straightened, a flash of pride surging through her as she took in the woman's awestruck expression. The bakery was a testament to their shared vision, a perfect blend of Jingles' whimsy and her own meticulous attention to detail.

Jingles stepped forward, his signature grin firmly in place. "Welcome to the North Pole Bakery! Is there anything in particular that catches your eye?"

The woman's gaze darted from the shimmering gingerbread houses to the delicately frosted sugar cookies, each one a miniature work of art. "It's all so beautiful," she murmured, her voice tinged with wonder. "How do you create such intricate designs?"

Holly exchanged a glance with Jingles, a silent conversation passing between them in the space of a heartbeat. This was their moment, a chance to share their passion with someone who truly appreciated the magic they'd created together.

"It's a labor of love," Holly said, moving to stand beside the woman. "Each piece is crafted with care, from the initial sketch to the final sprinkle of glitter."

Jingles nodded, his eyes sparkling with mischief. "And a little bit of North Pole magic, of course. We like to think that every treat carries a touch of holiday enchantment."

The woman laughed, the sound ringing out like sleigh bells in the cozy space of the bakery. "Well, you've certainly enchanted me. I'll take a dozen of those gingerbread cookies and one of the small houses. They'll be perfect for my daughter's Christmas party."

As Holly began packaging the woman's order, her mind drifted to the countless hours she and Jingles had spent perfecting their recipes, their laughter and banter filling the kitchen as they worked side by side. It was in those moments that she'd fallen in love with him all over again, his playful spirit and unwavering support a constant reminder of how lucky she was to have him in her life.

Jingles caught her eye as he carefully nestled the gingerbread house into a box, his smile softening into something tender and intimate. In that moment, Holly knew that no matter what challenges lay ahead, they would face them together, their love as unshakable as the very foundations of the North Pole itself.

The woman's voice broke through her reverie, her tone warm with gratitude. "Thank you both so much. You've made my day brighter just by being here."

Holly felt a lump form in her throat, her heart swelling with emotion. This was what it was all about, she realized - bringing joy to others, one shimmering treat at a time. And with Jingles by her side, she knew that joy would never fade, as constant and enduring as the North Star itself.

As the woman departed, the bell above the door jingling merrily in her wake, Holly turned to Jingles, her eyes shining with a mix of love and pride. "We did it," she whispered, her voice thick with emotion. "We've created something truly special here."

Jingles reached for her hand, his fingers lacing with hers in a gesture that felt as natural as breathing. "We have," he agreed, his gaze locked with hers. "But the best is yet to come, my love. With you by my side, I know that every day will be filled with magic and wonder."

And as they stood there, hand in hand, surrounded by the glittering fruits of their labor, Holly knew that he was right. Their story was just beginning, and with each new chapter, their love would only grow stronger, a shining beacon of hope and joy in a world that so desperately needed it.

As the sun dipped below the horizon, painting the snow-covered streets of Frostyville in a warm, golden glow, Holly and Jingles stepped out of the North Pole Bakery, their hearts full and their spirits high. The crisp evening air carried the faint scent of cinnamon and sugar, a reminder of the day's sweet successes.

Hand in hand, they strolled through the picturesque village, their laughter echoing off the frost-kissed storefronts.

The twinkling lights strung along the eaves winked at them, as if sharing in their joy.

"I can't believe we're just days away from our wedding," Holly mused, her eyes sparkling with anticipation. "It feels like a dream come true."

Jingles grinned, his mischievous eyes alight with excitement. "Speaking of dreams, I've been thinking about our grand exit. What if we add a glitter cannon? Imagine the looks on everyone's faces when we make our final farewell in a burst of shimmering magic!"

Holly couldn't help but laugh, her heart swelling with affection for her playful partner. "Oh, Jingles, you and your grand ideas! I love your enthusiasm, but let's keep the glitter contained to the bakery, shall we? I'd hate for our guests to be finding sparkles in their hair for weeks!"

Jingles chuckled, pulling her closer and pressing a kiss to her rosy cheek. "Ah, my sensible Holly, always keeping me grounded. But you have to admit, it would be a sight to behold!"

As they continued their walk, the conversation turned to the details of their impending nuptials. The guest list, the menu, the flowers - each element a reflection of their shared love and creativity.

"I can't wait to see you walk down the aisle," Jingles whispered, his voice softening with emotion. "I know you'll be the most radiant bride Frostyville has ever seen."

Holly felt her cheeks warm, a fluttering sensation filling her chest. "And I can't wait to begin our next chapter together, as husband and wife. With you by my side, I know that every day will be filled with love, laughter, and a sprinkle of magic."

Their steps slowed as they approached their cozy cottage, the warm light spilling from the windows a beacon of comfort and belonging. As they stood on the threshold, Jingles turned to face Holly, his expression suddenly serious.

"Holly, I want you to know that no matter what the future holds, my love for you will never waver. You've brought so much joy and purpose to my life, and I promise to spend every day cherishing and supporting you."

Tears pricked at the corners of Holly's eyes, her heart so full it felt ready to burst. "Oh, Jingles, I feel the same way. You've taught me to embrace life's little moments of magic, and I can't imagine facing any challenge without you by my side."

They sealed their declarations with a kiss, the warmth of their love a shield against the chill of the winter night. And as they stepped inside their home, ready to face the final preparations for their special day, they knew that their story was far from over.

For in the enchanted world of Frostyville, where hearts were full and magic was real, Holly and Jingles had found their happily ever after - a love that would endure, as timeless and everlasting as the spirit of Christmas itself.

The setting sun painted the snow-covered streets in a warm, golden glow as Holly and Jingles locked up the bakery for the day. Their breath formed wispy clouds in the crisp air, mingling with the sound of their laughter as they discussed the final preparations for their upcoming wedding.

"I think we should add more silver bells to the centerpieces," Holly mused, her gloved hand intertwined with Jingles'. "It would tie in nicely with the glittery snowflake theme."

Jingles' eyes sparkled with mischief. "What if we add a glitter cannon for our grand exit?"

Holly raised an eyebrow, picturing the explosion of sparkles raining down on their guests. She had to admit, it would make for a memorable and magical moment.

"Hmm, it could work," she said slowly, "but we'd have to make sure it's non-toxic glitter. And aim it away from great-aunt Maple's hairpiece!"

They both burst out laughing at the thought, their voices echoing merrily down the lamp-lit lane. As they continued walking, Holly's mind drifted to all the little details that still needed finalizing - the cake flavors, the seating chart, the enchanted ice sculpture...

But gazing over at Jingles, his auburn curls peeking out from under his jaunty red hat, she felt a sense of peace wash over her. No matter what minor hiccups may arise, their love was the real magic that would make the day perfect.

"I can't wait to marry you," she said softly, giving his hand a gentle squeeze.

Jingles brought her hand up to his lips, pressing a tender kiss to her knuckles through the knit fabric of her mitten. "Not as much as I can't wait to marry you, sugarplum."

As they rounded the corner onto Peppermint Lane, their cozy cottage came into view, smoke curling invitingly from the chimney. Holly's heart swelled with contentment. Here, with Jingles by her side, was exactly where she wanted to be - not just for Christmas, but for all the days and years to come.

Epilogue: Sweet Promises

One Year After Their Wedding...

The bell above Sugarplum & Evergreen's Magical Confections tinkled merrily as Holly pushed open the door, her arms laden with fresh baking supplies. The warm, spice-scented air enveloped her like a hug, and she couldn't help but smile at the sight before her. Her husband Jingles, his hat slightly askew, was putting the finishing touches on their latest creation – a three-tiered anniversary cake that seemed to defy gravity, with delicate sugar snowflakes spiraling up its sides.

"Careful with those spinning sugar sculptures, my husband," Holly called out, setting down her bags. "Remember what happened with Mrs. Peppermint's birthday cake?"

Jingles looked up with a grin, a smudge of powdered sugar on his cheek. "That was one time! And I maintain that the exploding candy rockets added a certain... festive flair."

"Is that what we're calling it now?" Holly laughed, crossing the room to wipe the sugar from his face. She paused to admire her wedding ring, which perfectly matched the one she'd presented to Jingles that snowy evening at the Frostyville Train Station, where she'd gotten down on one knee with a ring pop in her hand (and thankfully, a real ring in her pocket).

Their shared laughter filled the cozy shop, mingling with the scent of gingerbread and peppermint. In the two years since their famous gingerbread house creation in the town square, Holly and Jingles had turned their combined talents into Frostyville's most beloved bakery. Their reputation for creating magical confections had spread throughout the North Pole, drawing visitors from as far as Candy Cane Lane and Mistletoe Mountain.

The walls of their shop were lined with photographs documenting their journey – the gingerbread house that had brought them together, Holly's surprise proposal at the station (captured perfectly by their friend Tinker, who'd been hiding behind a candy cane pillar), their magical wedding day, and countless moments of joy shared with their growing family of customers. Their original gingerbread house still stood proud in the town square, preserved under a magical dome, a testament to the love story that had begun with sugar and spice.

"Can you believe it's been a year since our wedding?" Holly mused, spinning her wedding band. "Sometimes I still can't believe you said yes when I proposed."

Jingles wrapped his arms around her waist, pulling her close. "As if I could have said anything else! Though I still maintain that using a ring pop was simultaneously the bravest and most ridiculous thing you've ever done."

"Hey, I was working with what I had!" Holly defended, remembering how she'd panicked when her original plan to propose during the Winter Wonderland Festival had been derailed by a runaway chocolate sleigh incident. "Besides, you cried when you tasted it and realized I'd somehow engineered it to taste like your grandmother's famous hot chocolate."

"Because that's when I knew for certain I was marrying a genius," Jingles replied, kissing her forehead. "Though I have to say, reality has been far more interesting than any dream could be. Remember last week when we had to chase that enchanted gingerbread man all the way to the Frosted Forest?"

Their reminiscing was interrupted by a familiar jingling of bells outside. Through the frosted windows, they could see Santa's sleigh landing in the town square, right next to their original gingerbread house. The magical dome protecting it sparkled in the eternal twilight of the North Pole, the enchanted sugar never melting, the colors as vibrant as the day they'd created it.

"Speaking of Santa," Holly said, straightening Jingles' hat, "we should finish up here. The Winter Wonderland Festival planning committee meets in an hour, and we still need to present our ideas for this year's centerpiece."

Jingles' eyes lit up with that familiar spark of creativity that Holly had come to both love and fear. "Oh, don't worry about that, my sweet wife. I've been working on something spectacular – picture this: a life-sized chocolate castle with working drawbridge and..."

"No rocket boosters," Holly interrupted firmly, though she couldn't hide her smile. "I've been your wife for a year now, and I know exactly where this is going."

"But what about just a tiny one? For the drawbridge?" Jingles pleaded, giving her his best puppy-dog eyes. "I've been working with Tinker, and we've almost perfected the candy cane propulsion system!"

Holly shook her head fondly, reaching up to kiss him. "We'll discuss it at the meeting. But first, help me unpack these supplies. Mrs. Claus's cookie exchange is tomorrow, and we still need to make twelve dozen sugar plum swirl cookies."

As they worked side by side in their warm, sweetly scented shop, Holly couldn't help but marvel at how perfectly their lives had blended together. Marriage had only strengthened their bond, with Jingles' wild creativity balancing her careful precision, his spontaneity complementing her planning. Every day brought new adventures, new challenges, and new opportunities to create magic together.

The shop had become more than just a business – it was a haven for dreams and wishes, where young elves would press their noses against the window displays in wonder, and where even the grumpiest of North Pole residents (looking at you, Frosty) couldn't help but smile. They'd created something special, something that went beyond mere confectionery.

As the eternal twilight of the North Pole painted the sky in soft purples and blues, Mr. and Mrs. Evergreen worked their magic. Sugar spun like silk beneath their skilled hands, chocolate swirled into impossible shapes, and every now and then, when their fingers brushed or their eyes met across the workbench, that same spark that had brought them together flickered between them, sweet as candy and warm as freshly baked gingerbread.

Later that evening, as they locked up the shop and walked hand in hand toward the town square, the original gingerbread house glowed softly in the gathering darkness. They paused to admire it, as they did every evening, remembering the moment that had started their journey toward becoming the Evergreens.

"You know," Jingles said softly, pulling Holly close, "I think we should recreate it for our first anniversary celebration. But maybe with a few minor improvements..."

Holly raised an eyebrow. "Define 'minor improvements.'"

"Well," he grinned, "I was thinking about these fascinating candy fireworks I've been developing..."

Holly's laughter echoed through the square, bright and clear as sleigh bells. "Oh, Jingles Evergreen, what am I going to do with you?"

"Love me forever?" he suggested, his eyes twinkling like the stars above.

"Forever and a day," Holly replied, standing on tiptoe to kiss her husband. "Though I reserve the right to veto any explosive decorations."

As they walked home through the gently falling snow, their joined shadows dancing in the magical light of the North Pole, both Holly and Jingles knew that they had found something sweeter than any confection they could create. Their love story, which had begun with a simple gingerbread house and a surprise proposal at a train station, had blossomed into an adventure neither of them could have imagined – one filled with laughter, magic, and just the right amount of chaos to keep things interesting.

And as for their anniversary celebration? Well, let's just say that Frosty McFrosterson kept a fire extinguisher handy, just in case. After all, when it came to the Evergreens, you never knew quite what kind of magic might unfold.

BOOK 2

Chapter 1 Sweet Beginnings

The scent of cinnamon and nutmeg drifted through the frost-kissed windows of Holly's cottage bakery, a warm beacon against the perpetual winter wonderland of Frostyville. Outside, delicate snowflakes pirouetted past the candy-striped awning, each crystal catching the golden glow from within. Holly stood at her weathered wooden workbench, her fingers dusted with powdered sugar as she carefully measured ingredients for her legendary sugarplums.

"A pinch of magic, three drops of moonlight essence, and just a whisper of peppermint frost," she murmured, consulting her grandmother's recipe book. The ancient tome lay open before her, its pages crisp with age and decorated with generations of festive marginalia. Each annotation told a story of Christmases past, of triumphs and mistakes, of wisdom handed down through time.

The brass bell above the door chimed merrily, and Holly's heart skipped a familiar beat. Without turning, she knew who had entered—the slight jingle of bells that accompanied each step was as distinctive as a fingerprint.

Christmas on Peppermint Lane

"Working late again, Mrs. Jinglebells?" The voice was warm and teasing, filled with the kind of affection that could melt even the coldest North Pole night.

Holly felt her cheeks flush pink as she turned to face her husband of six months. Jingles stood in the doorway, his green uniform dusted with snow, his pointed ears slightly red from the cold. His eyes sparkled with the same mischief that had first caught her attention at last year's Snowflake Festival.

"These sugarplums won't make themselves, Mr. Jinglebells," she replied, trying to maintain a serious expression but failing as a smile tugged at her lips. "And with the festival just two weeks away..."

Jingles crossed the room in three quick strides, wrapping his arms around her waist from behind and resting his chin on her shoulder. "Ah yes, the famous festival where you'll defend your title as the Sugarplum Queen. Though I must say, you've already won the crown in my heart."

Holly rolled her eyes at the cheesy line but leaned back into his embrace nonetheless. "Save the sweet talk for after I perfect this batch. The recipe needs to be absolutely perfect this year. The competition is going to be fiercer than ever."

"Is that worry I detect in the voice of Holly Evergreen-Jinglebells, the most talented confectioner in all of Frostyville?" Jingles reached around her to swipe a finger through the bowl of powdered sugar, earning himself a playful slap on the hand.

"It's not just about defending the title," Holly said, her voice growing serious. "The festival is different this year. Bigger. More elaborate. Did you see the new pavilion they're constructing in Town Square?"

Jingles nodded, his bells chiming softly. "Hard to miss it. Mayor Kringle is determined to make this the grandest

Snowflake Festival in Frostyville's history. Something about attracting tourism from the Southern realms."

Holly turned in his arms, leaving dusty sugar handprints on his uniform. "And you? How are the preparations for the elf games coming along?"

A shadow of concern flickered across Jingles' usually cheerful face. "Well, about that..." He stepped back, running a hand through his hair—a nervous habit Holly had come to recognize. "The Council has assigned me a... partner for organizing the games this year."

"A partner?" Holly's eyebrows rose. "But you've always handled the games solo. You're the best games master Frostyville's ever had!"

"Apparently, with the festival's expanded scope, they felt additional expertise was needed." Jingles tried to keep his tone light, but Holly could hear the underlying tension. "His name is Frost. He's from the Northern Lights Division, specializes in 'innovative entertainment solutions,' whatever that means."

Holly wiped her hands on her apron, studying her husband's expression. "And you're not happy about this arrangement."

"It's not that," Jingles said quickly—too quickly. "He seems... capable. Very capable. Perhaps too capable." He forced a laugh that didn't quite reach his eyes. "Did you know he orchestrated the Crystal Kingdom's Millennium Celebration? Apparently, it was quite spectacular."

"Well," Holly said, reaching up to straighten his slightly crooked hat, "I'm sure between the two of you, this year's games will be absolutely magical. Now, make yourself useful and help me pack up these preliminary batches. They need to be delivered to the Council for approval tomorrow morning."

As they worked side by side in comfortable silence, Holly couldn't help but notice how Jingles' shoulders remained tense, his usual fluid movements slightly rigid. She knew her husband well enough to recognize when something was bothering him, but experience had taught her that pushing him to talk before he was ready would only make him retreat further into himself.

The kitchen clock chimed midnight, its face depicting a miniature Santa Claus whose beard grew longer with each hour. Holly stifled a yawn as she placed the last batch of sugarplums into a crystal container, each candy gleaming like a precious gem.

"These look perfect," Jingles said, holding one up to the light. The translucent candy caught the glow of the enchanted lanterns, sending rainbow reflections dancing across the walls. "May I?"

Holly nodded, watching as he popped the sugarplum into his mouth. His eyes widened, then closed in obvious pleasure. "Holly, these are... different. In a good way. What did you change?"

"Just a slight adjustment to the moonlight essence ratio," she said, pleased by his reaction. "I was thinking about how the festival always brings out everyone's inner child, that sense of wonder and possibility. I wanted to capture that feeling in the taste."

Jingles opened his eyes, gazing at her with such tenderness that her heart fluttered. "You never cease to amaze me, you know that? The way you understand the magic of Christmas, how you can translate emotions into flavors..."

The moment was interrupted by a sharp knock at the front door. Holly and Jingles exchanged puzzled looks—visitors at this hour were unusual in Frostyville, where most residents adhered to strict schedules to maintain toy production quotas.

"I'll get it," Jingles said, already moving toward the door. Holly heard it open, followed by a blast of cold air and a voice she didn't recognize.

"Ah, Jingles! Excellent, I hoped I'd find you here." The voice was smooth as polished ice, with an accent that suggested extensive travel through the magical realms. "And this must be the famous Holly Evergreen-Jinglebells. Your reputation precedes you, my dear."

Holly turned to find herself facing a tall, strikingly handsome elf with hair the color of fresh snow and eyes like frozen silver. He wore an elaborate coat of midnight blue, decorated with patterns of frost that seemed to shift and change in the light.

"Frost," Jingles said, his voice carefully neutral. "What brings you here at this hour?"

"Inspiration strikes at the most inconvenient times, doesn't it?" Frost swept into the room with the grace of a winter wind, his eyes taking in every detail of Holly's workshop. "I had some absolutely brilliant ideas for the games that simply couldn't wait until morning. And when I saw the lights on here..." He paused, inhaling deeply. "My word, what is that divine aroma?"

"Holly's signature sugarplums," Jingles answered, moving to stand beside his wife. "For the festival competition."

"Ah yes, the famous sugarplums!" Frost's eyes lit up. "I've heard tales of their legendary status even in the Crystal Kingdom. Would it be terribly forward of me to request a sample? Purely in the interest of cultural exchange, of course."

Holly hesitated, glancing at the carefully packed containers. These were meant for the Council's approval, and the recipe was still in development. But refusing would seem inhospitable, especially to someone who would be working closely with Jingles.

"Of course," she said, selecting a single sugarplum from her test batch. "Though I should warn you, this is just a preliminary version."

Frost accepted the candy with an elegant bow, examining it with the air of a connoisseur before placing it on his tongue. His reaction was immediate and dramatic—his eyes widened, and a look of pure delight transformed his features.

"Extraordinary!" he exclaimed. "Simply extraordinary! The complexity of flavors, the perfect balance of sweetness and magic... My dear Holly, you've managed to capture the very essence of Christmas in a single bite. No wonder you're the reigning champion."

Holly felt herself blush at the effusive praise, even as she noticed Jingles' posture stiffen beside her. "Thank you, but as I said, it's still a work in progress."

"Modest as well as talented," Frost said, his silver eyes twinkling. "Jingles, you're a fortunate elf indeed." He turned his attention back to Holly. "I don't suppose you'd be willing to share your expertise? The games this year will feature several culinary challenges, and your insight would be invaluable."

Before Holly could respond, Jingles cleared his throat. "It's getting late, and Holly has an early meeting with the Council tomorrow."

"Of course, of course!" Frost stepped back, adjusting his elaborate coat. "Where are my manners? I apologize for the intrusion." He produced a business card that seemed to be made of actual ice, offering it to Holly. "Please, do consider my request. I believe your participation would add an extra sprinkle of magic to the festivities."

After Frost had departed in a swirl of snowflakes, Holly turned to find Jingles staring at the closed door, his expression troubled.

"Well, he's certainly... impressive," she said carefully.

"Isn't he just?" Jingles replied, his voice uncharacteristically sharp. Then, seeing Holly's surprised expression, he softened. "I'm sorry, love. It's been a long day. Let's get these packed up and head home."

As they prepared to leave, Holly couldn't shake the feeling that their comfortable routine had just been disrupted by more than just festival preparations. The ice card in her apron pocket seemed to pulse with a subtle energy, and somewhere in the distance, she could have sworn she heard the sound of sleigh bells laughing.

Chapter 2 Frost and Fire

Morning arrived in Frostyville with a symphony of tinkling icicles and the distant chorus of early-rising elves preparing for another day of Christmas magic. Holly stood before the full-length mirror in their bedroom, adjusting her formal presentation apron—a beautiful creation of crimson silk embroidered with golden snowflakes that Jingles had given her as a wedding gift.

"You look perfect," Jingles said from the doorway, two steaming mugs of peppermint hot chocolate in his hands. He crossed the room and handed her one, pressing a kiss to her temple. "The Council would have to be under a serious enchantment not to approve your sugarplums."

Holly accepted the mug gratefully, inhaling the rich aroma. "I just can't shake the feeling that something's missing. The recipe is good, yes, but is it festival worthy? Is it special enough to defend the crown?"

"Holly." Jingles set his mug down and turned her to face him, his hands gentle on her shoulders. "Your sugarplums don't just taste magical—they are magical. You put your heart into every batch, and that's something no other confectioner can replicate."

She smiled up at him, drawing strength from his unwavering faith in her abilities. "What would I do without you?"

"Probably get a full night's sleep instead of staying up late experimenting with moonlight essence ratios," he teased, then glanced at the clock. "Speaking of which, we should get going. Your meeting's in thirty minutes, and I need to meet Frost at the game grounds to review his proposed changes."

Holly noticed the slight tightening around his eyes at the mention of Frost's name. "Are you sure you don't want me to come with you after my meeting? An extra pair of eyes might help with the planning."

"No, no," Jingles said quickly—too quickly. "You focus on your presentation. Besides..." He hesitated. "Frost can be a bit... intense. Very focused on his vision. It's probably better if we sort out the technical details first."

Holly studied her husband's face, noting the careful way he was choosing his words. "Jingles, if something's bothering you—"

"Nothing's bothering me," he interrupted, forcing a brightness into his tone that didn't quite ring true. "Everything's fine. Perfect, even. Now come on, we're going to be late."

The walk to the Council chambers was beautiful but tense. Fresh snow had fallen overnight, transforming Frostyville into a glittering wonderland. Holiday decorations adorned every lamppost and storefront, and the new festival pavilion rose in the distance like a palace made of ice and light. Yet Holly couldn't help but notice how Jingles kept glancing at his pocket watch, his steps quick and hurried.

They parted ways at the Town Square, Jingles heading toward the game grounds while Holly continued on to the Council building. She watched him disappear into the crowd, noting how his usually jaunty walk seemed more determined than cheerful.

The Council chambers were housed in an ancient structure that resembled a giant gingerbread house, complete with candy cane columns and frosted windowpanes. Holly took a deep breath, squared her shoulders, and pushed open the massive peppermint-striped doors.

Inside, the Council members were already assembled around their crescent-shaped table. Seven of Frostyville's most distinguished elves, each representing a different aspect of Christmas magic, regarded her with varying degrees of interest. At the center sat Mayor Kringle, his white beard rivaling Santa's own in both length and majesty.

"Ah, Mrs. Jinglebells," Mayor Kringle boomed, his voice as rich as hot cocoa. "Right on time. We're eager to sample this year's festival submission."

Holly stepped forward, carefully removing the crystal containers from her basket. As she arranged them on the presentation table, she launched into her prepared speech about the inspiration behind the recipe, the careful balance of traditional and innovative elements, and the specific magical properties she'd incorporated.

The Council members listened attentively, nodding at appropriate intervals. When she finished speaking, there was a moment of anticipatory silence as each member selected a sugarplum for tasting.

Holly held her breath, watching their expressions. There were thoughtful nods, raised eyebrows, and contemplative mmms. Mayor Kringle closed his eyes as he savored his piece, his impressive eyebrows drawing together in concentration.

"Remarkable," he said finally, opening his eyes to fix Holly with a penetrating gaze. "You've managed to capture something quite special here. The way the flavors evolve, telling a story with each taste... Most impressive."

Relief flooded through Holly, but it was short-lived.

"However," Councilor Evergreen (no relation) interjected, "we must consider the competition. This year's festival is drawing participants from all the magical realms. The Crystal Kingdom's entry, in particular, is rumored to be quite... revolutionary."

"Indeed," added Councilor Mistletoe, adjusting her spectacles. "We've received word that they're sending their most renowned confectioner, Master Icicle himself."

Holly's heart skipped a beat. Master Icicle was a legend in the magical culinary world, known for his innovative techniques and spectacular presentations. She'd studied his methods, dreamed of apprenticing under him before settling in Frostyville.

"Perhaps," Mayor Kringle said thoughtfully, "this is an opportunity rather than a challenge. Mrs. Jinglebells, what would you say to a collaboration?"

"A collaboration?" Holly repeated, confused.

"Yes. As it happens, Master Icicle's protégé is already here in Frostyville. I believe you've met him—Frost?" The Mayor's eyes twinkled. "He's quite impressed with your work, and his experience with Crystal Kingdom techniques could add an interesting dimension to your recipe."

Holly felt as though the floor had suddenly shifted beneath her feet. "I... that is... my recipe is a family tradition, passed down through generations..."

"Of course, of course," Mayor Kringle said soothingly. "We're merely suggesting an exchange of ideas. The festival is about bringing different magical traditions together, after all. Think of it as a cultural bridge."

Before Holly could respond, the chamber doors burst open with a gust of winter air, and Frost himself swept into the room, his timing so perfect it seemed almost orchestrated.

"My sincerest apologies for the interruption," he said, bowing deeply to the Council. "But when I heard that Holly's presentation was this morning, I simply couldn't resist." He turned to Holly, his silver eyes alight with enthusiasm. "I hope you don't mind, but I spent half the night thinking about your remarkable sugarplums and had some ideas I simply had to share."

Holly noticed how the Council members straightened in their seats, their attention shifting from her to the newcomer with obvious interest. Even Mayor Kringle leaned forward, his expression eager.

"Please, Frost," the Mayor gestured welcomingly. "We were just discussing the possibility of collaboration."

Frost produced an elegant crystal flask from his coat pocket. Inside, a liquid shimmed like captured starlight. "This is an essence we use in the Crystal Kingdom for our most prestigious confections. When combined with traditional Christmas magic..." He glanced at Holly. "Well, perhaps a demonstration would be more convincing?"

Holly felt trapped. To refuse would appear ungracious and possibly damage her standing with the Council. But accepting meant deviating from her grandmother's recipe, from generations of family tradition. And what would Jingles think?

"I..." she began, but Mayor Kringle was already nodding enthusiastically.

"An excellent suggestion! Mrs. Jinglebells, why don't you and Frost work together on a sample batch? We can reconvene tomorrow morning for a tasting."

It wasn't really a question, despite its phrasing. Holly recognized a Council directive when she heard one. "Of course," she said, managing a polite smile. "That would be... illuminating."

As the Council members filed out, chattering excitedly about the potential collaboration, Frost approached Holly with that same graceful movement that seemed to leave swirls of frost in his wake.

"I can't tell you how excited I am about this opportunity," he said, his voice warm despite its icy undertones. "Your talent combined with Crystal Kingdom techniques... we could create something revolutionary."

Holly clutched her empty basket, using it as a subtle barrier between them. "I should really discuss this with Jingles first. He's expecting me at the game grounds—"

"Oh, Jingles is quite busy at the moment," Frost said smoothly. "We spent the early morning reviewing my proposals for the games, and he's currently overseeing the construction of the new ice maze. Fascinating design, if I do say so myself. Shall we head to your workshop? Time is of the essence, after all."

Holly felt oddly disconnected, as if she were watching herself from a distance as she nodded and followed Frost out of the Council chambers. This wasn't how she'd expected the morning to go at all. She needed to talk to Jingles, to sort out the jumble of emotions clouding her thoughts. But Frost was already striding ahead, talking animatedly about crystal enhancement techniques and magical fusion theory, and she found herself hurrying to keep up.

Meanwhile, across town at the game grounds, Jingles stood in the center of what would soon be the most elaborate ice maze in Frostyville's history, feeling about as useful as a chocolate teapot in summer. Frost's "proposals" had effectively transformed the traditional elf games into a spectacular but unrecognizable event.

Christmas on Peppermint Lane

"Mr. Jinglebells?" A young elf apprentice approached, looking nervous. "We've got a problem with the enchanted ice blocks for the maze walls. They're... well... they're singing."

Jingles pinched the bridge of his nose. "Singing?"

"Yes, sir. Crystal Kingdom harmonies. Very pretty, but they're causing the nearby snow sculptures to dance, which is making the toy testing ground rather... chaotic."

"Of course they are," Jingles muttered. This was exactly the kind of magical overflow he'd worried about when he'd seen Frost's plans. Traditional Christmas magic didn't always mix well with other realms' enchantments. But Frost had insisted his calculations were perfect, and the Council had been so impressed with his presentations...

"Sir?" The apprentice shifted uncomfortably. "Should we stop construction until Mr. Frost returns?"

The question stung more than it should have. This was supposed to be Jingles' project. He'd run the elf games successfully for decades. Now he couldn't even handle basic construction issues without Frost's intervention?

"No," he said firmly. "We'll handle this ourselves. Show me where the resonance is strongest."

As he followed the apprentice through the half-built maze, Jingles couldn't shake the feeling that he was losing his grip on more than just the games. The thought of Holly presenting her sugarplums to the Council that morning had been nagging at him. He should have been there to support her, but Frost had scheduled an early meeting that somehow stretched into urgent construction oversight.

Frost. Everything seemed to revolve around Frost lately. His innovative ideas, his Crystal Kingdom connections, his elegant manner and strategic timing. Even Holly had seemed impressed by him last night, though she'd tried to hide it.

A crash from the toy testing ground interrupted his brooding. Several mechanical reindeer were performing what appeared to be a waltz through the equipment setup, scattering elves and half-finished toys in their wake.

"Right," Jingles said, rolling up his sleeves. "Let's sort this out before—"

"Before what, my friend?" Frost's voice rang out across the grounds. Jingles turned to see him approaching with Holly beside him, and something cold that had nothing to do with the weather settled in his stomach.

"Holly?" Jingles said, trying to keep his voice neutral despite his surprise. "How did the Council meeting go?"

"Wonderfully!" Frost answered before Holly could speak. "In fact, we're on our way to her workshop now. The Council has approved a special collaboration between us for the festival competition. Crystal Kingdom techniques combined with traditional Frostyville magic—it's going to be spectacular!"

Jingles looked at Holly, who seemed unable to meet his eyes. "A collaboration?" he repeated. "That's... unexpected."

"The best innovations often are," Frost said cheerfully, apparently oblivious to the tension. "Now, about these singing ice blocks—a simple resonance adjustment should do the trick. Holly, shall we continue to your workshop? Time is rather precious."

Holly finally looked at Jingles, her expression a mix of apology and uncertainty. "I'll explain everything later," she said softly. "Tonight?"

Jingles wanted to object, to pull her aside and talk now, to understand what was happening to their carefully built life. But another crash from the toy testing ground demanded his attention, and by the time he looked back, Holly and Frost were already walking away, their heads close together in discussion.

The singing ice blocks seemed to hit a particularly mournful note, and Jingles couldn't help but sympathize.

Chapter 3 Cracks in the Ice

Holly's workshop had never felt less like home. Crystal vials and elaborate equipment from the Crystal Kingdom now shared space with her grandmother's well-worn baking tools, and the familiar scent of Christmas spices competed with the sharp, clean smell of Frost's magical essences.

"The key," Frost was saying, measuring out drops of his shimmering liquid with precise movements, "is to maintain the core of your original recipe while enhancing its magical properties. Think of it as adding facets to an already beautiful gem."

Holly watched as he added the drops to her basic sugarplum mixture. The dough immediately began to glow with an ethereal light, tiny sparkles dancing through it like captured stars. It was beautiful, she had to admit—but was it still her grandmother's recipe?

"Now," Frost continued, his excitement palpable, "if we adjust the moonlight essence ratio as you did before, but filter it through this crystal matrix..." He produced what looked like a delicate ice prism from his coat.

"Wait," Holly interrupted, frowning. "How did you know about my moonlight essence adjustment? I never mentioned that specifically."

Frost's hands stilled for just a moment before he continued working. "Didn't you? I must have noticed it in the taste then. I have quite a refined palate when it comes to magical confectionery."

Something about his tone made Holly uneasy, but before she could pursue the question, the workshop door opened to admit a blast of cold air and a harried-looking Jingles.

"Holly, do you have a moment?" he asked, then noticed Frost. "Oh. You're still here."

"Still making progress!" Frost replied brightly. "Holly's natural talent combined with Crystal Kingdom techniques is producing remarkable results. Would you like to see?"

Jingles ignored him, focusing on Holly. "Could we talk? Privately?"

"We're actually at a rather crucial stage in the process," Frost began, but Holly was already removing her apron.

"Of course," she said, relieved for the interruption despite her interest in the magical fusion taking place. "Frost, would you mind..."

"Say no more!" Frost stepped back from the workbench with an elegant bow. "I'll use this opportunity to check on the game grounds. The singing ice blocks should have settled by now, but one can never be too careful with resonance harmonics."

After he'd gone, Holly and Jingles stood in awkward silence, the glowing sugarplum mixture casting strange shadows on their faces.

"So," Jingles finally said, "a collaboration?"

Holly sank into her grandmother's old rocking chair, suddenly exhausted. "It wasn't exactly my choice. The Council... they were impressed with my recipe, but with Master Icicle entering the competition..."

"Master Icicle?" Jingles' eyebrows shot up. "Since when is he involved?"

"He's coming to judge the festival competition. Apparently, it's part of Mayor Kringle's plan to make this year's festival more prestigious." Holly ran a hand through her hair, dislodging a sprinkle of sugar. "The Council thinks combining my traditional recipe with Crystal Kingdom techniques will give us an edge."

"Us?" Jingles' voice was uncharacteristically sharp. "Or you and Frost?"

Holly looked up at him, startled by his tone. "What's that supposed to mean?"

"I don't know, Holly. You tell me. First he shows up at midnight to 'share ideas,' then he happens to be at your Council presentation, and now he's practically taken over your workshop."

"That's not fair," Holly protested, even as a small voice in her head acknowledged the strange timing of Frost's appearances. "The Council assigned him to work with me, just like they assigned him to work with you on the games."

"Yes, and look how well that's going," Jingles said bitterly. "Do you know what the game grounds look like now? It's all crystal this and resonance that. The traditional games we've had for centuries apparently aren't 'innovative' enough."

"Jingles..." Holly stood, reaching for him, but he stepped back.

"I saw how impressed you were last night," he continued, the words tumbling out as if he'd been holding them back for too long. "The way you looked at him when he tasted your sugarplum, how you blushed at his compliments."

"I was being polite!" Holly felt heat rise to her cheeks again, but this time from anger. "And as I recall, you didn't exactly object to his presence then."

"Because I was trying to be professional! But now he's everywhere, changing everything, and you're just going along with it!"

"What choice do I have?" Holly demanded. "The Council has made their expectations clear. And maybe... maybe some change isn't such a bad thing. The festival is evolving, Jingles. We can't just keep doing things the same way forever."

As soon as the words left her mouth, she knew they were the wrong thing to say. Jingles' face closed off, his usual warmth replaced by something cold and distant.

"No," he said quietly. "Apparently we can't. I should get back to the game grounds. I'm sure Frost has more 'improvements' planned."

"Jingles, wait—"

But he was already gone, leaving behind only the faint jingle of bells and the scent of peppermint that always clung to his clothes.

Holly sank back into the rocking chair, fighting back tears. The glowing mixture on her workbench pulsed gently, like a heartbeat, sending sparkles of light dancing across the ceiling. It was beautiful, yes, but as she looked around her transformed workshop, she wondered if beauty was worth the price of tradition—and trust.

A light knock at the door made her quickly wipe her eyes. "Come in," she called, expecting Frost's return.

Instead, her grandmother's oldest friend, Mistletoe Mary, poked her head in. Her eyes widened at the sight of the Crystal

Kingdom equipment, but she said nothing about it as she entered, carrying a steaming mug.

"Peppermint tea," she said, pressing the mug into Holly's hands. "With a dash of comfort magic. You look like you could use it, dear."

Holly accepted the tea gratefully, inhaling its soothing aroma. "Is it that obvious?"

"Only to someone who's been around as long as I have," Mary said, settling her plump form onto a nearby stool. "I remember when your grandmother faced similar challenges during her time as Sugarplum Queen."

This was news to Holly. "Grandma never mentioned any challenges. She always made it sound so... magical."

Mary's laugh was like tinkling bells. "Oh, it was magical, dear. But magic comes in many forms, and not all of them sparkle like Crystal Kingdom starlight." She glanced meaningfully at the glowing mixture on the workbench. "Sometimes the most powerful magic is in the simplest things —like love, trust, and tradition."

"But the Council wants innovation," Holly said, voicing the worry that had been gnawing at her since the morning meeting. "They want something spectacular."

"Hmm." Mary reached into her apron pocket and pulled out a small, wrapped candy. "Try this."

Holly unwrapped what appeared to be a simple butterscotch. The moment it touched her tongue, she was flooded with memories: her first Christmas in Frostyville, learning to bake with her grandmother, the day she met Jingles at last year's festival, their wedding day...

"That's..." she blinked back fresh tears. "That's incredible. How did you..."

"Your grandmother's recipe," Mary said softly. "No Crystal Kingdom enhancements, no spectacular light shows.

Just pure Christmas magic and love." She patted Holly's hand. "Sometimes, dear, the most innovative thing we can do is remember what matters most."

Holly stared at the empty wrapper, then at her transformed workshop, understanding slowly dawning. "I've been so focused on winning the competition, on impressing the Council... I forgot why I became a confectioner in the first place."

"And why is that, dear?"

"To bring joy," Holly said, rising from the chair with renewed purpose. "To create something that makes people feel the magic of Christmas in their hearts, not just their eyes."

Mary smiled, her eyes twinkling. "Now that sounds like the Holly I know. And perhaps like something a certain games master might understand?"

Holly's heart clenched at the thought of Jingles and their argument. "If he'll still talk to me."

"Trust in love, dear," Mary said, standing with a slight groan. "It's the strongest magic we have." She headed for the door, then paused. "Oh, and Holly? Your grandmother had a saying about spectacular displays: 'All that glitters is not gold—sometimes it's just frost on the window.'"

With that cryptic remark, she departed, leaving Holly alone with her thoughts, the glowing mixture, and a decision to make. Outside, the sun was setting over Frostyville, painting the snow in shades of pink and gold. Somewhere in that winter wonderland, her husband was probably still wrestling with singing ice blocks and crystal resonance harmonics, his own Christmas magic being overshadowed by someone else's sparkle.

Holly looked at her grandmother's recipe book, then at Frost's crystal equipment. The Council wanted innovation?

Well, perhaps it was time to show them what real Christmas magic could do—magic born of love, tradition, and trust.

She reached for her apron, her mind already working on a plan. But first, she had an important stop to make at the game grounds.

BOOK 3

Chapter 1: A Perfect Plan Gone Awry

Holly Winters-Bells stood in her cozy kitchen, the warm December morning light streaming through frost-kissed windows. The aroma of gingerbread and peppermint hot chocolate filled the air as she prepared breakfast for Jingles. Their second Christmas as a married couple was approaching, and she wanted everything to be perfect. Lately, though, something felt different – a subtle shift in her body that she couldn't quite explain. Even the scent of her beloved baked goods sometimes made her stomach flutter in unexpected ways.

"Darling, have you seen my pointy shoes?" Jingles called from upstairs, his voice carrying that musical lilt that still made her heart skip after all this time. "I've got an early meeting with the Council of Holiday Magic, and you know how particular they are about proper elf attire."

Holly smiled, despite the wave of queasiness that had been her constant companion for the past week. "Check under the bed! That's where they ended up after last night's impromptu dance party."

Their home, a charming Victorian-style cottage on Candy Cane Lane, was decorated for the season, with twinkling lights casting a magical glow on the fresh snow outside. Holly had spent the weekend arranging everything just so – garlands of fragrant pine and holly berries draped along the banisters, magical ornaments that changed color with the mood floating on the Christmas tree, and Jingles' collection of enchanted bells tinkling softly in the morning breeze.

She flipped the gingerbread pancakes, adding a dash of her secret ingredient – ground star anise and a pinch of magic sugar that made them sparkle. The cast iron griddle, a wedding gift from Mrs. Claus herself, sizzled pleasantly. But as she bent down to retrieve the maple syrup from the lower cabinet, another wave of dizziness washed over her.

"Found them!" Jingles announced triumphantly, practically dancing down the stairs in his signature way – half-skipping, half-floating. His red and green striped socks (mismatched, as always) barely touched the ground. He paused at the bottom, his pointed ears twitching with concern as he noticed Holly's pale face. "Sugar plum, are you alright?"

Holly straightened up, forcing a bright smile. "Just fine! Probably just tired from all the holiday preparations." She didn't want to worry him, especially not today. They had been planning this Christmas for months, determined to make it even more special than their first as newlyweds.

Jingles wasn't entirely convinced, but the smell of breakfast drew him to the kitchen table, where Holly had already set out their favorite holiday china – the ones with dancing snowmen that actually moved across the plates when filled with hot food. He adjusted his collar, smoothing down his formal elf jacket with its intricate golden bells sewn along the lapels.

"The Council wants to discuss the annual Wish Enhancement Protocol," he explained between bites of pancake, his eyes lighting up with that mischievous sparkle

Holly had fallen in love with. "Apparently, some of the younger elves have been experimenting with unauthorized wish combinations. Last week, someone tried to merge a snow wish with a cookie wish, and now we have a neighborhood in Minnesota where it's raining snickerdoodles."

Holly laughed, then quickly pressed a hand to her mouth as the sound made her head spin slightly. She pushed her own plate away, untouched. "That actually sounds delicious, though probably not very practical."

Jingles reached across the table, taking her hand. His skin always felt like velvet-wrapped sunshine, warm and soft despite the winter chill. "Are you sure you're okay? You've barely touched your breakfast, and you never skip your morning pancakes."

"I'm fine, really," Holly insisted, though her stomach churned traitorously. "Just excited about our plans for tonight. Are you sure you want to try the Ancient Christmas Wish Spell? It sounds a bit... unpredictable."

The spell had been discovered in one of the dusty tomes in the Frostyville Library's restricted section. It promised to enhance a couple's understanding of each other by allowing them to experience each other's magical abilities for twenty-four hours. Holly had been hesitant, but Jingles was convinced it would be romantic – and helpful for their future together.

"Trust me, sugar plum," Jingles winked, his bell-tipped ears jingling softly with the movement. "What could possibly go wrong?"

Holly looked at her husband, taking in his confident grin, the way his eyes crinkled at the corners when he smiled, the slight dusting of magical sparkles that always seemed to follow him around. She loved him more than anything, but sometimes his enthusiasm for magical experimentation made her nervous.

After all, she was still learning to control her own baker's magic, which had developed unexpectedly after their marriage.

The grandfather clock in the hall chimed eight times, its mechanical birds emerging to sing a chorus of "Deck the Halls." Jingles jumped up, nearly knocking over his hot chocolate. "Sweet candy canes, I'm going to be late!" He rushed to Holly's side, placing a kiss on her forehead that left behind a trace of sparkles. "I'll see you at the bakery later? Don't forget, we need to gather all the ingredients for the spell before sunset."

Holly nodded, trying to ignore the way the room seemed to tilt slightly. "I'll have everything ready. Just be careful at the Council meeting. Remember what happened last time you got too excited and accidentally turned all their formal robes into ugly Christmas sweaters?"

Jingles grinned unrepentantly. "They needed some holiday cheer! Besides, some of them still wear those sweaters." He grabbed his pointed hat from the coat rack, which obligingly bent down to reach his height. "Love you, sugar plum!"

With a theatrical twirl and the cheerful jingling of bells, he disappeared in a shower of silver sparkles, leaving behind the faint scent of candy canes and his half-eaten breakfast.

Holly sank into her chair, finally allowing herself to acknowledge how strange she'd been feeling lately. It wasn't just the dizziness or the queasiness – her magic had been acting oddly too. Yesterday, she'd tried to frost a batch of sugar cookies, and instead of the usual delicate swirls, the frosting had arranged itself into tiny dancing snowmen that refused to stay still.

She glanced at the calendar hanging on the kitchen wall, where she meticulously tracked everything from special orders at Holly's Holiday Bakery to magical anomalies. Something tugged at the edge of her consciousness, a realization trying to break through, but before she could grasp it, the magical doorbell chimed with the sound of sleigh bells.

"Coming!" she called, pushing herself up from the table. Whatever was going on with her body would have to wait. They had a big night ahead, and she had a feeling their second Christmas as a married couple was about to become far more interesting than either of them had planned.

Chapter 2: A Dash of Doubt, a Pinch of Magic

The morning rush at Holly's Holiday Bakery was in full swing, the enchanted bell above the door playing a different carol with each customer's entrance. The scent of fresh-baked goods – snickerdoodles dusted with color-changing sugar, peppermint bark that actually barked, and Holly's famous mistletoe macarons that caused anyone who ate them to float briefly – filled the air with sweet promises.

But today, even the familiar comfort of her beloved bakery couldn't settle Holly's churning stomach. She stood behind the counter, one hand pressed against the cool marble surface for support, while her assistant manager, Pepper Peppermint, handled the register with characteristic efficiency.

"That's one dozen Christmas light cookies that actually twinkle, and a loaf of cinnamon swirl bread that sings carols when you toast it," Pepper announced cheerfully to a customer, her candy-striped hair bouncing as she moved. She shot Holly a concerned glance. "Holly, maybe you should sit down for a bit? You're looking a little pale – well, paler than usual, and that's saying something for someone who works with flour all day."

Holly waved off her concern, though the suggestion was tempting. "I'm fine, really. Just need to finish decorating Mrs. Claus's special order for the North Pole Ladies' Society meeting." She turned back to the elaborate gingerbread castle she'd been working on, but the sight of the royal icing made her stomach lurch unexpectedly.

The bakery, usually her haven of comfort, felt overwhelming today. The magical warming spells that kept the display cases at perfect temperature seemed too intense, and even the cheerful tinkling of the sugar bells that floated near the ceiling grated on her nerves. She'd already had to step away from the kitchen three times this morning when various scents became suddenly unbearable.

"At least let me make you some of that special tea my grandmother swears by," Pepper insisted, already reaching for the jar of dried herbs she kept behind the counter. "It's perfect for... well, for times like these." She gave Holly a knowing look that made Holly's heart skip a beat.

Before Holly could respond, the door burst open with a chorus of "Joy to the World," and Jingles bounded in, trailing his usual sparkles and bringing with him a gust of crisp winter air. His cheeks were flushed with excitement, his formal Council attire slightly askew.

"Sugar plum! You won't believe what happened at the meeting!" He practically danced to the counter, then paused, his expression shifting from excitement to concern as he took in his wife's appearance. "Holly? Are you feeling worse?"

"I'm fine," Holly insisted for what felt like the hundredth time that day, though she couldn't help leaning into his touch when he reached across the counter to cup her cheek. His hand felt cool against her warm skin, and for a moment, she allowed herself to close her eyes and just breathe in his familiar scent of peppermint and magic.

"You're not fine," he said softly, his bell-tipped ears drooping slightly with worry. "Maybe we should postpone the spell tonight..."

"No!" Holly straightened up, perhaps too quickly as the room swam slightly. "No, I've been looking forward to this. You were so excited about it, and I want to understand your magic better. Besides, it's only for twenty-four hours, right?"

Jingles still looked uncertain, but before he could argue, the bakery door chimed again. This time, it was Mrs. Frost herself, the elegant owner of Frostyville's premier ice sculpture gallery and one of Holly's most particular customers.

"Holly, darling!" Mrs. Frost glided to the counter, leaving a trail of delicate ice crystals in her wake. "I simply must have three dozen of your snow crystal cookies for tomorrow's gallery opening. The ones that release actual snowflakes when you bite into them? They complement my ice sculptures perfectly."

Holly nodded, already reaching for her special order notebook, but the movement caused another wave of dizziness. She gripped the counter tighter, feeling the smooth marble anchor her as the room threatened to tilt.

"Actually, Mrs. Frost," Pepper stepped in smoothly, "I can help you with that order. Holly was just about to take her lunch break, weren't you, Holly?"

Before Holly could protest, Jingles had come around the counter and taken her elbow. "Perfect timing! I brought us a picnic basket from that new café on Mistletoe Lane – you know, the one run by the retired sugar plum fairy? We can eat in your office and I'll tell you about the Council meeting."

Holly allowed herself to be led to the back of the bakery, through the kitchen where her enchanted mixing bowls were happily whipping up the next batch of magical meringues, and into her small but cozy office. The room was decorated with photos of their wedding day – including one of the moment they'd discovered Holly's latent baking magic, when their wedding cake had suddenly sprouted wings and tried to fly away.

Jingles helped her settle into her oversized armchair, the one she'd enchanted to always feel like a warm hug, and began unpacking the picnic basket. The aroma of tomato soup – her favorite comfort food – filled the room, along with the scent of grilled cheese sandwiches made with Mrs. Claus's secret recipe bread.

"Small bites," he advised, setting up their lunch on her desk with uncharacteristic care. "And if anything doesn't appeal to you, don't force it. I got a variety of options."

Holly's heart swelled with love for her husband. For all his mischievous nature and occasional magical mishaps, he always knew exactly what she needed. "Thank you," she said softly, accepting a mug of soup that was exactly the right temperature. "Now, tell me about the Council meeting. Did they approve the new wish protocols?"

Jingles perched on the edge of her desk, his feet dangling in their mismatched socks (today it was one with prancing reindeer and one with breakdancing snowmen). "Well, that's the interesting part. They're concerned about the increasing number of unauthorized spell combinations in Frostyville. Apparently, there's been a surge in magical experimentation ever since... well, ever since you developed your baking magic after our wedding."

Holly paused with her spoon halfway to her mouth. "What do you mean?"

"It seems you've inspired quite a few non-magical residents to believe they might have latent magical abilities too. The Council is worried about potential magical accidents." He ran a hand through his already tousled hair, making his bell-tipped ears jingle. "That's actually why I'm even more excited about trying the Ancient Christmas Wish Spell tonight. If we can show them that controlled magical experimentation can be beneficial..."

Holly set down her soup, her appetite suddenly vanishing again. "Jingles... are you saying you want to use our Christmas celebration as a test case for the Council?"

His eyes widened. "No! Well, not entirely. I mean, it could help our case, but that's not the main reason. I really do want to understand your magic better, and I want you to experience mine. Don't you think it would be amazing to know exactly what it feels like to be each other, even just for a day?"

She wanted to say yes, wanted to match his enthusiasm, but something held her back. Maybe it was the way her body had been feeling lately, or maybe it was an instinct she couldn't quite name. "What if something goes wrong?"

"Nothing will go wrong," he assured her, reaching out to take her hand. His fingers intertwined with hers, warm and reassuring. "I've studied the spell thoroughly. It's perfectly safe, and it only lasts twenty-four hours. Plus, think how much fun it will be! You can experience what it's like to have elf magic, and I can try my hand at your baking magic."

Holly tried to smile, but another wave of nausea chose that moment to roll through her. She closed her eyes, taking deep breaths until it passed.

"That's it," Jingles said firmly. "We're postponing the spell. You're clearly not feeling well, and-"

"No," Holly interrupted, opening her eyes with determination. "You're right. It's only twenty-four hours, and it could be wonderful. Besides, I've already gathered most of the ingredients we need." She managed a small smile. "Though you might want to handle the magical mistletoe – the smell of it has been making me feel strange lately."

Jingles studied her face for a long moment, his expression uncharacteristically serious. "Promise me you'll tell me if you start feeling worse? We can stop the spell preparations at any time."

"I promise," Holly said, though something fluttered in her stomach that had nothing to do with nausea. She picked up her soup again, forcing herself to take small sips. "Now, tell me more about this snickerdoodle rain in Minnesota..."

As Jingles launched into an animated retelling of the Council meeting, complete with magical illustrations that danced in the air above her desk, Holly tried to push aside her growing sense of unease. After all, what could possibly go wrong with a simple Christmas wish spell?

But as she watched her husband gesture enthusiastically, sending tiny sparkles showering across her paperwork, she couldn't shake the feeling that their second Christmas as a married couple was about to become far more complicated than either of them had imagined.

Chapter 3: Whispers of Wonder

The afternoon sun cast long shadows through the frost-covered windows of Holly's Holiday Bakery as Holly and Jingles began gathering ingredients for the Ancient Christmas Wish Spell. The bakery was closed now, the last customers long gone, leaving behind only the lingering scents of the day's baking and the soft hum of magical kitchen equipment settling down for the night.

Holly stood in her experimental baking room, a special space she'd created for testing new magical recipes. The walls were lined with shelves of enchanted ingredients – bottles of liquid starlight, jars of crystallized wishes, and bags of sugar that sparkled with different emotions. In the center of the room stood her prized possession: a massive copper mixing bowl that had been blessed by Mrs. Claus herself.

"Let's see," Jingles murmured, consulting an ancient scroll that sparkled faintly in the fading light. "We need essence of northern lights, three strands of tinsel from the original Christmas tree, and... oh! A pinch of first snow from this year." He looked up at Holly with twinkling eyes. "Good thing I always keep some in my pocket!"

Holly managed a smile, though the mere sight of the magical mistletoe hanging in the corner made her stomach churn. She'd been avoiding that corner all day, which was unusual – normally, she loved the sweet, festive scent. "What else do we need?"

"Something borrowed, something blue... wait, no, that's for weddings." Jingles squinted at the scroll. "Ah, here we go! We need a tear of joy, a laugh crystallized in winter frost, and – most importantly – a memory of our first Christmas together."

As if on cue, the copper mixing bowl began to hum softly, its surface reflecting the twinkling lights that floated near the ceiling. Holly reached for a jar of crushed candy cane dust, but her hand trembled slightly, causing the jar to slip. Jingles caught it with a quick wave of his hand, his elf magic surrounding the jar with sparkling silver light.

"Careful, sugar plum," he said softly, setting the jar on the counter. His pointed ears twitched with concern. "Are you sure you're up for this? You've been off-balance all day."

Holly took a deep breath, steadying herself against the counter. The smooth marble felt cool under her palms, grounding her. "I'm fine. Just tired from the holiday rush." But even as she said it, another wave of dizziness washed over her. The room seemed too warm, too full of competing magical energies.

Jingles stepped closer, his natural peppermint scent mingling with the bakery's sweet aromas. "Holly," he began, his voice serious, "there's something different about you lately. Your magic feels... changed."

She looked up at him, startled. "What do you mean?"

"Well, when you frosted those sugar cookies yesterday, they didn't just dance – they created their own little snow flurries. And this morning, the gingerbread pancakes were humming Christmas carols. Your magic has never done that before."

Holly bit her lip, remembering other strange occurrences she'd noticed but tried to ignore. The way her magical measuring spoons had started working twice as fast, the sugar crystals that formed heart shapes without her instruction, the cookie dough that kept trying to wrap itself around her in a hug...

"Maybe we should consult the Council before trying the spell," Jingles suggested, his bells jingling softly with worry. "Or at least talk to Mrs. Claus. She might know-"

"No," Holly interrupted, more firmly than she'd intended. She softened her tone at Jingles' surprised expression. "I mean, we've planned this for weeks. It's supposed to be special – just us. And you said yourself the spell is safe."

Jingles studied her face for a long moment, his expression unusually thoughtful. Finally, he nodded. "Alright, sugar plum. But promise me one thing?"

"Anything."

"If anything feels wrong – even slightly – during the spell, you'll tell me immediately. No trying to be brave or pushing through it. Deal?"

Holly managed a small smile. "Deal." She reached for a different jar, this one filled with rainbow-colored sugar crystals that chimed like tiny bells when shaken. "Now, where were we?"

They worked together in comfortable synchronization, measuring and mixing ingredients in the copper bowl. Jingles added three perfect snowflakes from his pocket (he always carried a collection, claiming you never knew when you might need emergency snow). Holly contributed a tear of joy she'd collected during their wedding day, carefully preserved in a crystal vial.

As they worked, the magic in the room began to build, creating swirls of colored light that danced around them like aurora borealis. The copper bowl hummed louder, its surface beginning to glow with a warm, golden light.

"Now for the memory," Jingles announced, pulling out his favorite holiday handkerchief – the one with tap-dancing reindeer embroidered in the corners. "Ready?"

Holly nodded, though her heart was racing with more than just anticipation. Together, they leaned over the bowl, hands clasped. Jingles touched his wand to their joined hands, and a silvery strand of memory began to form – their first Christmas morning as a married couple, when they'd woken up to find their Christmas tree had grown candy canes and their stockings were singing carols in harmony.

The memory dropped into the mixture with a musical chime, and the contents of the bowl began to swirl faster, creating a miniature whirlwind of sparkles and light. The scent of Christmas magic – pine needles, cinnamon, starlight, and something indefinably magical – filled the air.

But as the magical energy built, Holly felt another wave of dizziness, stronger than before. The room seemed to spin, the magical lights blurring together. She gripped the edge of the counter, trying to stay upright.

"Holly?" Jingles' voice seemed to come from far away. "Holly, what's wrong?"

She tried to answer, but the words wouldn't come. The last thing she saw before the room went dark was Jingles' worried face, his bell-tipped ears jingling in alarm, and the copper bowl's contents beginning to overflow with uncontrolled magical energy...

Chapter 4: When Magic Goes Sideways

Holly awoke to the sensation of tingling all over her body, as if she'd been dusted with fairy lights. The first thing she noticed was that she was floating several inches above the floor of her experimental kitchen. The second thing she noticed was that Jingles was not floating – which was decidedly unusual for an elf.

"Sugar plum!" Jingles rushed to her side, his movements oddly earthbound. "You're awake! I was so worried when you fainted, and then the spell mixture exploded, and now everything's..." He gestured helplessly at himself, then at her.

Holly tried to respond, but instead of words, a shower of silver sparkles fell from her mouth. Her eyes widened in alarm. She concentrated, trying again: "Jingles, why am I floating?"

"Well," he began, running a hand through his hair – which, Holly suddenly realized, had lost its magical shimmer, "it seems the spell worked. Just... not exactly as intended. When you fainted, I tried to stop it, but the magic had already begun, and with your unusual magical signature lately..." He trailed off, looking sheepish.

Holly managed to will herself back to the ground, though her feet kept trying to lift off again. The room smelled different to her now – she could detect individual strands of magic in the air, like separate notes in a symphony. The scent of peppermint was particularly strong, but for the first time in weeks, it didn't make her queasy.

"Jingles," she said slowly, "did we switch powers?"

As if in answer, the cookie dough she'd left on the counter suddenly rose up and formed itself into a perfect Christmas tree shape, then collapsed into a heap. Jingles stared at it mournfully.

"I tried to keep it together while you were unconscious," he admitted. "But I can't seem to control your baking magic at all. Everything I've touched either falls apart or..." He gestured to the far corner, where what appeared to be a gingerbread house was performing an enthusiastic tap dance routine.

Holly felt a hysterical laugh bubble up inside her, emerging as a cascade of musical notes that formed a brief chorus of "Jingle Bells" in the air. "So I have your elf magic, and you have my baking magic? For twenty-four hours?"

"That's the thing," Jingles said hesitantly, his now-sparkle-free ears drooping slightly. "When the spell mixed with whatever's been affecting your magic lately... I'm not entirely sure it will wear off in twenty-four hours."

The words hit Holly like a snowball to the face. She felt her feet leave the ground again as panic set in, and had to concentrate hard to stay earthbound. "What do you mean, you're not sure?"

"Well, normally the spell is very straightforward. But your magic has been acting strangely for weeks now, almost as if..." He paused, a look of dawning realization crossing his face. "Holly, when was the last time you checked the magical calendar?"

Holly blinked, trying to remember through the fog of recent queasiness and fatigue. "I've been too busy with holiday orders to... why? What does that have to do with anything?"

Jingles was already hurrying to the magical calendar hanging on the wall, the one that tracked not just dates but magical energy patterns in Frostyville. His eyes scanned the shimmering notations, widening as he reached the current date.

"Holly," he said softly, turning back to her with an expression of wonder, "your magical signature hasn't just been changing – it's been doubling."

"Doubling?" Holly repeated, not understanding. Then it hit her – the morning sickness, the changing magic, the strange cravings for candy canes dipped in pickle juice that she'd been too embarrassed to mention. "Oh... Oh!"

She floated upward again, this time with shock, and Jingles had to gently pull her back down. Around them, the magical energy in the room began to swirl in response to her emotions, creating tiny whirlwinds of sugar and sparkles.

"You mean I'm..."

"Pregnant," Jingles finished, his face breaking into a brilliant smile despite their predicament. "And based on these magical readings... with twins."

Holly felt the room spin again, but this time it wasn't morning sickness – it was pure, overwhelming joy mixed with panic. "Twins? But then... what does that mean for the spell? And the bakery? And Christmas is in three days!"

As if responding to her distress, every cooking implement in the room began to vibrate. Jingles quickly wrapped his arms around her, anchoring her both physically and emotionally. Despite lacking his usual magical sparkle, his touch still felt like home.

"It means," he said gently, "that we have an even more special Christmas ahead of us than we planned. We'll figure out the spell – we always do. And as for the bakery..." He glanced at the tap-dancing gingerbread house, which had now been joined by a chorus line of cookie cutters. "Well, we might need to put up a sign saying we're experimenting with some... unique holiday offerings."

Holly couldn't help it – she laughed, sending a cascade of snowflakes and jingle bells through the air. "Unique is one way to put it. But Jingles... we're going to be parents!"

"To magical twins," he added, his eyes twinkling despite his currently non-magical state. "Mrs. Claus is going to be thrilled – she's been hinting about wanting to knit baby booties that never get lost in the snow."

Holly started to respond, but was interrupted by a loud POOF! from the corner. They turned to find that the gingerbread house had apparently taught itself to juggle candy canes.

"Maybe we should call the Council," Holly suggested, watching as more baked goods began to take on lives of their own. "Or at least Mrs. Claus? Someone must know how to handle a magical power swap complicated by unexpected magical twins."

Jingles nodded, ducking as a tray of sugar cookies went flying past, attempting an aerial ballet. "Probably a good idea. Though..." He grinned suddenly, that familiar mischievous glint in his eye. "We might want to do something about your floating first. And maybe figure out how to stop me from accidentally bringing every pastry in the building to life?"

Holly tried to look stern, but it was difficult when she was slowly rotating in mid-air. "This is exactly why we should have checked with the Council before trying an ancient spell."

"Where would be the fun in that?" Jingles reached up to catch her hand, pulling her back down to earth once again. "Besides, think of what a story this will be to tell the twins someday – how their parents accidentally switched magical powers right before finding out about them."

As if in agreement, the copper mixing bowl began to play a cheerful lullaby, and all the animated baked goods paused their various performances to sway in time to the music.

"We're going to need to baby-proof the bakery," Holly realized suddenly. "Can you imagine magical twins getting into the enchanted ingredients?"

"We can start planning tomorrow," Jingles assured her. "Right now, I think we should focus on getting through the next twenty-four hours – or however long this spell lasts – without turning all of Frostyville's Christmas treats into a performing arts showcase."

Holly nodded, then immediately regretted it as the movement sent her floating toward the ceiling again. As Jingles reached up to help her down, she caught sight of their reflection in the copper bowl – her with Jingles' magical sparkle, him with flour on his nose and a distinctly non-magical appearance. They looked ridiculous, and yet...

"I love you," she said softly, sending inadvertent hearts made of light floating through the air. "Even when your Christmas surprises go completely sideways."

"I love you too, sugar plum," Jingles replied, attempting to brush the flour off his nose but only succeeding in adding more. "And our Christmas surprises always work out in the end. Even if the path there is a bit... unconventional."

Around them, the bakery hummed with mixed-up magic and the sound of tap-dancing treats, while outside, the first stars of evening began to twinkle over Frostyville. Their second Christmas as a married couple might not be going according to plan, but as Holly floated in her husband's arms, watching sugar cookies perform Swan Lake in the corner, she couldn't help thinking it was perfect in its own way.

After all, what was Christmas without a little chaos, a lot of love, and just the right amount of magical mayhem?

Here are some ideas to make your home cozy and warm with Christmas decorations:

Living Room

1. **Twinkling Lights**: Drape soft white or warm yellow fairy lights around the windows, mantels, or bookshelves for a soft, magical glow.
2. **Festive Throw Pillows**: Add pillows with Christmas patterns (like reindeer, snowflakes, or plaid) in warm tones of red, green, and cream.
3. **Chunky Knit Blankets**: Toss chunky knit or faux fur blankets over the couch for a cozy and inviting touch.
4. **Holiday Candles**: Use candles with Christmas scents like cinnamon, pine, or vanilla, placed in decorative holders or lanterns for ambiance.
5. **Garlands with Greenery**: Drape garlands made of faux or real greenery around door frames, mantels, or staircases. Add pinecones, berries, or small ornaments for extra detail.

Dining Area

1. **Table Runner**: Use a rustic burlap or plaid table runner with a centerpiece of candles, pine sprigs, and small ornaments.
2. **Chair Decorations**: Tie festive ribbons or mini wreaths to the backs of chairs for a charming detail.

3. **Christmas Place Settings**: Use holiday-themed plates, napkins, and glassware. Top each plate with a small sprig of greenery or a candy cane tied with ribbon.

Kitchen

1. **Holiday Mugs**: Display Christmas-themed mugs on a mug tree or open shelf.
2. **Festive Towels**: Swap out everyday kitchen towels for ones with holiday patterns.
3. **Hot Cocoa Bar**: Create a small hot cocoa bar with jars of marshmallows, candy canes, and hot chocolate mix, decorated with mini lights or a garland.

Bedroom

1. **Cozy Bedding**: Add flannel sheets or a quilt in Christmas colors or patterns.
2. **String Lights**: Hang string lights around the headboard or along the ceiling for a soft, romantic glow.
3. **Mini Tree**: Place a small Christmas tree on a nightstand or dresser, decorated with mini ornaments or fairy lights.

Hallways and Entryway

1. **Lit Up Entryway**: Hang a lighted garland around the front door or entryway mirror.
2. **Seasonal Doormat**: Add a festive doormat with a Christmas design.
3. **Festive Hooks**: Hang stockings, wreaths, or decorative scarves on hooks.

Small Touches

1. **Pine-Scented Diffusers**: Use diffusers or essential oils with pine or cranberry scents for a holiday feel.
2. **Holiday Figurines**: Place figurines of Santa, snowmen, or reindeer on shelves or side tables.
3. **Warm Rugs**: Use plush or faux fur rugs in living spaces to make the floor feel warmer.

Windows

1. **Window Clings**: Apply frosted snowflake or Christmas-themed window clings.
2. **Hanging Ornaments**: Use ribbons to hang ornaments at varying lengths in front of windows for a unique display.

Overall Ambiance

Keep the lighting warm and soft by using dimmer switches or candles.

Play soft Christmas music in the background to complete the cozy atmosphere.

If you have a fire place that's extra special.

Christmas scented candles, incense, essential oils in a burner. You can also simmer a pot on he stove with cinnamon sticks, orange slices, cranberry, star anise and cloves! I prefer a small crockpot.

These decorations can make your home feel like a warm and magical holiday retreat your guest will feel at home in and you will enjoy throughout the season!

Links to finding festive scents I use:

https://www.amazon.com/Winter-Premium-Grade-Fragrance-Oils/dp/B00CAFC98E

https://www.amazon.com/Holiday-Premium-Grade-Fragrance-Oils/dp/B01MYTO3T4

https://www.amazon.com/SALKING-Scented-Fragrance-Essential-Diffuser/dp/B0B799SDDM

https://www.thedipper.com/
(This company has the best incense with strong long lasting 3 hour burns. I purchase the bundle packages and their Balsam Pine smells like a real Christmas tree.)

Here are some fun and creative Christmas DIY craft ideas to bring holiday cheer to your home:

1. Mason Jar Snow Globes
- **Materials**: Mason jars, small figurines (like trees or snowmen), faux snow, hot glue, and glitter.
- **Instructions**: Glue the figurines to the inside of the jar lid, fill the jar with faux snow and glitter, then screw the lid back on. Turn the jar upside down for a snow globe effect.

2. Pinecone Ornaments

- **Materials**: Pinecones, ribbon, white paint or glitter, and glue.
- **Instructions**: Paint the tips of the pinecones white or apply glue and sprinkle glitter to mimic snow. Attach a ribbon loop to hang on the tree.

3. Christmas Tree Garland

- **Materials**: Twine, felt, scissors, and hot glue.
- **Instructions**: Cut felt into shapes like trees, stars, or stockings. String them onto twine, securing with glue, to create a festive garland for your mantel or tree.

Christmas on Peppermint Lane

4. Holiday Candles

- **Materials**: Plain candles, cinnamon sticks, ribbon, and glue.
- **Instructions**: Glue cinnamon sticks around the outside of the candle and tie with a ribbon. Light them to enjoy the warm glow and cozy scent.

5. Handmade Christmas Cards

- **Materials**: Cardstock, stamps, stickers, markers, and ribbon.
- **Instructions**: Decorate blank cardstock with festive designs like wreaths, snowflakes, or reindeer. Add a personal message for a heartfelt touch.

6. Sock Snowmen

Materials: White socks, rice, rubber bands, buttons, and fabric scraps.

Instructions: Fill a white sock with rice, tie sections with rubber bands to form a snowman shape, and decorate with buttons, fabric scraps, and a marker for the face. A fun project to do with the kids!

7. Christmas Wreath

- **Materials**: A wreath form (foam or wire), greenery, ornaments, ribbons, and glue.
- **Instructions**: Attach greenery and ornaments to the form, securing with glue. Add a large bow for a festive finishing touch.

8. Popsicle Stick Ornaments

- **Materials**: Popsicle sticks, paint, glue, and embellishments.
- **Instructions**: Arrange and glue sticks into shapes like stars, snowflakes, or reindeer. Paint and decorate as desired, then add a ribbon to hang.

9. Advent Calendar

- **Materials**: Small paper bags, clothespins, twine, and markers.
- **Instructions**: Number the bags 1–24, fill each with a small treat or note, and hang them on twine using clothespins.

10. Glittery Candle Holders

- **Materials**: Glass jars, Mod Podge, glitter, and paintbrushes.
- **Instructions**: Coat the inside of a glass jar with Mod Podge, sprinkle glitter inside, and let it dry. Add a tealight for a sparkly glow.

11. Personalized Stockings

- **Materials**: Plain stockings, fabric paint, and embellishments.
- **Instructions**: Use fabric paint to write names or holiday patterns on the stockings. Add pompoms or sequins for extra flair.

12. Felt Christmas Tree

- **Materials**: Green felt, smaller felt pieces, and Velcro.
- **Instructions**: Cut a large tree shape from green felt and smaller shapes (like ornaments, stars, and presents) from other colors. Attach Velcro to let kids "decorate" the tree.

13. Cinnamon Stick Reindeer

- **Materials**: Cinnamon sticks, googly eyes, red beads, and glue.
- **Instructions**: Glue cinnamon sticks into a triangle, add googly eyes and a red bead for the nose, and attach a string to hang.

14. Paper Snowflakes

- **Materials**: White paper and scissors.
- **Instructions**: Fold and cut paper into intricate snowflake patterns. Tape them to windows for a wintry look.

15. Candy Cane Wreath

- **Materials**: Candy canes, ribbon, and glue.
- **Instructions**: Arrange candy canes into a heart-shaped wreath and glue them together. Add a festive bow at the top.

16. Wine Cork Reindeer

- **Materials**: Wine corks, twigs, googly eyes, and red pom-poms.
- **Instructions**: Use wine corks for the body and head, twigs for antlers, and decorate with eyes and a red pom-pom nose.

17. Christmas Lanterns

- **Materials**: Empty tin cans, a hammer, and a nail.
- **Instructions**: Punch holes in designs (like stars or trees) around the can. Place a tealight inside for a glowing lantern effect.

Christmas on Peppermint Lane

18. Homemade Gift Tags

- **Materials**: Cardstock, stamps, markers, and ribbon.
- **Instructions**: Cut cardstock into tag shapes, decorate with festive patterns, and punch a hole to tie onto gifts.

19. Ribbon Christmas Trees

- **Materials**: Green ribbons, wooden sticks, and glue.
- **Instructions**: Tie ribbons in descending lengths onto a stick to form a tree shape. Attach a star at the top for a cute ornament.

20. DIY Photo Ornaments

- **Materials**: Small photos, clear ornaments, and glitter.
- **Instructions**: Insert photos and glitter into clear ornaments. Seal and hang them for a personalized touch.

Here are more ideas for meals, treats and ideas for parents to do with kids during Chrstmas break

Main Dishes:
A classic herb-crusted prime rib with au jus and horseradish cream, perfect as a showstopping centerpiece
Honey and orange-glazed ham with whole cloves and brown sugar crust for those who prefer pork
For a non-traditional option, consider a whole roasted salmon with dill and lemon, which can be served hot or cold

Side Dishes:

Garlic and rosemary roasted potatoes with a crispy exterior and fluffy inside
Green beans almondine with caramelized shallots and toasted almonds
Brussels sprouts roasted with bacon and maple syrup
A festive wild rice pilaf with dried cranberries and pecans

Appetizers:

Baked brie wrapped in puff pastry with cranberry compote and walnuts
Smoked salmon blini with dill cream
Spiced nuts and a cheese board with seasonal fruits

Desserts:

> Traditional Christmas pudding with brandy butter
> A yule log (bûche de Noël) with chocolate ganache and meringue mushrooms
> Spiced apple and cranberry pie with vanilla ice cream

Main Dishes:

> Tender pot roast slow-cooked with carrots, onions, and potatoes - the kind that fills the house with wonderful aromas all day
> Mom-style roast turkey with sage and butter under the skin, served with homemade gravy from the drippings
> Grandma's special meatloaf wrapped in bacon with a sweet glaze, perfect for smaller gatherings

Comfort Side Dishes:

- Creamy mashed potatoes loaded with butter and a touch of sour cream
Old-fashioned green bean casserole with crispy onions on top
Sweet potato casserole with brown sugar and marshmallows
Homestyle macaroni and cheese with a crunchy breadcrumb topping

Family Favorite Appetizers:

> Deviled eggs decorated to look like little Santa hats

Sausage balls made with Bisquick - a Southern Christmas morning tradition
  Cream cheese and pepper jelly dip with crackers
  Grandma's special cheese ball rolled in pecans

Down-Home Desserts:

  Classic sugar cookies decorated with colored frosting and sprinkles
  Warm apple pie with a scoop of vanilla ice cream
  No-bake chocolate oatmeal cookies (the kind that never quite set right but taste amazing)
  Snickerdoodles dusted with cinnamon sugar
  Fudge made from grandma's recipe

Breakfast Ideas:

  Make-ahead breakfast casserole with eggs, sausage, and cheese
  Cinnamon rolls baked fresh Christmas morning
  Hot chocolate with marshmallows and candy canes

  French toast casserole with eggnog and pecans, prepped the night before
  Christmas morning breakfast pizza with scrambled eggs, sausage, red and green peppers
  Gingerbread pancakes with whipped cream and maple syrup
  Biscuits and sausage gravy - perfect for a crowd
  Eggs Benedict with ham instead of Canadian bacon for a Christmas twist

Cheesy hash brown casserole with crispy top Breakfast enchiladas with red and green salsa
Belgian waffles with cranberry compote and whipped cream

Sweet Treats:

Cranberry orange scones with vanilla glaze
Christmas tree-shaped pastries made from puff pastry and Nutella
Red velvet waffles with cream cheese drizzle
Sticky buns shaped like a Christmas wreath
Peppermint hot chocolate muffins
Apple fritter bread with cinnamon streusel

Lighter Options:

Yogurt parfait bar with red and green fruits, granola, and honey
Christmas smoothie bowls with kiwi and strawberry toppings
Overnight oats with cranberries and pistachios
Fresh fruit arranged in a Christmas tree shape

Make-Ahead Options:

- Breakfast strata with spinach, mushrooms, and Swiss cheese
Overnight cinnamon roll bread pudding
Mini quiche cups that can be reheated quickly
Freezer-friendly breakfast burritos with festive red and green peppers

Easy Christmas Cookies:

> Sugar cookie cutouts they can decorate with frosting and sprinkles
> "Stained glass" cookies using crushed hard candies
> Peanut butter blossoms with chocolate kisses
> No-bake chocolate oatmeal cookies they can help mix
> Rice Krispy treats made festive with red and green sprinkles

Fun Breakfast Projects:

> Pancakes they can help decorate to look like Santa, reindeer, or snowmen
> Christmas tree toast (spread with cream cheese and let them decorate with fruit)
> Hot chocolate stirring spoons made by dipping plastic spoons in melted chocolate
> "Elf" smoothies layered with red and green fruits
> Cinnamon roll Christmas trees they can help shape

Simple Snacks They Can Assemble:

- Pretzel rod "magic wands" dipped in chocolate and sprinkles
  Rudolph apple slices (apple slices with peanut butter, pretzels for antlers)
  Christmas trail mix they can measure and mix
  Banana snowmen on popsicle sticks
  Fruit candy canes (alternating strawberries and bananas)

Fun Food Crafts:

    Gingerbread house decorating (you can buy kits to make it easier)
    Ice cream cone Christmas trees (decorated with green frosting and candies)
    Marshmallow snowman pops
    Graham cracker "gingerbread" houses
    Christmas wreath made from cereal and marshmallows

Safety Tips:

    Have kids wear aprons and wash hands first
    Adult supervision for any heating/melting
    Use plastic knives for younger children
    Have ingredients pre-measured for very young kids
    Keep a step stool handy for better counter access

Holiday Making & Crafting:

    Create salt dough ornaments for the tree or to give as gifts
    Make paper snowflakes to decorate windows
    Build a gingerbread house (or graham cracker house for easier assembly)
    Create paper chain countdowns to Christmas
    String popcorn and cranberries for tree garlands
    Paint pinecones to look like Christmas trees
    Make homemade wrapping paper using stamps and paint

Cozy Indoor Activities:

>Have a Christmas movie marathon with hot chocolate and blankets
>Read Christmas stories by the tree
>Build a blanket fort and decorate it with holiday lights
>Create a Christmas scavenger hunt around the house
>Set up an indoor "snow" play area with cotton balls
>Write and perform a family Christmas play
>Have a Christmas carol karaoke night

Holiday Learning Fun:

>Practice writing by helping kids write letters to Santa
>Learn about holiday traditions from around the world
>Make simple Christmas cards for family members
>Practice counting with advent calendar activities
>Learn Christmas songs in different languages
>Create a family holiday recipe book together

Outdoor Winter Activities:

>Go on a winter nature walk collecting pinecones and holly
>Make snow angels and snowmen (if you have snow!)
>Hang homemade bird feeders on trees
>Take a evening walk to look at neighborhood lights
>Have a candy cane hunt in the backyard
>Create winter obstacle courses

Holiday Kindness Projects:

    Make cards for a local nursing home
    Bake cookies for neighbors
    Create care packages for those in need
    Clean out toys to donate
    Make thank you cards for community helpers

ABOUT THE AUTHOR

Ladies and gentlemen, step right up to "Where the Magic Happens" - a literary circus that'll make your bookshelf do backflips!

Meet Patti, the ringmaster of this wordy wonderland! She's not just an Executive Producer; she's a word-wrangling wizard, conjuring up an animated TV series based on "ELLIOT FINDS A HOME." It's the tail-wagging tale of a thumbs-up pup and his silent sidekick, proving that you don't need words when you've got opposable digits and a heart of gold!

Hold onto your bestseller lists, folks! This Polygon Entertainment superstar has hit the USA TODAY jackpot and Amazon's #1 spot more times than a cat has lives. With 7 dozen books under her belt, she's got more genres than a chameleon has colors. From Urban Fantasy to Horror, she's been spinning yarns longer than your grandma's knitting needles!

But wait, there's more! Patti's life is like a celebrity bingo card:

She rocked "Romper Room" at 4, probably making the other kids look like amateur rompers.

She rubbed elbows with Captain Kangaroo and Mr. Green Jeans. (No word on whether the jeans were actually green.)

She shared a train ride and a sandwich with Sidney Poitier. Talk about a meal ticket to stardom!

She high-fived President Nixon at the circus. Who knew the circus could get any more political?

She went to school with David Copperfield. We assume she didn't disappear during attendance.

She roller-skated with pre-famous John Travolta. Grease lightning, indeed!

She sipped cocoa with Abe Vigoda. Fish never tasted so sweet!

When she's not busy being a literary legend, Patti's juggling roles faster than a circus performer. Teacher, grandma, furparent - she does it all with a smile that could light up a haunted house.

Speaking of haunted houses, meet the "Queen of Halloween" herself! This Wiccan High Priestess is stirring up stories spookier than a skeleton's dance moves. Her books are flying off the shelves faster than witches on broomsticks, so follow her on social media or risk missing out on the hocus-pocus!

So, come one, come all, to Patti's phantasmagorical world of words! It's more exciting than a roller coaster, more magical than a rabbit in a hat, and more diverse than a box of assorted chocolates. Don't be shy - step into the spotlight and join the literary party where the pages turn themselves and the stories never end!

www.ingramcontent.com/pod-product-compliance
Lightning Source LLC
LaVergne TN
LVHW041753060526
838201LV00046B/993